About the Author

Born in Jaipur, Parul Mehta Patel grew up in Delhi and Mumbai, India. Parul has a love for creativity and art, writing poetry since she was a child, painting, and Indian classical singing. Parul has also always enjoyed reading books. Her parents encouraged her in her pursuits, and filled their home with books to feed her joy. Parul earned her Bachelor's degree in Commerce and Economics from Bombay University in Mumbai, India, followed by a stint in journalism for Cine Blitz magazine, until she moved to the United States. In the USA Parul obtained her Master's degree in Human Development from Pacific Oaks College, California, and went on to earn a second Master's in Marriage and Family Therapy and a Doctorate in Marriage and Family Therapy, both from Alliant International, California. She currently is in private practice where she sees clients for psychotherapy, and she also supervises students at a university.

Over the last few years, Parul gave in to the irrepressible need to write a book. That book evolved into Meera, her debut novel.

Parul lives with her husband and daughter in California.

Meera

Parul Mehta Patel

Publishing Facilitation: AuthorsUpFront

The Write Place
A Publishing Initiative by Crossword Bookstores Ltd.
Umang Tower, 2nd Floor, Mindspace, Off Link Road,
Malad West, Mumbai 400064, India.

Web: www.TheWritePlace.in
Facebook: TheWritePlace.in
Twitter: @WritePlacePub
Instagram: @WritePlacePub

*This book is dedicated to my parents Asha
Mehta and Bharat Mehta –
You remain my lighthouse in the storm.
Thank you for everything!
Specifically,
Mom, for instilling in me the love of stories, and
Papa, for instilling in me the love of discipline.
Without these, Meera would not have happened!*

And now I have a story to tell...

CONTENTS

Part III: Reasons And Realities

Epilogue: Two Years Hence
Stories Within Stories

PART I

Childhood And Challenges

1

Meera Myna Dutt

'When did I become such an expert at deception?' I sank to the floor on my knees, sat very still beside the king size bed and rested my forehead on the polished wood of the end table as I pondered the question. Despite my stillness and the solid familiarity of the wood, nothing eased the knot in my stomach.

I was five years old, so young and innocent, when Super was born. But very soon it dawned on me that this new beloved child was taking over what was previously my sole role and position. With my small hands clenched in tight fists, my eyes threatening to spill over with tears, probably for the first time in my life I felt anger. Back then I didn't even know what I felt was called anger. It felt strange in my little body, still plump with baby fat, to be dethroned by my brother's birth.

The scene is etched in my memory. I stood in a corner watching the parade of adults pour their sweet adoration over the child in the crib. I wanted him to disappear, so I planned to bury him in the back yard when no one was watching. It wasn't that I wanted to harm the baby; I just wanted him to vanish so that life could be restored to the way as I had known it all my five years. I didn't want this new-baby-brother person to ruin everything. But it seemed like it was already too late.

It was then that he had first noticed me. I was five and he was nineteen years old; an unusually kind nineteen. He saw me and said, "Hi, beautiful lady. What are you doing hiding in the corner like that?" I didn't know I was a lady, let alone beautiful. He casually hoisted me over his shoulder, and galloped like a horse out of the room saying, "Let's go find something fun." We went to the pantry in Grandma's big mansion and snuck chocolate fudge bits out of the big box. It was such a forbidden pleasure to stuff eight fudge bits into my mouth. I couldn't control my giggles. In that moment I decided I loved Ari Jana. Even his name meant something befitting: lion heart. Ari was my savior; and in a way my brother's savior, because he extinguished my anger and I forgot my plan to bury Super.

Ari Jana was Grandma's neighbor. He lived in the mansion next door with his three brothers and three sisters. He was the youngest, born to his parents by surprise after they were done raising their six. He was fed and bathed by his mom, but then mostly left to fend for himself – he would tag along with any sibling who would allow it that day. Perhaps it was this experience that made him sensitive to my plight. Regardless of what made him notice the five-year-old bundle of rage that fateful day, it won him my undying loyalty.

Ari, Ari, Ari… Little did I know that a few decades later, his name could be my undoing.

* * *

My maternal grandmother, whom we all called Nani, lived in Jaipur in India. Jaipur is the sultry city of my childhood summers. A romantic city of indelible tenderness and unfathomable mysteries. Jaipur is called 'Pink City' because of the colour of the old buildings and fort walls still standing in the marketplace. It is impossible to feel that life is ordinary in Jaipur. It is magical, and I believe visitors leave a bit of their hearts – and a bit of their dreams – in Jaipur, which adds to the colour and depth of the city's soul.

At the beginning of each summer, I said goodbye to my father – Papa, who was the shining beacon of light in my life – and I dutifully held on to my mother's sari to board the flight from Delhi to Jaipur. I hated airplanes. They were strange, stuffy, oddly shaped containers with wings, with people sitting in them like tinned cookies, all neat in a row, soon to turn stale. Besides, I hated leaving Papa alone in Delhi. Who would cook his favorite foods? Who would excitedly anticipate his return from work each evening? Wouldn't he be lonely all alone? But the broad smiles and open arms of Nani and my various aunts and uncles waiting to receive us at the airport inevitably succeeded in distracting me from my concern. We always got a large reception at the airport in Jaipur. Times were different then and the idyllic days spent in Nani's Magic Mansion, surrounded by family, food and fun were extraordinary.

During the Jaipur summers after Super's birth, everything changed. Super had clearly come to destroy my perfectly ordered world. I learned how to sulk and be moody. I also learned that someone other than Papa could be important to me. Ari became a highlight in my life for two unforgettable summers. I spent the days playing with Rita and the rest of my cousins in the big lawns behind Magic Mansion, but a half hour each evening at five belonged to Ari, who always came by to meet me. Of course, Ari was ever the gentleman and played with us all, but I knew that it was me who was his special little friend. He often got me the dried mango slices I loved. He kissed both my cheeks, swung me on his shoulders, and sometimes he tickled me until I begged him to stop. He would then have to leave for his clandestine meeting with his girlfriend. But he never called her a lady, like he did me.

"Why do you have a girlfriend, Ari?" I asked him one day.

"Because you are too young yet, Meera," he responded with a wink. I didn't know exactly what he meant by that, but it sounded good. It seemed to mean that he would not have a girlfriend when I was older. I didn't like sharing him with some girlfriend. I'd rather we played all evening.

I ultimately accepted Super as a part of the family. With Papa in Delhi and Ari in Jaipur, Super's invasion didn't matter as much anymore, because my life felt full. Besides, I was a lady. I was special. Unfortunately, this happy existence wouldn't last long.

Two summers later, when I was seven and Ari twenty-one, he left. Ari moved with his parents and two sisters to Mauritius. The rest of his siblings were older and had their own families in various parts of the world. Ari's father got some apparently desirable work opportunity in Banko Mauritius and when he asked his remaining family for their vote, all but Mrs. Jana voted to go. Even my Ari wanted to go.

"But Ari," I spluttered when I found out they were moving at the end of that summer. "What about your girlfriend?"

"I know, Meera. It's kind of sad for her. But it was over anyway."

"Why?" I said. "Don't you love her?"

"You are too young to understand. I care for her. But it's over for me. She will be fine, don't worry."

"Why?" I insisted. Even though I didn't like the whole girlfriend thing at all.

"I don't know," he said with a serious expression. "Sometimes things end. I will miss *you* much more. I am sadder about not seeing *you* every summer, my special friend. Will you take good care of yourself and know that you are very, very cool?"

"Ari, then don't leave me."

"We will always be friends, Meera." And with that he ended the conversation firmly, and turned and walked away.

I didn't understand. How could he just leave? Didn't he know it was just wrong? Didn't he care? I stomped off and refused to talk to him after that. I was so angry and broken-hearted. I sulked my way through the next two weeks and though I still waited anxiously for Ari's evening visits, I also resented them. I liked that I got a chance to be angry around him and not talk to him when he dropped by. But I became even more furious each evening when I looked at him and remembered that he was leaving forever.

The Jana family came to say goodbye the evening before they left. I refused to come out to the living room where they sat tearfully drinking *chai*, spicy hot Indian tea, the forever comfort drink. Ramukaka, our old and faithful cook had made *chai* like he did every day for the adults, and with this he served a fried Indian snack – *chakri* – made of rice flour and spices. I hid in the bedroom I shared with my favorite cousin Rita. Because the bedroom door opened into the formal living room, I could hear them talking.

"Yes, there is no place on this planet like India, Bhaijaan." Mr. Jana said to Ram Uncle. "But when an opportunity such as this one comes along, what is one to do?"

One is supposed to be loyal, I answered in my mind. Didn't these stupid adults know even this much?

"Yes, some decisions in life are difficult," answered Ram Uncle, "but you have to do what you have to do."

What does that even mean? I made a mental note to ask Ram Uncle after I decided to stop sulking.

"Meera will miss our Ari. She adores him. He is like a big brother to her." That was fat Mrs. Jana.

"Oh yes, she will. She is so fond of him. It is very sweet." My mother this time. And they continued with their senseless chatter.

There was a knock on the bedroom door. Ari had come to say bye. "What do you want?" I grunted.

"Meera, I am leaving late tonight. I just want to say bye and wish you good luck with school and all. I know you are mad at me. But it's going to be alright."

I wanted to open the door and let him give me his trademark warm hug, and swing me on his shoulders and gallop around the house, but I was determined to hold my ground. And with that same determination, I delivered my carefully rehearsed one sentence speech, "I know this is a bad word and I am not supposed to say it, but Ari, I *hate* you."

And that was my last sentence to him for over two decades.

* * *

The several years following that made up my 'post-Ari era'.

For months after Ari had left I became sullen and quiet, often brooding on the swing on the back porch of our home in Delhi. I swung back and forth, sometimes for hours, humming something I made up as I went along. I also liked pottering around in the mud in our garden. I made little mud houses. Sometimes I dug, and if I discovered a worm, I watched it intently, trying to determine its life-purpose. If I found a colony of ants, I curiously watched their uniformity and seeming adherence to a unified goal. I discovered the pleasure of books and would get lost in them, pretending to be living the life of a character in the story instead of my own.

Mostly he was annoying, but I even warmed up to Super a bit. It was his innocence, and the way deep dimples formed on either side of his mouth when he smiled. I played with him occasionally and I knew it made Mom and Papa happy to see us together. Our game usually consisted of me throwing his colored plastic shapes a short distance away and him making his way over to retrieve them, bursting into giggles when he did. His delight at getting a plastic shape was infectious. He'd clap his plump hands with triumph and glee. He was two then, and the centre of my mother's existence. I didn't mind too much. Mostly I wanted to be left alone to read, or brood, or continue my explorations in the mud, or to play with my neighborhood friends. Unless Papa was around, that is. Papa was the only person who could turn me into a giggly young child again. Papa, who told me enthralling stories of Robin Hood's clever stealing from the rich and giving to the poor. Papa, who sang me to sleep at night. Papa, who had the warmest hug and the heartiest smile. Papa, who loved me unconditionally. Now that Ari was gone, Papa was the only one left on that high pedestal in my heart.

* * *

It is the autumn after Ari's departure, and we have a week off from school. Mom has been complaining that we never take the time to enjoy our own city, so we plan to spend my school break at home in Delhi. And in the process, we get stuck with an unwanted visitor.

"Monty is coming to stay here for a week. You really need to clean your room, Meera. And I want you to be a good host, and talk to him. I don't want you keeping to yourself all the time," Mom warns.

Monty is Shaun Uncle's son. Shaun Uncle is Papa's childhood friend. I've heard many stories of the mischief Shaun Uncle and Papa got up to in their college days. Papa told me about the time they both peed in a glass jar and then let their prissy roommate think it was body oil and apply it all over himself. I'm not sure if Mom approved of Papa telling me this story, but I found it delightful. Shaun Uncle has a hearty laugh and his eyes shine with kindness and mischief even now. I like him a lot, but I am not sure about his mean looking son. Monty is very fair and plump with small eyes. He looks like his mother.

I skulk off to clean my room. It is not fair that whenever someone comes over, Mom flies into a flurry of activity, cooking and cleaning and generally barking orders at whomever she can catch. This time she even tells Super to put away all his toys in the toy tub. What's the problem with things the way they are? Like Monty could ever notice all this effort through his too-small eyes! He probably also has a too-small brain, I think, but then I stop myself because I know this is a mean thought. I say Lord Krishna's name to ward off the mean thought, just like Nani taught me.

Monty arrives that evening. I am thankful my bedtime is nine and I am not forced to interact with him for longer than thirty minutes that night. He looks just as mean as before, but not as plump as I remember. He is thirteen and thinks he can boss me around. His laugh sounds more like a mouse squealing in pain, than anything else. I stifle a giggle at my thought: Monty the mighty mouse. Tomorrow will be painful, because I'll have to spend all day with him. Monty's parents have gone to Kodaikanal with his sister to settle her into her new boarding school. They will pick him up a week later, on their way back.

"Meera, are you asleep?" Mom leans over me to check. I keep my eyes closed. She runs her hand over my face, lifts her fingers to her lips and kisses them. This is the loving gesture that I've seen both Mom and Nani do, many times. I keep very still and will her to leave. I like being alone in my room, so I can pretend. Sometimes I am a sailor on a ship, sleeping through a storm. Sometimes I am a princess escaping from her wicked step-mother, hiding in a tent in the woods. Sometimes I am a detective lying low in my hideout, waiting for something to happen. And sometimes I am Robin Hood in a Sherwood Forest treehouse. I drift off to sleep that night pretending that rather than my autumn break in Delhi, it is summer in Jaipur and Ari is going to visit me tomorrow evening.

* * *

"I always win Monopoly. Are you sure you want to play with me?" Monty wanted to know.

I don't want to play with you, stupid; Mom's making me. "We can play Monopoly. Unless you want to play something else…." Because he seems to be too busy squinting at the ceiling, I go in my room and pull out the Monopoly box. We set up and play until Super waddles over, disrupting our game. It's boring playing with Monty anyway.

"Your brother is a brat," says Monty.

"No, he is not."

"Yes he is."

"No, he is not, not, not." I defend Super, my eyes tearing up.

"What's going on, kids?" Mom comes into the room with her eyebrows raised.

"Noorie Aunty, we were just playing. Everything's fine." Monty lies smoothly. Mom looks at me. I imagine I am evidence to the contrary, as my fists are clenched and my face feels hot. Monty looks at me too through his slit-like eyes, daring me to say anything, but I just nod mutely at Mom. Finally she turns and goes back to the kitchen saying, "Well, play nicely with each other. Tonight we are having pizza for dinner, so keep your appetites ready."

I stalk off as soon as Mom is out of sight. Super is happy playing with the little Monopoly pieces, and frankly, I don't care what Monty does with himself. I am done playing nice and babysitting him. He is a big, rude, bully and he is welcome to die of boredom, as far as I am concerned. All I will say to that is 'good riddance'.

That night Papa tells us more stories about the antics he and Shaun Uncle got up to, making me forget about my earlier troubles with Mighty Mouse Monty. I can't help but laugh at the things Papa and Shawn Uncle did when they were children. Even when I go to bed my head is full of the stories and it's hard to stop smiling... till I remember that this is only Day Two and I have four more days of Monty to endure.

The next morning, soon after Papa leaves for work, much to my dismay Mom looks like she is getting ready to go somewhere too. "Where are you going?" I ask, as I lounge on my parents' big comfortable bed. Their room is large and to me it always looks kind of cool and blue, even on a hot afternoon. The morning light is muted as it creeps in through the wooden shades over the giant windows. I can see the ferns outside, so green and lush, through the shutters. The large purple and blue mango print on the quilt on the bed is so familiar. I just love Mom and Papa's room. It feels comfortable and safe.

I enjoy the feel of the oft-washed soft Indian cotton on my bare legs as I stretch out on my stomach, watching my Mom complete her getting-ready routine: smoothing her hair after putting two drops of coconut oil on her palms and rubbing them together; sticking a medium-round red *bindi* on the centre of her forehead; and smiling at herself in the mirror. Though I usually feel so peaceful in here, today I am restless.

"I am going to see Kajal Aunty. Uncle has his surgery today and she is so worried. I want to keep her company while he is being operated on. I will be back in a few hours. Chandra Aunty is coming too with her little son, so I'll take Sagar with me and they can play together. Isn't that nice?" Mom calls Super by his real name: Sagar. Only Mom calls him Sagar. Papa and I – and the whole world too – call him Super, but mom thinks Sagar is too lovely a name to not use. She used to try to make us call him Sagar too, but she finally gave up. When he was born, Rita began calling him Super, because she kept forgetting his real name. And soon everyone was calling him Super. Maybe some people don't even know his real name...ha! I am secretly pleased about this.

"When will you be back?"

"I told you – in a few hours, Meera." She looks annoyed now. "But you have Monty here to play with." I cringe at that thought. Even though the maid Rabdai is always home, she is hardly any company. I wonder if Monty would want to play, or instead find some new way to harass me. I can't wait for the day that slit-eye leaves. Then I can go back to observing ants and reading without anyone judging me or what I do. I look at Mom, trying to find some argument to have with her, but I can't come up with anything. Instead, I idly think that she looks kind of plump, bursting out of her sari.

* * *

I lie down on an old deck chair covered with a thin cotton mattress on the back porch of our house, near the ferns. If I open my eyes, from that spot I can look into Mom and Papa's bedroom through their window. Half of our back porch is covered by a canopy and the other half, by trees. It's really quite lovely.

I sleep. I dream that Ari is on the back porch with me. We are playing Monopoly, sitting on either side of a long deck chair. He is laughing about something. I love his laugh. Suddenly, a big slimy snake begins to crawl up my leg. Ari's laughter starts to sound strangely scary. I look towards him, desperately trying to scream for help, but no sound comes out of my throat. The snake has slid all the way up to my thigh. My eyes are wide and I start to turn red with the effort of trying to scream. Where is my voice? To my horror, Ari's face contorts and as I watch, beautiful safe Ari is growing scales. He is slowly turning into the snake.

My eyes fly open. I instantly realize that I've been dreaming. But something is still crawling up my thigh. I scream and sit up to see whatever it is. I expect some large insect and hope that it's not poisonous. I've heard stories about how painfully insect poison can kill you. My eyes widen in shock. I can't move. The 'insect' is Monty. His hand was sliding up my thigh and now lies motionless on the deck chair, because I had pulled away. Monty has a strange look in his slit-eyes that scares me from the inside out. I know I must escape him somehow and jump up. I start to turn to run. But he is too fast. He grabs my ankle. As hard as I try, I can't scramble out of his grasp.

"Be quiet," he orders through tight lips.

"What are you doing? Why are you touching me?" I panic now. I know Rabdai is old and half deaf and will not hear me from inside the house, even if I scream. Monty is too big and strong for me to push away. His hand is still clamped around my ankle and I am sprawled on the deck chair after my failed attempt to escape.

"There are things you don't understand yet, Meera. Just be quiet and I will let you know when you can leave." With my other foot I push against the hand grasping my ankle. "Stop it, Meera, or I will hit you. Just be quiet." Is he going to try some science experiment on me to try to turn me into an animal or something, I wonder. Or maybe he will put mud and dirt all over me.

To my surprise, he sprawls right on top of me. His weight squashes me against the cotton mattress on the deck chair. I can't move my head. My cheek is pinned against the mattress by his shoulder. My head is forced to one side – I can see the purple and blue of the mangoes on the bedspread through the half open shutters of Mom and Papa's bedroom window. Monty's heavy legs are lying on mine, holding them in place, slightly apart. One of his hands is under my skirt and on my panties. He seems to be searching for something in my private parts. Why is he touching me there? What is he looking for? I narrow my eyes at the purple and blue splashes, desperately trying to see the shape of the mangoes, but I can't. I don't know why, but it makes me very sad. I start to cry. I wish I could see the shape of the mangoes, but all I can see through the tears in my eyes is a blur of purple and blue.

Monty is squirming on top of me and making strange noises. It sounds like he's panting. Suddenly he stops and kind of presses down hard on me with his whole body. Is he dead? I don't know how long he lies like that. It could be one minute or thirty. I can't tell because all the while I'm trying to see the mangoes through my tears.

Suddenly, he gets up, holds my side-turned face and pulls so that I look at him. He's breathing hard, and his eyes look everywhere, but not at me. He seems afraid of something, or maybe embarrassed. He glances around and then says, "Look, this is our secret. Don't tell anyone what we did, okay? People don't understand some things, so just don't tell anyone anything. And if you do tell anyone, even one person, I will kill you. I have a bottle of poison and I will make you drink it. Okay?" I nod without making a sound. What am I supposed to not tell? What have we done? "Anyway, you are too small and you don't even have knockers," Monty says smugly. "I did you a favour. Now you will learn about real life and stop counting your silly ants, or whatever you do. Go to the bathroom and wash your face. I don't know why you are crying. Stupid."

I don't know either why I am crying, and I don't know how he knows about the ants. It seems silly that not being able to see the mangoes on the bedspread is making me cry. I can't tell him that's why I'm crying. Besides, I should not be crying in front of Monty anyway. I rub my eyes very hard and get up off the deck chair. My body feels heavy and hurts. I don't say anything. I just slowly walk into the house.

* * *

For the rest of Monty's stay I try to keep close to either Mom or Papa. Monty wants me to play Monopoly with him, but I fake a stomach ache. The next day, he finds me alone in the hallway and squeezes my buttock hard. I run to the kitchen and hear him sneer.

I am not sure what he did to me that day on the back porch or why, but I don't like to think about it. I look okay, and it's not like my skin is turning green or anything like that. But I worry anyway. What if whatever he was trying to do didn't work the first time and he'll try it again to make sure it works? Or maybe it will have a delayed effect and something will happen to me after he leaves. Still, I can't wait for him to go. I pray to Lord Krishna that Monty didn't give me leprosy or cancer, because I know those things are really bad. In a documentary I saw in school last year, I learned that when people get leprosy, their skin gets white spots and they start losing feeling in those spots. I find some white spots on my arm and I poke them with one of Mom's safety pins to check. To my relief it hurt, and bled. I don't know how to rule out cancer though.

I am more sullen and quiet than usual. Papa asks if I am alright. "So far so good," I tell him. He looks at me with concern. I am afraid Monty may make me drink poison if I tell anyone, but I know Papa would protect me. I almost tell him about the afternoon Monty squashed me in the deck chair. But then, I can't tell him. I know that I am Papa's baby girl and I don't want to tell Papa anything that might upset him, or make him see me differently.

There was one more thing that happened before Monty left. Papa and Mom had taken Super to the doctor. I couldn't think of any reason to go with them. I decided I would be safe if I stayed indoors and watched TV, especially because Monty had stayed away from me for the last three days, so maybe he had lost interest in trying his tricks on me. Maybe it was because I don't have knockers... whatever that means. That's what he'd said that day on the back porch. Besides, I knew Rabdai was cleaning in the TV room, and Monty wouldn't do anything with someone else present – he wouldn't want anyone to know, he said I should not tell anyone. Mom and Papa said they would be back in half an hour.

"Where are you going?" I ask Rabdai.

"Need to use the bathroom," she mutters before disappearing down the hallway.

Right on cue, Monty appears. Was he waiting for this chance? I grab a cushion, holding it like a shield to protect myself. He sits down next to me on the couch.

"You should thank me, Meera." Suddenly he looks afraid. "You haven't told anyone, have you?"

"Am I going to get leprosy or cancer?" I blurt, as I shake my head and blink back tears.

Monty bursts out laughing. "You are stupider than I thought." Then suddenly he grabs my shoulders and brings his face very close to mine. Before I know what is happening, he starts doing the mouth-to-mouth thing they did in *Superman* when Mom made me cover my eyes. (I peeked, though.) His mouth is pressing down on mine and he is trying to open my mouth with his tongue and lips. It's really very nasty. I don't know why Superman and Lois Lane do this. My friend Bhavi told me that is how big people who are boyfriend and girlfriend kiss. It feels so yucky! I feel Monty's tongue in my mouth. It is leathery and dry, even though he is slobbering on my face. Just when I think I will vomit, he suddenly stops and scoots over to the other end of the couch. I am still trying to stop the vomit feeling when Rabdai comes back into the room and starts her cleaning again, with no idea what had just happened.

"That's wrong. I know children are not supposed to do that," I hiss at Monty, feeling safe with Rabdai in the room. "I know it's wrong."

He looks scared again. "Don't tell anyone!" he orders. "Or, like I told you, I'll make you drink poison."

"I am not afraid of you anymore, you bad person!" I jump up from the couch. "And don't ever do anything to me again!"

Just then I hear Mom, Papa and Super come back. To his utter shock and mine too, I spit at Monty before running into the bathroom to brush my teeth and wash my mouth out, several times. Monty leaves that evening. I avoid talking much with anyone. I just want him to be gone. Shawn Uncle tries to joke around with me, but I glare even at him. Later, after they are gone, and we've said our good-nights, I hear the faint sounds of Mom and Papa arguing about something in their room. I don't care as much as I normally would. Instead, I snuggle deeper into my bed and cover my head with my pillow. Everyone is tired that night. I am too, but my sleep is not restful.

* * *

I am surprised that it's already past ten in the morning when I wake up. I never sleep that late. Papa has left for work. In my pajamas, I go straight to the front room where Mom is sitting, sipping a cup of *chai*. Super is not around. He's probably playing in his room, or napping. I have to tell her.

I blurt it all out in a rush: "Mom, Monty did the lip-kiss on me and it was very dirty. And he also did something bad to me on the back porch. He lay on me and made some noises and he touched my panties and I think he was looking for something in my privates. I don't think he gave me leprosy, but I don't know if I got cancer." I said it all very fast, without stopping.

Mom stops drinking her *chai*, holding the cup up just before it touched her mouth. She stares at me. I can't tell if she is angry, or not. Her eyes are red, like she's been crying, or drinking too much wine, and her face looks blank and strange. Papa's eyes get red the next morning after he drinks alcohol at his work parties, but I've never known Mom to drink. Maybe she is sick. I wonder if she will have a fit and start frothing at the mouth like the woman in a TV show I once watched. I wonder if she cried because she argued with Papa last night. I don't want to ask. I just stare back at her, waiting. After several moments she blinks and smiles.

"Oh, you are a strange one! Come here, Meera." She wraps me in a hug. "You must not say such things about family or friends. How can you make such nonsense up? My dear, dear girl, I think you need to read some good books and take Lord Krishna's name so that you get good thoughts in your head. You must not say such a thing to anyone or about anyone. You understand? Now drink some water, wash your face and come eat something. I didn't wake you up early because you seemed tired yesterday. You know, you were grumpy at dinner. Come on, eat something and get into a good mood."

"But I am not making anything up, Mom. I am not making anything up." Hot tears prick at the back of my eyes.

"Meera, these are not good things to say. Why do you have to say such things?" Mom looks exasperated.

"But I didn't do anything. I tried to run away and stop him. And I am not making it up." I am crying now. "He said he would make me drink poison if I tell, so I waited till he left, just to make sure. And my skin has not turned green or anything, but I don't know if it's a kind of black magic that he did. And I don't know if I will get can... cancer." I sob.

"Oh Meera, you will not get cancer. And he does not have black magic powers. No one has done anything to you. Do you understand? Now I don't want you to talk about this nonsense to anyone else and I want you to forget such bad thoughts."

"But, Mom, it's true. Aren't you going to give me medicine? Will you do anything to him for what he did to me?"

"Look, *Raja-beta*," Mom tries to reason while using her special name for me. *Raja-beta* literally translated to English, means king-son. Papa's special name for me is Chinks, which doesn't mean anything. I prefer Chinks to king-son. "I promise that no black magic has been done to you. I want you to believe me – nothing is going to happen to you. You are fine. Go wash up and come to eat. You will feel much better then. And don't talk about this again."

I stomp off. There is nothing I can do or say. It feels as though a huge weight has been put on my shoulders. It almost feels worse than it did when Monty was doing those things to me. Why doesn't she believe me? Did I do something wrong? Is it my fault somehow that Monty did those things? And is Mom covering up for him? I wish Ari were here. Irrationally, I think all this would never have happened if he had been here. And if by chance it did happen, I could at least ask him all my questions and he would give me honest answers. It is his fault that I feel this way – lost and confused and very, very small. And I hate the mango print on the bedspread now. And I hate Ari even more.

2

Meera Myna Dutt

Today is the day I've been waiting for – I am finally thirteen years old. I am now a teenager and, officially, superior to Super. It's been five and a half years since the Monty incidents and I've changed. I am completely different from the person I was back then. I was a bit naive all that time ago. I now know that what Monty did to me is called molestation. I don't think about it much anymore.

I love spending time with Rini, my best friend since third grade. She and I have learned so much together, especially recently. For example, Rini and I know about adult things like sex – from the school library; from Karina who watched her mom and dad bathe together through the bathroom keyhole; and from Pala, Karina's older sister, who likes to educate us with pictures, books and actual stories of what she does with her boyfriend. I find it all very interesting, but filthy and disgusting at the same time. I don't really think about sex too much, except when Karina tells us stuff. Rini and I discuss our new-found tidbits of knowledge in hushed voices, knowing that it would be dangerous for the wrong ears to overhear us. It is kind of strange that adults go to such lengths to keep sex a secret from us. But we must indulge them in their thinking that they are hiding something, because they get upset if they realize we already know.

I still haven't told Rini about what Monty did to me. I don't think I will. Actually, I haven't told anyone after Mom told me not to, and I haven't brought it up again with Mom either. I think I avoid Mom most of the time now. If we try to talk, we end up arguing about anything and everything. I know I have to talk to her about eating, homework, bedtime and such. And I have to deal with her when Super and I fight. But other than these kinds of things, I avoid her. She tries to spend time with me, but she is usually too busy looking after Super and the house. Anyway, I'm glad she does not have too much time to spare. Besides, I'm busy with school, Rini, my world of make-believe and my books. The best thing Mom does for me is buy me dozens and dozens of books. It almost feels like a competition. Can I read faster than she buys them? Or does she buy them faster than I read them? For the books, I will always be grateful to her. The books let me forgive her a tiny little bit.

Papa is another matter. My Papa is a handsome and happy man, untouched by all things impure. He is never too busy for me, and usually he seems delighted to spend time with me. We go for walks together. That's our thing. We talk about constellations, philosophy, religion, my friends and his work. He is doing well at work. I heard Mom tell someone on the phone a few days ago that he has 'climbed the corporate ladder'. I am not sure exactly what the corporate ladder is, but I know it means that he is doing well at work. Mom and Papa don't seem to like each other much, so I am most grateful that she is glad for his progress. I say a silent thank you to Lord Krishna for this.

That being said, I am not sure what to do about Lord

Krishna. I know Rini does not believe in Him. She says she believes in 'good', not 'God'. But isn't Lord Krishna an embodiment of 'good'? So isn't it kind of the same thing? Besides, in the Krishna story, Lord Krishna is mischievous and I like that. I don't see much difference between good and God, but I won't admit this to Rini. It is safer to remain undecided regarding Lord Krishna's existence and powers. I don't want to fight with Rini and risk her grumpiness. But then neither can I really let go of my belief in Lord Krishna, though again I won't admit this to Rini.

Rini can get grumpy and moody sometimes. But though I don't like it, it is okay and I understand. She has an older brother, Raju, who is mentally disabled. Rini and her family find it insulting when it is called 'mental retardation'. They don't like to talk much about Raju or his condition. Raju goes to a special school, and Rini's parents are completely devoted to his care. Rini says that because Raju needs a lot of attention from their parents, they don't have a lot of time to spare for her. Rini understands this, but I think it makes her grumpy. It's because she always has to be the understanding one. I try to give her attention and include her in our family as much as I can.

I decide to think about all this later because it *is* my birthday after all, and I *am* supposed to enjoy my day. Mom bursts into my room and grasps me in a tight hug. "Happy birthday, my sweet child! I wish you lots and lots of joy and fun and success in the year to come." I cringe at her calling me 'child', but smile in response and dutifully hug her back.

"I am thir*teen. Teen.*" I repeat for emphasis. "That's almost an adult."

Papa is right behind her and I roll my eyes, communicating silently with him regarding Mom's cluelessness. But it feels celebratory and I am smiling in spite of Mom. Thirteen is a big deal. Super, my annoying eight-year-old brother, wants to wish me a happy birthday, and because I am in a very good mood this morning, I allow all the wishing and hugging they want. Unfortunately, today is a Thursday and I have school. I know we'll go out to dinner this evening to celebrate, as we always do on birthdays. Right now though, I can't wait to see Rini – even though I have to go to school to see her.

* * *

"Neel wants to tell you something." Praveen says to me in a hushed voice as Rini and I walk past him. Rini is the leader, and I am kind of shy, quiet and studious. I am not by any stretch the most popular girl in class, but I am still far from an outcast. I have earned respect for doing well in subjects like English, algebra and art. Rini and I have a handful of friends. These are stragglers who don't fit into any of the tighter groupings. Outside our handful, when someone wants to address either Rini or me, mostly they talk to her. And I am happy to let her respond on my behalf too. During lunch, Rini and I walk around the school grounds, chatting. Sometimes one of the stragglers joins us, but I like it best when it's just Rini and me. I am very surprised to hear that Neel wants to tell *me* something. Neel is one of the more popular boys in our class. I've heard some of the girls have a crush on him.

In our eighth grade class, Zohra is the only one who has a boyfriend so far. Zohra began shaving her legs when we were all in sixth grade. She was the first to do that. We were fascinated and would want to feel the little hairs when they grew back. She used to be coy with the boys when most of us still hated them. Now, however, many of the girls shave or wax their legs, arms, upper lips, armpits and goodness knows what else. Rini and I don't do that yet. I want to wax my legs, but Mom won't let me. Rini doesn't care because she is Rini – the good, steady, solid girl who does not care about frivolous things or outward appearances. Rini is pretty and sweet, but once she starts talking, the boys realize how sensible and practical she is, and back away. As for me, I am perceived as too quiet and strange to be handled by anyone except Rini.

"Meet us behind the big tree in the yard at lunch," Praveen instructs. I glance around, but no one seems to have heard. I nod mutely and move away.

* * *

"I think we should absolutely not go, Meera. It could be dangerous," Rini says responsibly. "They could be planning to play a prank or something. Besides, it's not safe to meet boys alone like that."

"But it's only in the school yard. They can't do anything that bad. They would know they could get caught," I try to convince her.

We are standing under the butterfly tree, debating furtively. This is the tree in the front of the school building under which we buried the butterfly Zohra killed when we were in sixth grade. Zohra wanted the color from the butterfly wings and, to our horror, she pinched the butterfly until the yellow of the wings came off on her fingers. We'd been too late to save the butterfly. It made Rini and me sad. We shrouded the poor discarded butterfly in two leaves, dug a small grave at the base of the tree and buried it. Then, with tears in our eyes, we'd decorated the top of the grave with flowers. We had even said a small prayer, because at that time Rini believed in Lord Krishna too. Since then, we feel that the butterfly's soul hovers near the tree and watches over us. We come to the butterfly tree to think or to argue our differences. We believe that if we argue under the butterfly tree, we will resolve our differences and walk away hand in hand. Today's decision is a tough one though.

"You are too rash, Meera. Why do you need to know what Neel wants? Who cares? It is risky, I am telling you," says Rini for the tenth time. "I don't think this is a good idea at all. Why did that stupid Praveen have to say anything to begin with?"

"He was just giving me the message. Let's go, Rini. Let's find out. I swear we can run faster than they can. And if he tries any prank, we'll just run back into the yard where every-one's playing. Okay? Aren't you curious? Come *on*." I drag her before she has time to think it through.

We make our way to the yard and slowly approach the big tree at the far end. It is away from the area where everyone plays. If someone is standing behind the tree, they can be completely blocked from view from the other side. My heart is beating so loud I am worried that Neel and Praveen may hear it. What if they aren't even there? I just realize Rini and I are holding hands, and that gives away our nervousness. When we reach the tree, I let go of her hand and walk to the other side. My palms are sweaty and I can hear my heart pound. There they are. Praveen and Neel, standing with arms crossed, leaning against the tree.

"Thanks for coming," Neel starts.

I stand still. When it's evident that I am not going to respond, he glances at Rini. "Hi, Rini." Turning back to me, he says, "I hope you both don't mind that I asked you to come here, Meera. I just wanted to say something."

"Go ahead." I nod, positioning my feet in a run-ready state just in case this turns out unpleasant. I glance at Rini, wanting to make sure she is ready to scoot too. Ever cautious, she is all set, and I suspect she has been ready to run since the moment we got here.

"I... um. It's nothing important, I mean it *is* important, but... it's not like it's something like that. It's kind of a surprise... maybe... for you. Like a... um... you know how it is."

Neel is not making much sense and I am surprised to hear him speak like this. He is one of the best speakers in elocution class, so it's even weirder. Praveen nudges him from behind and whispers something urgent-sounding.

"Um... I wrote something. It's just that I'm a bit... um." He smiles almost shyly. "Meera, it's just um... without you I am like a rose without its thorn... I mean a thorn without the stem... Oh gosh, I am not saying this right. You are the rose in the poem, and I'd just really like to kiss you." He claps his hand over his mouth, looking as shocked and wide eyed as I feel.

"What do you mean, Neel?" Before I know it, Rini is at my side.

"I like you, Meera." Neel continues looking at me. "I hope you like me. And I am sorry I said that previous thing about the... um... kiss."

"B... but aren't you going to trick us? Is this the trick?" I am confused now.

"No, I mean it. It's not a trick. I really like you." Neel looks earnest. He takes a folded paper out of his pocket. "Look here, I wrote the rose poem. You are like a rose, Meera."

"He really likes you. As in the *love* kind of like." Praveen defends Neel.

"But why?" I ask.

"Because you are so sweet and quiet and pretty; And because I just like you. I know I am younger than you are, but only by five months, you know." Neel makes his case.

I am not sweet or quiet, I think in my head. And I'm not pretty either. This is really awkward.

"We need to think about things." Rini saves the day and I love her for stepping in. She grabs my hand and we head back towards the populated area of the yard.

* * *

"We have something to tell you kids." Papa says quietly in the midst of my birthday dinner at Rangoli that evening. "You are having another brother or sister."

What! Really? What is today? A day for shocks? What does he mean? I didn't know my birthday was going to be so explosive. First, Neel likes me, and I don't even know what to do about *that*. And now they are having another *baby*? *Really!*

"As in, Mom's pregnant?" I ask to confirm that I understood right. Super seems oblivious to the life-altering aspect of this news.

"Yes," says Papa. "So now you kids have to help Mom with chores."

No wonder she has been looking even plumper than usual. I am not sure what to think. Super is annoying enough; we don't need another baby. Mom has no time for anything as it is, and I don't think she is very mentally stable, because she has mood swings and emotional outbursts. I am busy studying and I now have the Neel dilemma to sort out too. On top of that, Papa and I have our routine and Super is just plain stupid. So who is left to care for this new baby?

"I don't think it's a good idea, Papa." I say, matter of fact.

Papa looks silently at me for a moment. "We will manage." I think he is willing me to keep quiet. And for Papa I hold my tongue and don't argue.

"Are you excited?" Mom asks, smiling.

"Sure," I say. "Congratulations."

Like Super, she seems oblivious, but Papa is watching me intently. The food doesn't taste as good as usual.

* * *

"Meera, what is worrying you?" Papa has come to my room, sits by my bed and strokes my hair back from my forehead, the way I like. Papa's hand on my head is the most calming thing ever. I feel tears prick at my eyes.

"She can't take care of another baby, Papa." I am talking about Mom. *She couldn't even take care of me,* I want to add.

"She will be fine, Chinks," Papa calls me by my favorite name. "Sometimes things happen for a reason and we have to accept them as God's gift to us. Maybe this child is God's gift to us. Things have a way of working out. Don't worry. I am here and, between you and me, we are a pretty tough team."

We *are* a tough team. "Will you love the new baby more?" I ask.

"Meera, the happiest day of my life was the day you were born and nothing will ever change that." Papa answers.

"I hope it's not a boy like Super."

Papa laughs. "Super is a good kid."

"How old were you when you liked a girl for the first time?" I change the subject.

"Does someone like you?" The laughter is gone from Papa's voice.

"Um... no, it's Rini." I lie. "We think *maybe* someone might like her. But we are not sure about anything right now. It's a very big maybe. I'll let you know." I regret it as soon as I say it. Papa thinks of Rini as another daughter. Rini looks upon Papa as the attentive father figure in her life, because her own father is so busy with her brother all the time. Papa will worry about this now.

"You both are very young. There will be a right time for you to explore such things. But not yet. Yours is not the age to get involved with boys. You know girls mature much before boys. Boys your age don't know what they want. You give Rini good advice. And if she wants to, she can talk to me. You know that, right?"

"Yes, Papa." I dutifully say. I love my Papa so much that it is the singular most powerful feeling I have. But I have to explore my own world too. I think Mom and Papa's marriage makes them both unhappy. That's why I have to take care of Papa. Loving Papa and Rini is easy. But I don't know about love of the romantic sort... the sort that Mom and Papa are supposed to have, but don't seem to. And I don't have time for it. There is a lot I have to mull over. New baby, Lord Krishna, Papa... My list is long and I can't spend too much time on Neel and his absurd proposal. That night, after a very long time I dream about someone I even forgot I had forgotten. Ari is in my dreams again.

* * *

"Meera, you have to say no to him. I know Neel is good looking, but really, we are not ready and you know if your parents find out, it won't be good," Rini advises at lunch the next day.

"But I want to know how it feels to kiss." I giggle. I don't tell Rini that I used her name to deflect Papa's questions. I feel guilty about it, but push it to the back of my mind.

"Shut up," she giggles back. "Be serious, stupid. It is dangerous to do such things. Let's wait till we are older. My mom told me she waited till she got married."

"After my mom's baby comes, I think I'm going to be busy, so I better try the kiss now, before the baby." I am laughing like a lunatic now, but I can't quite pinpoint what I find so funny.

"Meera, be serious!" Rini scolds, though she herself is laughing.

"Okay, okay. What do I tell him? I feel so strange in class. I mean can you believe it! A poem about a rose – who does that these days?" I say, though I secretly think it is very sweet. In fact, the thing I like the most about the Neel episode is the poem. It is the most romantic thing anyone has ever done for me. Actually it is the only romantic thing anyone has ever done for me, except when Ari called me a beautiful lady. But then I quickly and sternly remind myself that I probably don't believe in that kind of love anyway.

"Yes, the poem is uncool," Rini confirms. "I think you should write a note saying, *'Thank you, but no thank you'*."

"Should I sign it 'With *love*, Meera'?" I giggle.

"Oh, the poor boy will not know what to do!"

Finally, Rini pushes me to write the note. It says:

Dear Neel,

Thank you for the nice things you said. I think you are quite nice.

I am sorry, but right now I can't be your girlfriend or anything.

And right now I can't kiss either.

It's just not cool in my family right now.

Plus, I will be busy, because I am having a new brother or sister soon.

Thanks.

Meera

After I write it, I am not sure about all the 'right nows', but Rini says its fine, and we slip it in his desk.

Later that day, we are all at our desks for journal writing. I sit at an angle one row behind Neel and so I spy him reading the note hidden between the pages of his journal. He looks up and turns suddenly and catches my eye. I am embarrassed and I look away. I think there is a tear in his eye, but it must be my imagination. No thirteen-year-old boy cries over a girl, right?

* * *

Laila Myna Dutt is born in the summer of 1985, when I am thirteen-and-a-half and Super is eight-and-a-half years old. India is recovering from the Golden Temple shootout, Indira Gandhi's assassination and the riots that shook not only Delhi, but the entire country. Indira Gandhi's handsome son Rajiv Gandhi is appointed as the new prime minister and he brings fresh new hope.

Just like Laila brings fresh new excitement to my life. She is the most beautiful, most exquisite, most pure baby I have ever seen. I thought it would be like when Super was born, but it's not. I love this baby so much. She's mine. I've decided that Papa and I are the main caregivers for Laila. I feel fiercely protective of her. As long as I am around, she will only feel happy and comfortable. She will never feel neglected. She will never be hurt like I was. And she will never know how it feels to not be believed.

I rush home from school each day, eager to see Laila. I change her diaper. I feed her milk. I read to her and play with her. And I watch the wonder that is my little sister. She is smart and strong-willed from the start. She is a strong baby too; she has a good grip and kick. Her first word is my name – 'Mia' is how she pronounces it. *Mia.*

Rini is almost as fascinated with Laila as I am. She comes home with me whenever her mom lets her. Laila loves Rini and me. Actually, Laila loves everybody. And everybody loves Laila. Even Super, who, besides taking apart all the remote controls and pens in the house, is generally engrossed in his toy cars and helicopters, but stops what he is doing for Laila. She is a happy baby and almost never cries.

Mom is grateful that Laila is such a good natured baby, but she is lost somewhere in her own world and is glad to hand Laila over to me as soon as I return from school. Rabdai and Mom enjoy Laila, but I think she tires them out in the mornings. They both look relieved when I come home. Then Laila and I are lost in our world and at times, Super joins us too. Sometimes we make Super a dog and Laila gets to ride around on his back. Sometimes we just play with her little blocks and dolls. I never tire of playing with Laila, or feeding her, or changing her, or bathing her. She is my little live doll.

Papa too is caught in Laila's spell. His eyes light up when he sees her. I am not jealous though. Laila is too small, too precious and too loveable for me to be jealous. Besides, she is mine, so of course Papa better love her.

It is not odd then that I am by Laila's side, a fiercely protective sister, when Monty visits with his family. Nobody catches on that I won't let Monty hold Laila, stepping in between, making an excuse that she needs to be changed, when she is being passed around. Mom makes a joke about how I'm so maternal with Laila, even more than she is. But I see in Monty's eyes that he knows exactly what I am doing... and why.

Monty catches me in the hallway as I am bringing Laila back. "Meera, I just want to say hi and see how you are. I got you colouring pencils from Singapore during my trip. I gave them to Noorie Aunty for you." He knows I understand now what he did to me. He is cautious, wanting to gauge me. Perhaps he feels apologetic. It is too late, though. He has no business being in my home or in my life now.

"Go away, Monty," is all I can manage through gritted teeth. I don't know how to say the things that are in my head. I don't want him to exist. At the same time, I don't want to acknowledge my thoughts about him – the memories or my anger. And I certainly don't want his colouring pencils from Singapore. It is so much easier to focus on the good things, the easy things in life. Now that I have Laila, there is an important purpose to my days.

Fortunately, Laila brings a previously unknown peace, joy and sense of balance to me. In fact, her existence has cast a magical glow on us all, a delicate yet tenacious shield protecting us. I figure that the rumblings of the past have been put to rest.

But little do I know that trauma and grief, and deep-seated primal feelings are not resolved until they *are* resolved. Feelings may be packed away, but they don't just disappear. In spite of Laila, I have a growing darkness inside me. I don't know what this is from, but I know I didn't have it before the Monty incident, or rather before the experience of telling Mom and her not believing me. The only way to fight darkness is to shed light on it – but I don't know this, so I fight to keep the darkness in the dark.

3

Ari Hasan Jana

I love Mauritius. It is beautiful – the beaches, the freedom, the air, the freedom, the women, the freedom. Did I mention the freedom?

Do I miss Jaipur? I don't miss anything or anybody. The food perhaps, not the people though. I'm unattached to attachment. Attachments and expectations create misery. I'm glad I got away from the trappings of Jaipur's suppressive society. My ex-girlfriend Renu should have seen that I am not the attachment type. Mmm… I am so glad about the 'ex' factor. It was becoming stifling. I understand that some people want the commitment thing and Renu wanted more from our relationship after two years together. But she could not accept that I'm just not the type. I didn't have to make up excuses for breaking it off with Renu. The move did it for me. Happily, I was acquitted without a trial. I'm sorry she felt so badly but… oh well… there are always casualties in love and war. It's not like I intended to hurt her, and I was clear that I didn't believe in commitment, monogamy or anything of that sort. I wish her well. She will recover. Everybody does, eventually. Right?

I admit I feel kind of sad when I remember sweet young Meera. It's those eyes and their innocence laced with some sort of pain, I think, or anger. Something drew me to her as if she was a kindred soul... but so young. It's just a fleeting thought. There is a lot to be done, a lot of life to be relished, dope to be smoked and parties to be enjoyed. Maybe I'll convince Dad that I'm old enough and responsible enough to get a motorbike. Then I'll have to find myself a job. Maybe Dad can set me up in Banko Mauritius with a super cute boss in a mini-skirt.

There are so many beautiful women here. For instance, Mrs Chichi – our neighbour – is much older, but quite attractive for her age. She has been eyeing me since we got here. Ha! But then I certainly am an eyeful.

I'm living it up and enjoying my existence. I will not repeat my siblings', or my parents' mistakes. Bhaijan, the mighty first born to my parents, would be stark raving mad if he got a glimpse into my mind. Bhaijan has written me off as a nut job as it is. My industrious brother is allowed his audacities and is respected in spite of them. How is that fair? Bhaijan is on his third marriage and has six children, three from the first and three from his current third wife. He tired of his first wife (admittedly, for good reason); he drove his second wife insane and now is enjoying the affections of his third wife, twenty years his junior and mother of three in just five years of marriage. No one gossips about him, though. He has money, and money gives power. As for my other two brothers and three sisters, none of them hit the jackpot. Each one succumbed to the dream of love and ended up unhappy. Either divorced or on their second marriages, which haven't proven to be an improvement over their first. Universally, they are still searching for fulfillment.

I will not succumb to money, power or woman. I know how to keep myself safe. Besides, I need to get on Mrs. Chichi's schedule; it might be good for me.

4

Meera Myna Dutt

I am in Super's room, helping him with his homework. He tops his class in math and science, but when it comes to book reports and creative writing, he bribes or guilts me into helping him. "Papa is having an affair." Super says.

I am shocked by this completely unanticipated declaration. "What? What nonsense! Where do you get such stupid ideas from?"

"I heard Mom say that."

"To whom?"

"Chandra Aunty, I think. It was on the phone."

"It is NOT true. She must be talking about a movie or something. You just got it mixed up."

"I am telling you, I heard it."

"You know Mom can get weird sometimes. She imagines things too."

"Okay." Super doesn't like discussing anything much. He is content with his five sentence discussions, but I'm not.

"What do you mean okay?"

"I said okay. Now can we finish my project? *Please!*"

"Seems like it doesn't bother you? What you heard."

"Yeah. It doesn't bother me."

Super is only eleven and too young for such things. It's

strange to me that he even knows the meaning of 'affair'… perhaps he doesn't know the full implication of the accusation. I hope he does not. Regardless, not much bothers him, but I fret about what he said.

More importantly, who will stop Mom from her mumblings about these things she imagines? Mom is often irrational and sometimes loud. In my opinion, she's always been slightly unstable, but after Laila's birth she has progressively become more and more ridiculous. I don't understand why Mom has fits of anger. She is loving and everything seems fine, and then suddenly she gets inexplicably angry. She directs her anger mostly at Papa. He is an easy target. She's unfair to him, and he silently absorbs it all without a single angry word in response. Though I am not surprised by Mom's affair accusation, it is a new low, even for Mom. I almost hate her. The problem is, I love her too. I have to be the shield for Papa and Super as much as I can. Thankfully Laila is untouched by all this, or so I think.

"If you believe it, then why doesn't it bother you?"

"It's his life. He should live it as he likes." Super shrugs.

"Well, he is not having an affair, and you should not think about it." I feel suffocated.

"I don't think about it. Maybe *you* should stop thinking about it."

Knowing Super, he will probably never bring it up again. As for me, I will probably never forget it. I could confront Mom, but it is not worth it, especially with Nani unwell, and my impending trip. I take deep breaths and turn to his homework.

* * *

I am so excited to be on my first flight alone. I am going

from Delhi to Jaipur. But even though I am sixteen, I still can't help the butterflies in my stomach. I check my handbag, probably for the eleventh time, to ensure that I have my ticket. I check the departure board again and then look at my watch. I hope the flight lands on time.

I feel the stir of anxious anticipation. I hope Nani recovers from her pneumonic cough soon. Mom sounded worried. I can't wait to see both her and my cousin Rita. I haven't seen them for nearly two years. I wish Papa and Laila were with me. Though I've always liked my Jaipur trips, I've never liked the part about leaving Papa behind. And now I feel that way with Laila too. This is the first time I will be away from my charming little two-year-old sister who cried when they dropped me off at the airport. I hope Mom does not have her anger outbursts, and nothing dramatic happens while I am gone. Mom and Laila will be joining me in Jaipur in a week.

I notice that my knuckles are white from clutching the strap of my handbag. I remind myself that I am supposed to enjoy this first time experience and not fret about my family, and purposefully loosen my grip, straighten my back and keep my eyes on my book, feeling very small in the large Delhi airport full of busy-looking strangers. Finally, I hear the boarding call. The flight attendant has been asked to look after me because I am flying unaccompanied. The flight is uneventful, and I feel about a foot taller with my new-found confidence after flying solo.

I excitedly spot my aunties. My eyes keep searching, but I don't see the person I am looking for.

"Rita had to go to her school for some special summer project she is doing," my aunt gently explains. "And Nani is coughing less and sitting up in bed now."

Rita picked her school project over seeing me? This is, after all, my first trip back since Laila's birth. I try to smile, but there is a lump in my throat. Rita and I have been close since we were toddlers, inseparable during each summer of our childhood. We shared almost everything. That doesn't change if we don't see each other for two years, does it?

My aunties are chatting away, oblivious to my thoughts. I robotically respond to the standard inquiries and comments about how I've changed. Laila and Super are fine; and Mom and Papa are fine too. Everyone's health is alright. Yes, I have gained some *curves*; yes, I am wearing *bras* now (but do we have to talk about that?). School is going well; everyone keeps busy; everyone gets along. We reach Magic Mansion and, before I know it, I am in Nani's room, by her large bed, engulfed in her hug. Grandmas have a special kind of love reserved for only their grandchildren. And it is in endless supply. To my embarrassment, I feel tears prick at my eyes and I try to swallow them away. Nani is the best... and sometimes I forget that. Around her, I don't mind being a child.

"Come on, Nani," I say. "Back in Delhi everybody is worried about your health, but you look hale and hearty to me. You look like you could go dancing in your mini-skirt tonight. Why are you making everyone worry by staying in bed?"

Nani laughs as I strike up my usual jovial and impudent banter with her. "Meera, you have not changed one bit." I love teasing Nani and I know she enjoys it. Nobody else talks to her in this manner. Rita is too proper for impudence, and she does not know how much joy Nani gets from this.

"Nani, you have to get up, out of this bed and shake your you-know-what to feel even better. And what is this oldies hairstyle you have? Let's get you a nice trendy haircut today."

She's laughing and I'm on a roll. I even turn around and wiggle my butt to show her what I mean.

Nani is laughing so much that she starts coughing, so I stop. "Meera, tell me – why have you not come to see your Nani in two years?"

"I am sorry, Nani. I should have come sooner. After Laila, it's been busy. School is awful. They give us so much work, I don't know what they are thinking. We are kids, not machines! Laila is so big now, Nani. You will see her in a week when Mom and she come. I know you saw her in Delhi, but you will be amazed. She is so smart, strong and beautiful. The complete package!"

"As are you, Meera... as are you," Nani says.

It is wonderful to be back. I have missed Jaipur so much. Now if only Rita would come back and tell me how she messed up my arrival day in her head, or else she would never have missed picking me up, all would be fine in my world right now. But in my oblivion I don't even suspect that this is the summer that will change everything between Rita and me forever.

* * *

I have washed up and settled in. It is time for dinner and still there is no sign of Rita. This is ridiculous. And then suddenly, there she is standing by the door. Twirling her long single braid around her finger, wisps of hair framing her lovely face. My cousin has always been so delicate, so feminine looking. She brings up the image of a fragrant petal, soft and pink, with a dewdrop balanced on it. She is beautiful. When I was younger, I would try to imitate her style. But I gave up, convinced that I looked comical in my attempts. I resigned myself to just admiring her.

She has a half smile on her lips and a dreamy look in her eyes. She looks somehow different. Older? Lovelier? I don't understand this change, but I feel it standing like a wall between us, challenging the familiar.

"Meera, Meera, oh Meera!" She sounds somewhat dramatic.

"Rita, where have you been? It's been hours since I came. You didn't even come to the airport to get me," I say accusingly.

"I know, I know. I thought you might be upset by that. Look, I am sorry, Meera. But I have so much to tell you. You are not going to believe what's been going on. Let's go eat quickly and then go up to the terrace to talk. Okay? I promise you will understand."

Dinner is done and we are lying on our backs on thin cool cotton mattresses on the terrace. Rita has just told me about Jai, her *boyfriend*, and how much he *loves* her and she him. It sounds appalling to me that she would skip coming to the airport for a *boyfriend*. She promised I would understand, but I don't. I want to cry, and shockingly, I want to slap her. I want it to be like it was before. Rita and I used to be partners in everything – baking mud cakes in the sun, playing shop on endless afternoons with paper money and toys, attempting our first experiments in the kitchen together. I can't tell her she must take back the last ten minutes, because I am supposed to be happy for her... I think. So I just remain silent and keep staring at the stars up in the clear black sky. To distract myself from tears, I count the stars, looking for a falling one so I can make a wish. I would wish away all the pain of the whole entire world. I can feel a sulk settling on my face.

"Say something. You are so quiet."

"Mmm... just thinking." I stall.

"What are you thinking?"

"Well... have you kissed?"

"Meera! Really! Sometimes you ask such strange questions." Rita is exasperated.

"Well, have you?" I persist.

"Yes, of *course*. It is like floating and bubbles and melted ice-cream down your throat." Rita says dreamily.

"Nani is going to be so mad." It's nauseating that she kissed, and it's even worse, that she enjoyed it so much.

"How does Nani come into the picture? Nani is never going to know. Besides, I bet you that Nani did some wild and crazy kissing when she was young."

"Have you done anything more?"

"Meera, really? I am a responsible person, okay!" Rita pretends to be indignant. "Aren't you happy for me? I mean, Jai is *the* love of my life. I am lucky to have met him so young. Some people are lucky in love, you know. I am one of those."

"Yeah, I am happy for you. But I am still mad that you didn't come to pick me up. And you didn't tell me sooner about your *Jai*." I emphasize his name. I dislike him.

"I wanted to tell you in person. And today Jai wanted to meet at Coffee House, so I couldn't come to the airport. I didn't think you would mind. What's the big deal? We are here now and I've told you about Jai."

I lie still, silent, trying to think of what to say, and trying to understand why I am so upset. It sounds crazy that I am jealous of my cousin's boyfriend. Or that I feel cheated and betrayed by Rita. Though Rita is still Rita, she is also not, and things are all of a sudden completely, complicatedly different. How can I tell her that I feel so sure and so sad that we will never again have what we had?

"Jai wants to meet you. Tomorrow we will go to Coffee House and he'll be waiting for us there," Rita continues excitedly, oblivious to the despair I am feeling.

I don't respond.

* * *

Rita takes a full fifty-eight minutes to get ready. I am tired of waiting, but I keep silent. I've kept silent a lot since her disclosure about her relationship. It took me exactly eighteen minutes to put on my emerald green cotton t-shirt, jeans, flat black sandals, black eyeliner, lip gloss and small gold hoops. The natural brown highlights in my long wavy − and fiercely brushed back − hair show even more in the Jaipur sunlight. I think I too look quite pretty in the mirror, and that surprises me. Finally Rita is done. She is dressed in a pink tank, a light white sweater, jeans and white sandals. She has hoops in her ears too and her signature single long braid with tendrils of hair framing her face. She is stunning.

"How do I look?" she asks, smiling broadly.

"Like a piece of heaven." And she really does. But I have already decided that Jai is not worth looking so good for. Rita is mine and Jai has no business taking up those fifty-eight minutes that she could have spent sitting on the terrace and shooting the breeze with me, instead of being so caught up in looking perfect for him.

We leave for Coffee House. I dislike everything about this day. I don't want to go to Coffee House. I don't want to drink coffee. And I certainly don't want to meet Jai. Probably for the first time, I hide my true feelings from Rita, who seems oblivious in her excitement.

"He said he will be here by three. Fifteen minutes to go.

Let's find a nice corner table." I hate how Rita sounds so eager.

"Are you sure he knows I am coming?" I ask dismally, wishing I could turn around and walk out, leaving Rita to deal with her precious Jai.

"Yes, of *course*, silly. He asked to meet you. He wants to meet my closest, special-est cousin." She squeezes my hand. I feel even worse.

"What do you want me to say?" I ask.

"Just be yourself and don't be nervous. He is amazing. And you are going to love him. He puts everyone at ease."

"How old is he?"

"He's twenty-four." Rita says proudly.

"Ugh. That's old."

"Stop it. He's very handsome and very debonair, and I just adore him!" Her eyes glow when she talks about him.

"What does he do? I mean, does he work like a grown up and all that?" I ask.

"Yes, he has a real job. He's a manager at Ristaji. The builders, you know? He is the youngest manager in the team. And it's because he is so smart that he did so well." Rita can't stop praising him any opportunity she gets.

Suddenly, she lets out a squeal and waves her hand up in the air frantically. I turn to see the quintessential tall, dark mysterious looking stranger framing the door at Coffee House. As he strides over to our table, I grudgingly register that I didn't expect him to be this handsome, but something is amiss. Jai has just given Rita a customary kiss on her cheek and is holding out his hand to me. Some words have been spoken, but I am stuck in staring silence. Finally, Rita shakes me by the shoulder and says, "Meera, Jai is saying hello. Where are you lost?"

"Hello." I shake his hand without meeting his gaze.

"Well, sit and make yourselves comfortable." Jai commands. "What can I get you ladies to drink?"

We are already seated, dumbo! We tell him what we want and Jai-the-gentleman goes to get our drinks.

"Why didn't you tell me?" I angrily whisper to Rita.

"Tell you what?" She sounds bewildered.

"That he's so so... so..." But I don't have a chance to articulate my thoughts, because Jai is back at the table, smoothly sliding into the chair besides Rita. Though I appear calm on the outside, I am squirmy and uncomfortable inside.

Just as I think how glad I am that no one can peer into my head right now, because I am confused about why I feel so shaken, Jai asks me with fake politeness, "Are you hot, Meera? Your face is flushed." He looks amused. But when he sees the alarm on my face, he quickly adds, "It is a Jaipur summer though, so I don't blame you."

Rita on the other hand is oblivious and chattering away about goodness knows what.

"It's horrible," Rita is saying. "Just simply horrible how he dumped her. When she realized that he was two-timing her with her best friend, she swallowed an entire bottle of pills. Thank goodness they were vitamins and didn't do her much harm except for giving her a terrible stomachache. It took her six months before she was even able to crack a smile after all that." I have no idea who she is talking about.

"She should have known," Jai responds. "We all saw it clearly."

Rita gets up and mumbles that she needs to visit the ladies room. As she heads off, I have a sinking feeling in my stomach. I turn to look at Jai. Perhaps it's the first time I am looking him square in the face in the entire hour that we've been here.

"Meera, how long are you in Jaipur?"

"A couple of weeks," I mutter.

We are both waiting for Rita to return. I look around, and when I turn back to Jai, I see him brazenly ogling two girls sitting across the café. There is a leering look on his face that I recognize so clearly. In a flash I remember Monty, with his predator look. And I instantly know with certainty what ulterior motive Jai has, in pursuing Rita. I am as certain about this as I am about the sun rising each morning. I feel nauseated as the panic churns in my gut.

Jai turns back to me and I watch his expression change into one of realizing that I see him for what he is and is not – he is not the well-intentioned, polished, in-love gentleman he portrays; rather, he is a lustful, ill-intentioned guy, out to get laid. He knows I see through his fake boyfriend act, and he also knows that I know he knows. He seems to be mocking and challenging me at the same time. It is the progressive year of 1988, but there is no shortage of sleaze balls in our great country.

"Don't play with her, Jai." It slips out of my mouth on its own accord.

"Mind your own business." Jai shoots me a huge fake smile.

I can feel the color drain from my face. He clearly makes no attempt to hide his act from me, but still I am stunned by his rudeness. How dare he? He registers the shock on my face. Before I can retort, he turns and watches Rita cross the cafe to our table. "Hi, baby," he croons to her, smoothly slipping into his committed boyfriend role. "Meera and I were just discussing how we need to have more air conditioning in all public places in Jaipur." He looks at me with the confidence of a snake charmer, daring me to try to strip his façade. He knows that Rita is completely under his spell.

* * *

I can't sleep. I replay the events of the afternoon over and over in my head, trying to decide the best way to explain to Rita what happened. Rita believes with no doubt that Jai loves her. She wants to marry him. She said Jai is *the* love of her life. In some ways this is even worse than what Monty did. In the Monty episode, I was hurt. I don't think Monty fully understood the ramifications of what he was doing when he did it. But Jai knows exactly what he is doing. He knows he is playing with someone's love and trust. His is an intentional, deliberate move. And what's more, he is confident that he will not get burned in the process, while being indifferent as to whether anyone else burns. But will Rita believe me?

I sit bolt upright on my bed, my muscles tense, frozen in place. I don't know the words to say to Rita. How do I explain all this to her? How do I warn her that she has fallen in love with the façade he is portraying? That Jai actually is a smooth operator and is playing her. That he is not who he seems to be and that is a very dangerous thing.

* * *

The next morning at breakfast, Rita positively glows and is clearly gloating over some secret. I have a sinking feeling in my stomach. I am not fulfilling my responsibility as a sister and I must rectify that.

"I have to talk to you, Rita." I whisper, while Nani gives orders to the kitchen's head honcho, Ramukaka, who has become an undeniable part of the family.

"I have to talk to you too," declares Rita, bouncing on her chair.

I have a foreboding feeling. I chilly and notice goosebumps on my arms. I can't stomach my breakfast of *idlis*, the South Indian steamed rice cakes that Ramukaka has perfected to a science. I silently sip my *chai*.

After breakfast Rita and I sneak off to our secret basement greenroom (the corner room in the basement), where we go when we want privacy from the multitude of people in Magic Mansion. It has one window covered with a wire mesh over which thick ivy grows from the outside. The room is bathed in greenish light at all times of the day, because sunlight turns into this extraordinary hue as it seeps in through the foliage. The door is usually kept closed, but not locked. The greenroom stores various old large kitchen vessels, kitchen gadgets, big jute bags of grain, large bottles of dry lentils and dry spices for use through the year, and homemade pickles and sauces. Occasionally, when something from the greenroom is needed to refill the kitchen storage, it is accessed by someone under Ramukaka's instructions. But for the most part, the greenroom is empty of people.

"I'll go first, because I can't hold it in any longer." Rita explodes. "We did it." She is beaming. We are perched on two large jute grain bags. I love the warm smell of jute and grain and distractedly I take a deep breath in, trying to understand what Rita is saying. I am at a loss. Did what? Who we?

Seeing the blank look on my face, Rita continues. "We went all the way."

She appears to be waiting for a response from me. But when it becomes clear that I intend to remain silent, she explains further. "Jai and I had sex, silly. I gave him my virginity. This is how much I trust him. I am completely his now and he is mine. I am so happy and so in love, I can't even begin to tell you. It was beautiful. I mean it was kind of strange at first and I was shy and all. I didn't know exactly what I was doing. But Jai put me at ease. He is so good at everything. Even though it was his first time too, he was a natural. He is just amazing and I am so lucky."

"Rita, what have you done?" I suddenly wake up from my state of shock. "He does not love you. He is a player. How can you not see that?"

The colour drains from Rita's face. After a moment she says in a low voice, "I can't believe it, Meera. You are jealous of me. Just like Jai said. In fact, he asked me not to tell you because you would react with something like this. He was so right, yet again."

"No, no. You've got it wrong. Believe me. Jai is sleazy. He is a flirt and he is fooling you. When you went to the restroom at Coffee House, I just saw it on his face. I... I can't explain how, but I know. I know he is very handsome and charming. But you have to believe me, he is not who he pretends to be."

Rita looks undecided for a moment. I hold my breath. Then her expression settles into one of determination. "I am done with this topic, Meera. And for that matter, I am done with you. I don't need your jealousy. And for the record, I am disappointed with you." With that, she stalks out of the greenroom.

I am stunned. I am not sure how long I sit alone in the greenroom. I breathe in big gulps of air, warm with jute and grain. I think how beautiful the greenroom really is, and how many memories it holds of Rita and me. It has a full account of all our childhood summer secrets. Strangely, I want to apologize to the greenroom for today. Finally, a cascade of tears begins to flow out of my eyes. It feels like I am mourning so much, along with the loss of Rita's trust in me, along with the loss of my innocent childhood relationship with my beloved cousin. Somehow, I know things will never again be the same. Not even after Rita realizes how correct I am. I find myself thinking of the Monty incidents and all that I lost back then. I think of my mother's refusal to believe or even acknowledge what I told her about what Monty had done. Just like Rita refusing to believe me now. And then, unexpectedly, I think about Ari and his laughter.

5

Rita Hem Solanki

It is awful that Meera is jealous of me. I never expected it. Who would have thought she would make up such horrible lies about Jai! Little Miss Perfect. Just because she is a big city girl living in Delhi and all, does she think she knows everything about relationships? How nasty of her to make up such a lie! Jai loves me. I know that. And now he loves me even more after I gave him myself fully. I gave him what he asked for and I am sure he would never even think of anyone else.

I wonder what Nani thinks has happened between Meera and me. That old woman is very perceptive and she has to have noticed that Meera and I are avoiding each other. It is such a stark contrast to how we used to be: inseparable. Now I wake up early just so I can have my *chai* before she comes to the table. Anyone who doesn't respect Jai or my relationship with him does not deserve a place in my life. I hope Nani doesn't ask me what is going on. I am not ready to tell anyone about Jai. Not yet.

I do kind of miss Meera. If only she could have been happy for me. I think she was jealous from the first day I told her about Jai. He was so right about her. Anyway, I can't wait for her to go back to Delhi in three days. I can't wait for her to go. It gets awkward to go through the day avoiding her.

I almost spoke to her a few times out of habit, but then I remembered just in time that we are not speaking. How many excuses can I make to everyone about having to go out to do school projects? But at least that gets me out of the house and into Jai's arms.

It's so good to see Noorie Aunty and meet little Laila for the first time. It's easy to see how much Meera loves Laila. I wish we could all be sisters together. But Meera spoiled it all with her jealousy and lies. Thank goodness I have Jai.

Speaking of which, I better hurry down and make some excuse to head out.

I look in the mirror while I arrange my hair to make it look carelessly braided, with tendrils framing my face. This is how Jai likes it. All modesty aside, I look good. I've inherited Nani's good looks. I've been told so many times that I look exactly like her when she was my age, a fact established by all the black and white photos I've seen of her and Nana. She was a looker. No wonder Nana was so in love with her his entire life. And that's how Jai and I will be too.

I like my choice of clothes today – a cream, lacy fitted top and blue jeans. Simple. I look like a virgin! Ha! Let Meera be jealous all she likes.

"You look lovely, *beta*." I turn around to see Nani at my bedroom door. The door is ajar and Nani must've decided to peek in. I am blushing. Thank goodness Nani can't read my mind. Or can she?

"Hi, Nani. I have to run to school to work on the big summer project again. But I will be back soon. I promise I won't take as long as yesterday," I mumble.

"It seems like a very big project, Rita."

"Yes, yes. I am trying to get it done." I wonder if Nani suspects anything. I hope not.

"*Beta*, what is the matter with you and Meera? I don't see you both together anymore." She asks the question I have been dreading. A part of me wants to be a little girl again and tell my smart grandmother everything. The part that wants to curl up, cry and make up with Meera again. But then I think of Jai. And of how he would want me to be strong and to guard our secret. And so I just shake my head and blink back the tears.

"Nothing really. It's just that I am busy with the summer project and perhaps Meera expected me to have more free time. That's all. Everything will be fine, Nani."

"You both have always been so close. I don't like seeing you both avoid each other. Meera seems very glum and thoughtful too. I hope you resolve whatever it is that's bothering you both. Such relationships are too precious to lose. Did I ever tell you about how when I was young my best friend stopped talking to me over a man? Neither one of us ended up with that scoundrel, thank goodness. But I lost something very precious: my friendship. And that is one regret I still have today."

"Why are you saying all this, Nani?" She knows. The wise old woman knows. What am I to say?

"Rita, I have seen much of life. What Meera and you have is real. It is a true friendship, a history shared since birth. Don't throw it away."

I am silent.

"I will let you get ready now." And with that she's gone.

I realize that I am shaking a little. I take a deep breath and steel myself. I need to be my happy and sweet self for Jai. I take one last look in the mirror and hurry, trying to push away the thoughts blurring my vision, and the doubts weighing my heart.

6

Meera Myna Dutt

It's Friday evening and Super and I are going with Papa to *Khana Khazana*, the new restaurant that Mom heard good things about. Laila and Mom will stay home, because Laila has been sniffling with the start of a cold, and Mom wants to put her to bed early. I suspect Mom's glad to be rid of us for the evening so she can have some quiet time. Super, Papa and I have our own boisterous way when it's just the three of us. That particular day, after we are seated at *Khana Khazana*, Papa asks with a twinkle in his eye "Can you two keep a secret?"

"What? Of course!" I'm curious and jumpy. I wonder if he's going to talk about the affair. "But are you sure the secret is appropriate for Super too?"

Super just rolls his eyes at me, widens them and nods at Papa, grinning in a comical way.

"The secret is very inappropriate for this young man." Papa says grinning from ear to ear. Then he waves over our server and orders three glasses of sherry.

"Who's that for?" I'm bouncing on my seat like a hyperactive kid. I notice and stop myself.

"It's for the three of us." Papa announces, to my utter surprise. "I want you to be responsible drinkers when you do start drinking. And I certainly want to share your first drinks with you. We are going to have sherry tonight. But be sure to keep it our secret from even Mom. She would kill me if she finds out. And you can't talk about it at school either. Kids are not allowed to drink this, you know! But in different parts of the world that is not the case – like in France, in a region called Champagne, children grow up drinking champagne like water. So I'm trusting you both to be responsible with this one-time experience, which will remain between the three of us."

"Is that alcohol?" Super asks, his eyes still wide.

"Yes, it is." Papa answers seriously, but his eyes give away his smile.

Super leans over and gives Papa a hug, and his excitement is reflected in the grin that I can't seem to wipe off my face, not matter how mature I want to appear. "We won't tell a soul," I say, while Super nods effusively as the sherry arrives. Luckily, drinking laws in India, if any, are not strictly followed, and it is left up to parents to dictate the rules for their children. Besides, it's easy to bypass a law by slipping some rupees into the right palms. All these thoughts rapidly pass through my head as I pick up my elegant little glass of the auburn liquid. My fingers burn.

"Remember to slowly take a tiny sip, just enough to roll over your tongue. You don't have to finish your glass. Just get a tiny taste. Don't gulp it, or it will burn your throat." But it's too late, Super has taken a large swallow and is coughing. I put my glass back down and glare at him while patting his back.

"Papa said sip *slowly*, stupid."

Papa hands Super water, and his cough settles. "I will finish your glass, leave it," Papa says to Super.

"No, no. I want it." Super grabs his glass.

Papa is grinning. "All right, but be patient and sip very, *very* slowly. And always wait for the cheers." Papa raises his glass and Super and I follow suit, like I've seen in some movies. I can't wait to try my drink. "Cheers to the most wonderful family anyone can have," says Papa. We solemnly bring our glasses to our mouths and I take a tiny sip of my drink.

It's hot and molten on the tip of my tongue, but sends shivers through the rest of me. I don't know if the shivers come from the alcohol, or just my excitement. This time, Super takes his sip the right way too. The moment feels so perfect. Papa on one side of me and Super on the other. I'm willing to forgive Super his natural stupidity, as I feel an overwhelming surge of love for the two men in my life. I momentarily recall Ari, who had joined that status at one time, but he now feels like a distant dream.

Apparently I'm not the only one feeling this love envelop us. Papa asks, "Do the two of you know how important you are, and how much your Mom and I love you and Laila? With my three beautiful children by me, I can only be happy."

"Yep Pops, it's like how I'm most happy when I'm playing football with my friends." Super responds, inadvertently declaring the end of any serious conversation. I slap my forehead in mock exasperation as Papa and I laugh.

Soon enough, Papa has us giggling relentlessly at his elephant and ant jokes. I can visualize the cartoon ant and elephant getting into the car in black and white, as Papa proceeds with his joke. Super and I are in splits. I can't get my words out right. We each have had barely four or five tiny sips of our sherry, but the world already feels like the best place ever. Super and I don't finish our drinks that night. Papa finishes his before we head back.

Papa reminds us to act normal at home, not silly. And to not say a word about our sherry tasting to Mom, or anyone else for that matter. Super and I giggle furtively as we nod. I know I have the best Papa in the world.

"Thank you, Papa. Today is one of the best nights of my life," I manage to say, before I rush to my room to avoid running into Mom.

* * *

"Meera, you have a letter from Rita," Mom calls out. "It's nice of her to write to you. This is the first contact after whatever went on between you both in the summer. I don't know what happened, but whatever it was, you must let it go now."

It is painful to think about the summer. After that fateful day in the greenroom, Rita avoided me and I just continued feeling awful and remained sullen. There was nothing I could do. It was a relief that Laila came with Mom and was there for the last week of my trip. But even Laila could not make me forget for a long time what had happened between Rita and me. It felt like something in me broke and a piece of me hardened. I learned something about life, perhaps something that I should have figured out after the Monty incidents. What I learned, in all its excruciating reality, was that life is not always fair.

For some inexplicable reason, I'm not surprised to receive Rita's letter, but nevertheless, I hesitate to open it. The letter feels simultaneously heavy and fragile. I go into Papa's study, closing the door behind me. This is one room where Laila will not follow me. I perch on the windowsill in the study, the afternoon sun causing me to squint against its brightness. In the sunlight, I can see the floating dust. I take a deep breath and open the envelope.

* * *

Dec. 11, 1987

My dear Meera,

I want to say sorry and I want you to know what happened. I feel so awful. I feel awful for what you may have felt and for what I have gone through ever since. Three days before you left to return to Delhi I went to meet you-know-who. I will not write the name, as I have decided never to utter that name again. We were to meet at my school.

As you know, you and I were avoiding each other (which btw is entirely my fault). Nani had cornered me and was asking about what had happened between us. I thought it was safer for me to just leave home and get to school earlier than our meeting time and just wait for you-know-who there. Oh, I have been such a fool, Meera! I should never have ignored you or ignored your warning. Even though I had a nagging doubt, I just didn't want it to be true and so I chose to not believe you and to make you the lying villain. I am so sorry, my dear, dear sister.

Anyway, thank goodness I got there early that day. The school building is open during part of the summer for students who want to use the library and lab for summer projects. The library and lab are the only two open, along with staffed parts of the school building. And the school watchman Gurka-bhai is always there.

Gurka-bhai let you-know-who into the school building, because he knew him from the many times he had come to the school with me. I had told Gurka-bhai that you-know-who is helping me with one of my projects in the library.

Well, that day I thought I'd go and wait in the classroom where we usually met. I got there and I couldn't believe what I saw. He was with that Mohra girl from Nairobi who transferred to my school. I couldn't believe my eyes. He was on the same bench that he and I used to sit on and oh, you know, kiss and make out. (PS: I hope this letter is completely confidential on your end. I assume that now that you are sixteen you get to open you own mail. I did write confidential on the envelope.) They were kissing. I was so stunned, I didn't even feel pain. I was just numb for a while. Can you believe that – I walked up to them and slapped him! He hadn't seen me walking up and he was so shocked, he almost fell off the bench. Then I turned around and walked out.

When the tears came, Meera, they didn't stop for a long, long time. How could I have been such a fool? I actually saw my entire future with him. If you had looked at me those last two days before you left, you would have known something had happened. So I expertly avoided you. My pride was hurt too and I didn't want you to know. And I was very shaken to the core; I really wish I had not gone further – you know what I mean?

I won't bore you with the details of the subsequent days. Let me just say it was very hard and very heartbreaking.

It took me this long to muster the courage to write you. I want you to know how sorry I am. Thank you for trying to warn me, Meera. Please forgive me. I miss you and want you back.

Love,

Rita

* * *

Dec 16, 1987

My dear Rita,

I am so sorry that you went through something so painful. I wish it could have been different. Your letter made me cry. Why did you wait this long to tell me? I wish I could have been helpful somehow. What a cheat! What a dog you-know-who turned out to be.

I hope you are doing alright now. You have to forget about this and move on. You are a wonderful, beautiful person and I've missed you too. Thank you for writing to me. Of course I forgive you, Rita. And I can't wait to see you again.

Nani will be happy that we are friends again. I don't ever want to lose you.

Laila grows so fast. Each day she seems bigger. She is almost three now, and so much fun. Super's older (of course) and slightly more sensible (can you believe it?). At least he keeps to himself and is into his friends right now. I don't really know what he does half the time. Mom and

Papa are happy, because Super always stands first in his class. I am alright. Getting set for Junior College (can you believe it?). Rini and I are going to try getting into the same Junior College, but I don't know if we will. I hope we do. I am so happy to have you back, Rita.

Love,

Meera

There is a bittersweet feeling in me. I am sad and relieved, though I am also angry and indignant on Rita's behalf. On the one hand, I want to hug and comfort Rita, but on the other, I want to yell at her for not believing me and treating me the way she did. I want her to know it cost me something. Something in me irretrievably changed the moment she disbelieved me. My faith in the goodness of the world, in truth and justice, and in the permanence of bonds, shifted. I know my letter to her is sweet and forgiving. I don't know why I didn't express any of the bitterness. I guess I don't want to risk losing her friendship again. And maybe I thought she's been through a lot as it is.

I didn't realize that in the bargain, I sacrificed a bit of my authenticity with her.

7

Sagar Suraj Dutt

My father's dearly beloved childhood boxing guru's name is Suraj. That's why it's my middle name. But Meera and Laila's middle name is Myna. Myna was my paternal grandmother, Mayalata's pet-name. Myna actually is the name of a type of bird that sings very well. Meera and Laila can't sing too well though. Papa tried to get Meera to learn vocals when we were little, but she is not focused. I started learning the *tabla* years ago when I was five, and I could master it if I wanted. All that's needed is focus, practice and discipline.

Meera's okay and talented with her artwork and such, but in my opinion, she wastes her time and her smarts. Instead of spending so much time with her friends and our relatives, she could do something useful with herself. But her absolute biggest problem is that she thinks too much about everyone and everything. She worries, like Ma, and that takes up a lot of mental space and energy. Maybe girls are just made like that. I, on the other hand, observe and learn. I don't worry. If anyone has a problem, it's their problem, not mine. If there is anything I've learned in my thirteen years, it's this. And it is a very important lesson for happiness.

Laila is just sweet. I hope she learns from me, and doesn't

become a typical woman when she grows up. I wish she were a boy, but it's okay.

"Rohit is here to pick you up, Sagar." Mom calls. I run down the stairs and skid to a halt next to Rohit, who is standing near the landing, grinning from ear to ear. We are going out for dinner for Chintu's birthday. Rohit's driver is driving us to the restaurant, and we are going to be there unchaperoned, because Chintu's parents know the restaurant owners and so they are okay with it. *And girls are invited too.*

"Hi Rohit. Have fun today, kids," Meera calls out from the living room by the front door. I am secretly amused at Meera's stupidity sometimes, like her thinking we are kids. Or her getting all weird when I told her about the conversation I'd overheard about Papa's affair.

"Sure, Oldie!" I grin back at her.

"Shut up!"

"Oh, don't start, you two," Mom warns. "Rohit would you like something to drink?"

"No, thank you, Aunty."

* * *

I throw another stone up at Meera's window, while thinking about the fantastic evening. I got my first kiss, had my first beer and my first taste of meat. Though I've had sherry with Papa, that doesn't count. The chicken was delicious. I know Mom, Papa and Meera would throw a fit if they found out, but it's my choice what I want to eat. I've already missed out on meat for so long. As for the kiss – I am such a good kisser that Loveena didn't want me to stop. I know the perfect hiding place in the school yard to take her so that we can kiss after school. Hmm! Among the guys, some of them have snuck beer from their dads' glasses, and some of them are non-vegetarian, but I am the first to kiss. And now the guys are in awe of me. I throw up another stone, and finally Meera opens her window. "Open the door," I yell.

"You are so late." Meera grumbles as she lets me in.

Before I can answer, I start to gag. I run up to my room as fast and noiselessly as I can, Meera at my heels. I barely make it to my room and suddenly all the beer and the chicken comes out on the floor. Meera stands at my room door. "Ew. Gross. What did you eat?"

"I think the food was bad at the restaurant." I lie holding my belly and screwing up my face. I actually think it's the beer that's making me do this. I gulped down as much as I could, and I can't remember how much it was.

"Mom almost went out to pick you up from the restaurant, but I convinced her that she didn't have to go because Rohit's driver was going to bring you back. But she'll be crazy worried when she sees this mess."

"Let's clean it up." I manage to say before I gag and start to vomit some more.

"Idiot, go to the bathroom!" Meera whispers loudly.

"I think I'm done."

Meera complains non-stop, but brings up a bunch of rags and we clean the vomit. Mostly she cleans it, and I pretend to help. I have to be good for the football match tomorrow.

"Thanks, Meera. Good night."

8

Meera Myna Dutt

It is 'Rose Day' in college. On this day boys give roses to the girls they like and ask them out. It is a much awaited day, for it is when many college romances begin. Strategically it comes in January, at the start of the New Year, a time for new beginnings and just a month before Valentine's day. So the joke is that college infatuations begin in January, mature in February in time for Valentine's, and end in March, in time for the real studying to begin before the final exams in June. In our practical world, even Rose Day is designed to fit the exam schedule.

I don't expect a lot of roses or anything, but still I want to look nice today. I wear purple. Purple symbolizes royalty and sophistication and also magic and mystery; it is the combination of burning red and calming blue. It is simultaneously virginal and not. I can't think of any other colour that is tranquil yet passionate. My shirt is a soft purple with tints of light blue and pink woven into it; blue jeans complete the outfit. My hair needs ferocious brushing to try and tame the unruly curls a bit. I am far from the prettiest girl in college, but I look okay today. I feel happy for no reason and grin at myself in the mirror.

My college is well situated on a tree lined and shaded

street close to the city. The red brick buildings, the crowded corridors and the green of the shrubbery, all feel so familiar. I at last feel a sense of purpose besides Laila and my family concerns. I am not entirely clear what the purpose is, but it's something about being instrumental in shaping the future, and changing the world. I belong. I am a part of something, of some greater collective. It's separate from my family, and different from school, which never felt like my own. My world is now bigger. It doesn't even matter as much that Rini got into a neighbuoring college. In fact, there are some advantages – it forces me to talk to other people. It feels so good to be all of eighteen. Even Mom often asks me for my opinion on things, not treating me like a mere kid anymore.

"Meera, are you going out again?" Laila comes running to me. "Why do you have to go every day?"

"You will go to school too next year. You will have to go every day except weekends. You know, you are becoming a big girl too." Laila's charm has only grown and I can't believe she is already four years old.

"Have a good day, *Beta*," Mom calls out from the living room where she is drinking her *chai*. "I am taking Laila to the park later today."

"Thanks, Mom." I grab an apple and rush out.

* * *

A few minutes after I get to college, I receive a rose from Suraj. This is unexpected and oh, I am flattered. On the card he writes, '*I would love to take you out. Will you go out with me?*' He rushes off shyly right after handing me the rose with the card. I walk over to my locker feeling kind of cool because of the rose in my hand. There are a lot of roses in a basket left near the lockers. I bend to take a look.

Boys often leave roses near the lockers for the girls to find. There is a strict honour system by which no girl takes another's rose. Once a girl finds a rose addressed to her, it is up to her to approach the boy to thank him, which gives the boy the green light to ask her out. If a girl does not thank the boy, it means that she is not interested in going out with him.

I look through the roses in the basket. There is one addressed to Sangeeta, and several for Rani. There's none for me. Oh well! What did I expect? I straighten up and turn around, and there is Raj standing spookily close behind me, with a rose in his hand. He is so close I can smell his breath, and I hastily step back. He takes another step forward, towards me.

"This is for you, Meera," says Raj. "Would you like to go for a coffee?"

"Um… Thanks Raj. I… Uh… really I am flattered. Thank you. Can I uh… get back to you?" *He is so direct.*

"What's there to get back about? I would really like to take you out for a coffee. All you have to do is say yes."

He is pushy too. "Well, I have a class right now."

"Oh come on, you can miss your class. Not like you've never bunked classes before."

"Raj, really, I have to go. Thanks for the rose though."
"Is that a rejection?"

"Um…it's not like that. But I really have to go right now." *I am getting very uncomfortable.*

"Meera, can't you tell I like you a lot?"

"Raj, you are being pushy. I want to go."

"What do you mean pushy? Aren't you happy?"

Just then Girish walks towards me holding a rose. He hands it to me silently and walks away. Raj looks furious. I am beginning to question how stable Raj is, and right then Raj grabs my hand. "Look here, Meera. You need to go out with me."

I twist my hand, trying to get it out of his grip. I am livid. "Let go of my hand!" I order from between clenched teeth. "Leave me alone! I am not interested!" My reaction of utter fury is surprising, even to me.

Raj looks taken aback. "You are making a mistake. You will regret letting me go."

I walk away hastily, not looking back, three roses held tightly in my hand. There's a tightness in my throat and I have to blink several times to push back tears of anger. Thankfully, I don't encounter anyone until I get to my class. Instead of going in, I turn right and go straight to the college café. I find a corner table and wait for Rini, who is supposed to meet me here after her classes.

I sit at the table for a long time, willing myself to calm down. Raj should not have grabbed my hand. He has no right to do that. What makes him think he can touch another person so forcefully? Like Monty. I revert to my old habit and quickly say Lord Krishna's name under my breath.

By the time Rini finds me settled at a corner table in the café I have calmed down sufficiently to read through Raj's and Girish's Rose Day card messages. Both of them are variations of '*Hi, Meera, Happy Rose Day. This is for you, XYZ.*' Boring! I have received more roses than I expected, but not from the person I hoped would give me one. But then, why would Raul give me a rose anyway? I don't think he even notices me.

"What's up, Meera? Why are you slumped like that?" Rini says pulling back a chair to join me. She has three roses in her hand too.

"Just whatever. Nothing interesting," I mumble. "Who did you get roses from?"

"Akash, Vijay, Ronil. No one interesting."

This day has turned out worse than expected. We both sit silently. I order a fresh lime soda, again fighting down the urge to cry.

"You got three too." Rini goes through my cards.

I am silent and we continue to people watch from our corner café spot.

"May I join you beautiful ladies?" It is Raul. Raul has two roses in his hand and hands one to Rini and one to me. "Happy Rose Day."

This is the rose I have been waiting for, though I never expected I would get it. I can feel colour creep up my cheeks. Oh no, I must look red as a beetroot. I try to think cooling blue thoughts. Then I realize I need to thank him. He is already seated next to Rini and opposite me. Rini and he are talking and if her wide smile, head bobbing and laughter is any indication, she seems very entertained by what he's saying. *What is he saying?* Suddenly I blurt out, "Thank you." They both look at me. His eyes widen with amusement for a moment, before regaining their normal cool look. He politely nods.

"The pleasure is entirely mine."

The pleasure is entirely *his*! The *pleasure* is entirely his! The pleasure is *entirely* his! I want to knock myself on the head to snap out of this chant. But I can't do that in the café. I try to focus on what Rini and Raul are talking about.

"Yes, I read that notice. I can't believe it that they are making us take two papers a day this year. I am glad they at least made an advance announcement. But it still sucks."

"Well, people as smart as you both have nothing to worry about," Raul flatters.

"Yeah sure," Rini rolls her eyes good-naturedly. "It just means getting no sleep the previous night and having to cram enough information in our heads to fill two papers."

Even though Rini is in the neighboring college, they are affiliated and follow the same exam structure.

Rini abruptly looks at her watch. "Oops! Lost track of time. I have to run. I have to get back to help out a friend with one of her assignments. I promised. I'll see you guys later." And with that, she's gone.

Slowly, Raul turns his penetrating gaze on me.

"How many other girls did you give roses to?" I demand. I can't believe that came completely unsolicited out of my mouth. I can feel myself turning red again. I sound like a jealous tyrant from the island of desperation.

Raul grins and keeps looking at me for what feels like eternity. His gaze burns a hole right through my heart. How can anyone look so good?

"Sorry. Please forget I asked that. I don't know why I asked." I am surely very red now.

"Does it matter to you, Meera?"

"Um... no. Of course not."

"Well, it matters to me. So let me tell you. You are the only one... though technically, I did give Rini a rose too, but that's because she was right here with you. You are the only one I am asking out."

He is asking me out! "You are asking me out?"

Raul is still grinning. *Never before has there been a sexier grin in the history of the universe.* "Yes. Meera Dutt, will you please honour me with your lovely company and join me to watch Jurassic Park? It's playing right now at a few different locations and I thought we could go one afternoon, if you are okay with it."

It feels like a proposal. It *is* a proposal. I feel a tingling at the pit of my stomach, and I continue to stare at him.

"Are you going to answer? Or are you going to keep me waiting?" He is grinning even bigger now. He looks so confident.

"Raul, thank you. I would love to go."

* * *

We are at the movies. This is the first time I am out on a date alone with a boy, that too such a cute one. I am staring at his broad back and the way his hair curls over the collar of his t-shirt. I think he's almost a foot taller than me. Meera and Raul – it has a nice ring to it. Unexpectedly, he takes hold of my hand as he leads me, single file, through the crowded ticket booth area and up the stairs into the cinema. It feels exquisite. I am aware of only him and the feel of his grip. I wonder if he can hear my heart beat. With my pulse racing as it is, he can probably even feel it in my hand. He finds us centre seats and to my disappointment, lets my hand go as we sit down. I can still feel his touch on my skin. We are mostly silent.

"Can you see the screen clearly?" He asks as a tall man takes the seat in front of me.

"Yeah," I say.

"Would you like popcorn?"

"No, thanks."

"You and Rini are very good friends, aren't you?" He is trying to make conversation.

"Yes, we were in school together." I don't know what more to say. Thankfully, the movie begins.

About ten minutes pass and then Raul leans over and whispers, "May I?"

I give him the bottle of water in my hand.

"That's not what I want," he says, as he puts the bottle aside and gently takes my hand in his. I sit in absolute silence, not daring to move a muscle, as he intertwines his fingers with mine. He glances at me, but I keep staring ahead at the movie. It feels like the only parts of my body alive right now are my hand lying in his, and my exploding heart, and I don't want to do anything that might jeopardize either. And so we sit like that, in complete silence, for the remainder of the movie.

* * *

I am at Rini's. We are sprawled on her bed, chatting. I have not told her a word about Raul and me. It's been three weeks since *Jurassic Park*. It's difficult to hide this big recent part of my life from her. But I wanted to hold on to it for a while and not tell anyone. It's been my precious secret. After the movie, Raul and I had gone to Mondegar's Café in awkward silence.

There he told me how he's liked me for a while, how he loves my laughter, how he'd like us to date exclusively if I would consider it. I just could not believe that was happening to me. He looked so irresistibly shy at that moment. I sat on top of my hands to stop them from shaking, but I could do nothing about the butterflies in my stomach. I could not get any words out. I thought I was going to be sick. It was awkward. He took my silence to mean I was not interested. Then he had said that it was okay if I was not interested.

I had stuttered, but finally managed to say I would very much like to date him exclusively. It was only a week later that we'd kissed in his car. It was delicious – my first real kiss. It felt so right; like it was meant to be, like everything in the world was just right.

"Where are you lost, Meera?" Rini snaps her fingers as though to wake me up.

"Oh nothing, I'm sorry. I was thinking about Raul."

"Why?" Rini is suddenly very attentive.

"Well, I have something to tell you."

She remains silent.

I take a deep breath. Why is this so difficult? Rini is staring at me expectantly. "Raul and I are going out."

"How long has it been?" She does not bat an eyelid.

"Three weeks. He asked me out for a movie on Rose Day."

"And you tell me now?" She sounds angry.

"I am sorry, Rini." I can't think of any excuse for this. "Aren't you happy for me?"

"Sure."

"Why are you so mad?" "Why? You want to know *WHY*? BECAUSE YOU SHOULD HAVE TOLD ME ABOUT THIS! THAT'S WHAT GOOD FRIENDS *DO*! THEY *TELL* EACH OTHER. THEY DON'T WAIT THREE WEEKS AND SHOCK EACH OTHER LIKE THIS! And I thought you were my best friend. I am such a *fool*."

Rini is shouting. I am sitting up on the bed by now, confused. My hands are icy cold and tingly.

"I trusted you, Meera. I didn't think you would stab me in the back like this."

"Stab you in the back? What are you talking about? I just waited to tell you, that's all. I haven't done anything to stab you in the back." My eyes have pooled with tears. My face is burning and I wonder about the contrast between my hot face and icy hands. I try to understand Rini. Perhaps she feels betrayed in the same sense that I did when Rita told me about her and Jai. But I had not yelled at Rita or accused her.

"You should have *told* me. I don't know why you would do this to me." Rini is crying now too.

I am still trying to understand her reaction and seeing her tears, my anger melts away. I grab her shoulders. "Rini, please tell me what I have done wrong. I don't know why you are so upset. We are still best friends."

Rini continues to cry and refuses to look at me.

"Rini, please talk to me." I am feeling upset.

We sit in silence for a few minutes. Finally, Rini looks at me. "Meera, you can get anyone you want. I am ordinary looking..."

"No, you're not," I interject.

Rini stops me from saying anything more by holding up her hand. She continues, "If you don't already know it, you should. You can get anyone you want."

"Well, so I am going out with Raul. What is wrong with that?"

"I like him too."

"You *what?*" I whisper.

"You heard me."

"Oh!" I don't know what to say. I didn't expect this. Rini never has crushes. Rini, my good, steady, sensible friend, who scoffs at silly, wasteful things like college infatuations, fancies my boyfriend. Now what?

"Rini, I am sorry. I didn't know. Why didn't you say something about it? You never like anyone."

"Say *what?* There was nothing to say. And now he likes you anyway. Forget it. I am fine. I am always fine."

Rini and I don't have much to say to each other after that. There is awkward silence till I get up to go home, leaving the unspoken sisterhood of years shattered on her doorstep.

* * *

Rini and I don't call each other for almost a week. Then I give in and call her. We try to be how we've always been with each other, but something's changed. The centre of our comfortable, familiar friendship has irrevocably shifted to a very distant spot. And the harder I push to bring it back to centre, the more it shifts away.

I believe Rini tried too. But she gave up sooner than I did. In fact, I never gave up at all. I quietly believe we will find each other again. I don't ever want to not believe that. I can't imagine a life without Rini. And yet I get used to it.

9

Rini Rathode Mehra

I am jealous. Perhaps as her friend I should not be, but I am. How come things always go her way? It's always about her, and not me. I'm born in a family where my parents don't have the time or energy for me. Why did they even have me? They are completely, entirely occupied with Raju. On top of that I had to have a best friend like Meera, who's so full of herself. I've always been there for her, always been a good friend, and what do I get in return? This? How come she gets the guy I like? I can't be there for her this time. I can't watch the two of them hand in hand. I can't stand it. I can't smile and pretend I am happy for her. She can't have it all. She can't be the centre of attention every time.

I like Raul. He is the only boy I've liked in my entire life. He gave *me* a rose too. Would he have asked me out that day if I had not left the café? Would he have been my boyfriend by now? Maybe he would not have liked me anyway, because I'm so plain, but what if… I will never know. Why do I always get left behind? Meera… people like her. And now Raul likes her and is going to get to know her so well. I hate it. She could have had anyone. Why him?

And yet I miss her too. I hate missing her. She does not see me as an equal with my own needs, she sees me as just her support, her sounding board. Someone to talk to about her needs and wishes. I am tired of being the sensible one whose life revolves around Meera-the-great's more elaborate and glamorous one.

She has Laila and Super, and what do I have? Raju! What the heck kind of fairness is this? I don't want to be second wheel anymore; I don't want to be an appendage to Meera's perfect family. I don't want to see them; I don't like them.

I wonder where I will end up. I know Meera will have a fairy tale life with the picture perfect happy ending, in which she will have a handsome husband and two lovely children (neither of them disabled like Raju), as opposed to me. I don't even know if I will ever get married. Who would like me or want to be with me? Who would want to be tied to a plain looking girl with a disabled brother? People will always look at me and wonder if something is wrong with me. If it's genetic. Mom told me that after I was born she was asked the question, "Is she okay?" all the time.

Mom and Dad expect me to be successful. They want "the best" for me – that's what they keep saying. And I don't want to disappoint them. But *please!* If I'm so busy being the best, being everyone's everything, when do I get to be myself? I want to be cranky sometimes, throw a tantrum, and get what I want at least some of the time. Meera's best friend, Mom and Dad's perfect daughter, Raju's caring sister… I'm done. I resign from all these jobs.

I deserve to be happy. And I deserve to be heard. I have to get over Raul. Or else I just have to get him.

* * *

"Hello, Raul," I call him at ten at night.

"Is this Rini?" Raul sounds surprised.

"Have you read *To Kill A Mockingbird?*"

"Is that a trick question?"

It's as easy as that. And we talk till midnight. I don't flirt. But I don't avoid flirting either. If he flirts, I respond. We just talk about this and that. That's how it begins. And we talk most every night, then on. We don't mention Meera in our conversations. I don't know what I want out of this. It is enjoyable and that's the extent to which I am willing to think. For once, I am living in the moment and following my heart, not my brain. I am not going to worry about how this will end. I deserve this happiness. Don't I? For once, don't I?

10

Meera Myna Dutt

In the months that go by, I get closer to Raul. I try to replace Rini-time with Raul-time. It is not the same though. I miss my girl time so much. There are things I can't say to Raul the way I could to Rini, without the risk of being misunderstood. There are so many things I miss about her. I miss just sitting around in her room, or lounging with her in our patio. I miss our midnight snacks when we slept over at each other's places. I miss her smile. But most of all, I miss our conversations and our laughing together at jokes that nobody else would even understand.

Mom and Papa know something is wrong and about Rini. I finally tell them we had a fight, but add that I don't want to talk about it. They look worried, but respect my privacy. Mom finds it harder to suppress her curiosity, but Papa stops her from prying too much. Once, when I burst into tears at the dining table, it was Papa who thoughtfully stopped Mom from following me to my room. He says they are there for me if I want to talk, and if I don't, they will not force it. He says they love me.

Many things make me cry these days. For instance, almost everything Papa says makes me emotional, I can't understand why. I am fine with Raul though. In fact, he is the only person with whom I am cheerful and happy. I don't feel like interacting much with anyone else. Even Laila doesn't make me forget my worries, and I have to often force myself to smile for her. Only when I'm with Raul do I forget about the void left by Rini. Because when he's around, I don't have to think for myself. I let him take charge. And nowadays I don't like to think too much. We make out when we are alone. He wants to have sex but I don't, and so we stay away from actually doing it. I like making out, but not as much as he seems to like it. Sometimes I get bored. But I don't want to displease him, so I pretend I am enjoying it as much as him. What I like most is the attention, the power of knowing that I am so attractive to him. But sometimes I think of other things when he kisses me. Like the beach, or my ant-counting days, or Lord Krishna. Or I imagine sharing a sister-moment with Laila someday, describing my first real kiss to her. Sometimes I hear Mummy's or Papa's voices in my head, admonishing me for making out. But it's the worst when I hear Rini's voice saying, 'I like Raul too'. I don't know why I am distracted like this during my most intimate moments with Raul. Is this how love is supposed to be? Tinged with boredom and other thoughts? Do I truly love him? Or is it, like Rini would probably say, just infatuation which is slowly losing some of its charm? Whatever it is, my initial excitement about Raul is somewhat placid now. But still, I love knowing I have a boyfriend who finds me so attractive. I love feeling attractive. And I certainly don't let Raul know that my passions have cooled. For perhaps this is just how it is with me.

Life falls into a rhythm and if not happy, I am at least content. Exams come and go and the summer passes. Raul and I are really a couple and it's comfortable. Everyone in college knows. I mostly like it. Sometimes though, I long for the old days when I was single and felt like a carefree girl; the days when I didn't have to account to anybody, when I didn't have to pretend to be pleased or amused and laugh at jokes that are not funny, when I didn't have to care about how I dressed and whether my hair was freshly washed.

Raul is very particular about how he wants me to be. Usually I don't mind him telling me how he wants me to dress. But I do mind him telling me what to eat and when. Though I like to think that it is an expression of his love for me, isn't it also some sort of a violation of my independence? But I don't have Rini to talk to about it and I couldn't discuss it with anyone else. Strangely, Raul is not surprised that he never sees Rini and me together anymore. He has not asked me about her. Finally, one day when we cut class to just laze in his car, I ask him.

"Raul, do you know why Rini and I don't hang out anymore?"

"You had a fight."

"We did. But how come you've never ask me about it?"

"I don't want to upset you."

"I thought you'd be curious. Don't you want to know?"

"Only if you want to tell."

Raul does not sound like himself at all. Typically, he wants to know everything about me. I find it very odd that he is not curious about what happened. But I let it drop. It is a painful subject, after all.

* * *

Old hurts, if not healed, remain, but are set aside. From the outside, mine is the ideal college existence. It might seem odd that I'm so deeply affected by the thing with Rini, but I am. It feels like an essential part of my life has gone missing. And while I'm grateful that Raul is my escape, it also doesn't feel right that he is an escape. Like some people smoke or drink for their escape – Raul is mine.

Mom and Papa know about Raul now. Though reluctantly, and with initial objections, they too have accepted him as part of my life. He is welcome at our home. He plays with Laila, but for some reason neither Laila nor Super are very fond of him. I don't let that bother me.

There is a mysterious melancholy that persists in my existence now. But I don't want to examine this. I am happy escaping into Raul's embrace, even when it means relinquishing a part of myself. Escaping, after all, allows me to avoid facing whatever it is that makes me sad. Raul is the fix in my back pocket that relieves me, and I know Raul likes that role.

* * *

My teenage years fly by in a whirlwind. I am twenty now. It's been two years since Rini and I have spoken, two years since Raul and I have been together. It's been two years of growth and change. I've enjoyed and explored the unfamiliar territory of relationships, and I've learned that sometimes you become another person for someone else, and you don't even realize how. Raul is an integral part of my life now, but he seems restless to me. If I let myself think about it, I feel insecure. But whenever I bring it up, he reassures me that it's all my imagination.

* * *

Sunday evenings are family time. Usually we all gather around at home. Even Super, now a very anti-social fifteen-year-old, joins in. Sometimes, especially for Laila's benefit, Papa reminisces about when Super and I were younger, recounting amusing stories, and we all enjoy it. Sometimes Papa tries to discuss politics with Super and me, but we are not very good at it. Papa wants me to read the papers "and not just the headlines", he says. Mom gossips about people we know – neighbours and relatives – recounting tidbits she may have heard through her grapevine. Since Mom loves to read, sometimes she animatedly tells us about some "really good book" she has come across. I think we all relish this time together. Eventually, Mom always calls it a day, usually when Laila begins to yawn. It is during one such Sunday evening that the phone rings. I jump up and grab it. "Hello?"

"Hi, Meera," says the familiar voice on the other end. "Can we meet?"

"RINI?"

"I need to talk to you. Can we meet?"

My eyes are starting to fill up and my throat is tight. I turn away from Papa and the rest who are all silently pretending not to hear. I take the phone into my room. "Rini?" I can't believe it.

"Yes, Meera. It is me. Listen I want to say sorry, and so much more to you. Will you please meet me?"

"Mee... meet you?" I stammer.

"Yes. Will you?"

"Yes, of course. Thank you. I mean, *yes*. Where?"

"Let's meet tomorrow at the Coffee Café? Is two okay?"

"Yes. S... see you."

"Bye."

"Bye."

* * *

I have not told anyone that I am meeting Rini today. Mom and Papa asked about Rini's call. I told them that I was surprised to receive the call and that we had decided we would talk about things. I told them that I didn't want to talk about it at the time, but I would fill them in later. They didn't ask me anything further.

I sit at a corner table, at the Coffee Café by our college. So many important, life altering moments in my life that have occurred in coffee shops. My stomach is in knots. What will Rini say to me? I wish she would hurry up and come. I want to tell her how much I have missed her, but I think I should wait to hear what she has to say first. I intentionally wore a white t-shirt and blue jeans, because white stands for peace, and blue indicates calm. I very much want Rini back in my life. But what does she want? I notice that my fingers are uncomfortably tightly clasped around each other and I force myself to untangle my fingers and sit on top of them. I am ready to forgive anything, to forgo anything. At this moment, perhaps I would even forgo Raul.

"Meera, hi." Rini walks up to the table with a tight-lipped and somewhat sad smile. She is in a long skirt and top of pastel yellow. She looks the same. Her hair is longer and lies straight like a silk sheet down to her shoulders.

"Hi, Rini." I'm so happy inside. I wish I could just hug her.

There is an awkward, momentary silence. Then Rini, in true Rini fashion, takes charge.

"Meera, thanks for coming. There are things I want to talk to you about. But tell me, how are you? And how is everyone? Laila must be so big now."

I'm a bit disappointed by the small talk. Something tells me that she's stalling. "I am well. See?" I spread my arms. "Laila is six. Can you believe it! How are you?"

"I am okay. Really, thanks for coming."

"Of course I would come. I am glad you called."

"I don't know how you will feel after we talk. But I want you to know you mean a lot to me."

"You mean a lot to me too, Rini." And it's almost as if the two-year gap never existed. I swallow hard to push down the lump in my throat, and wait expectantly. Nothing she tells me can change the fact that I've never had a friend like Rini, and I don't think I ever will.

"Meera, I've missed you. I'm sorry. I am so, so, sorry." There are tears in Rini's eyes, and then I can't hold back either.

"I've missed you too Rini. And it's okay. Let's forget all the bad stuff." I am sniffing and smiling at the same time.

We sit like that for a few moments. I can't remember the last time I felt this happy. It was probably when Laila was born. Rini looks away and then down at her hands for a long time before she finally speaks.

"You don't know all that's happened, Meera. Maybe you won't be able to forgive me."

"Tell me. Tell me whatever is on your mind."

"I've done something I shouldn't have."

"You never do anything bad. Don't worry, and tell me whatever it is. Please don't worry so much."

"I am so sorry, Meera. I really am. And if I could turn back the clock two years, I would. I am so sorry." Her voice is cracking, and she seems so fidgety. I'm wondering what could make Rini this uncomfortable.

"I know. I would turn back the clock too, Rini. I've missed our time together."

"Oh, that's not it. What I'm trying to say is that I've been in touch with Raul."

Oh. I wasn't expecting that. "What! He never mentioned it."

"Raul and I have been talking on the phone ever since you told me you are going out with him. Ever since that day, we've been talking. Till about six months ago."

"What do you mean you've been talking?" This is confusing.

"Well, I called him that night after you told me you were dating. We began chatting. We didn't talk about you at all. We just chatted about stuff. After that, we had this weird understanding. Um... sorry... I have to get this out, okay? I'm sorry, okay, Meera? Most weekdays I'd call him at night and we talked, sometimes for a few hours. Sometimes we even flirted. I thought it was harmless. But it was not. If you both were going out, he'd tell me he was not available till eleven or whatever time. Then I would even call at that time. Some days we didn't end up talking. But most days we did."

Rini blurts all this out, her words tumbling over each other. Slowly, I start to understand.

My head is reeling. "Do you still like him?"

"No, I don't, Meera. I thought I liked him and maybe I did for a long time. But it didn't feel good. After each call I just felt so wrong inside. And it didn't feel good that he seemed fine with our arrangement, either. I knew I had to tell you. It's taken a long time, and I am sorry and I really hope you can forgive me."

Tears are running down her face now, and I notice a glimmer of sweat on her upper lip. It must take courage to tell me. I have to give her that, even while I despise this betrayal. A betrayal by my best friend *and* my boyfriend. "I don't know what to say."

She looks crestfallen, but she continues. "About six months ago, it hit me how wrong it really was. And I realized that I couldn't like someone like Raul. I knew I had tell you. You are too good for him. What he did was not fair to you. And what I did was not right, either. Oh, it was so wrong and I have learned so much, and I really feel so much regret. I realize I really do love you, Meera. And I will never again do anything to intentionally harm you. I am sorry. Slowly, six months ago, the calls began to stop. I have not spoken to him in the last three or four months at all. But it took me this long to gather my courage to talk to you." She looks down and a tear slides off her face onto her hand.

"Rini, I don't know what to say."

"Okay. I understand."

"Did you both ever meet up? Go on a date or something?"

"We met once."

"Was it a date? Did anything happen?"

"It was about six months ago. We'd been talking for a year and a half. We had talked a few times about meeting up. Finally, that day we met up for the first and only time, went for a drive, and parked at the park. We were just chatting, but it felt very uncomfortable and wrong to me even then. Of course I knew you both were together and he was going behind your back. Then he tried… to kiss me. At that moment I knew for sure this was all wrong and I had made a very big mistake. I knew I had to tell you, to explain."

"He tried to kiss you? Raul?"

"I am sorry, Meera. I can't say that enough."

"Is there more?"

"No."

"I need to go now, Rini."

"Can you forgive me?"

"I don't know."

"Okay, I understand. Whatever you decide, please just know that I really care, I'm really sorry, and know that I'm waiting. Anytime you want to talk I'm here. I... I know you may not want it, but I want our friendship back. I'll respect whatever you decide."

"I have to go, Rini. Bye."

* * *

Forgiveness is a funny thing, as is betrayal. Forgiveness happens the moment you realize that you are being stretched out to breaking point, but that you don't break. Your breaking point is not there. Forgiveness happens in that moment of realization. I wonder if the closest people are always the ones to betray. With me it's been Ari, Mom, Rita and now Raul and Rini. I wonder if the purpose of betrayal is to teach forgiveness. But I can't forgive Raul. I don't know what to say to him. It feels good to cry.

* * *

"Hi, Raul. I wanted to meet today because I have to talk to you about something." I wonder how I am able to keep my voice so calm.

"What's up, babe?"

"I know about you and Rini."

"Huh?" He sits up from his lounging position in the car. "What do you mean?"

"You heard me. I know about you and Rini. I know about the calls and about the meeting."

"She told you? Wow! I never thought... It was nothing, really. It didn't mean anything."

"It's even worse if it meant nothing to you."

"That's not what I mean. I mean... nothing will come out

right, right now. It's just that… what can I say? It's not as bad as it sounds to you. I don't know what she told you, but don't believe everything you hear. It was harmless."

"No it was not harmless."

"I love *you*, Meera."

"That's a bullshit kind of love. I'm done with you." Though my voice is calm, my nails are digging into my palms and I try to loosen my fists, because they begin to hurt.

"Please, baby. I'm sorry. I know you are angry. Let's wait till you calm down."

"Why did you, Raul? You should have thought about it before. The first month we got together is when you started your affair with her. Wow! I would never have imagined."

"It wasn't an affair. Nothing happened! And I don't want to lose you over something that really didn't mean anything to me."

I am now crying hot, angry, indignant tears. "Too late, Raul. We're done. Don't call me anymore, anytime." This chapter of my life is over. It has been a bittersweet chapter, teaching me a lot about life and relationships, but also exacting its pound of flesh.

* * *

I quietly walk home that evening, surprised that I feel a sense of relief. As I reach home and am about to walk in the front door, I hear raised voices coming from inside. I hurriedly unlock the door and walk in to see Super standing with his head bent, looking down at his feet. Mom and Papa are sitting at the table. Papa looks angry, and Mom is crying silently. The argument has stopped and they are quiet now.

"What happened? What's wrong?" I ask.

No one says anything for an eternity. "What happened?" I

try again. "Papa, say something. What's wrong?" I demand, louder this time.

"Ask Sagar what happened," Mom answers in a tearful voice. "He has been lying to all of us. Where did we go wrong? Tell me. What happened for him to do such a terrible thing? Just because we are trusting parents, he thinks he can do anything?"

"Super, tell me." I turn to him, wanting to know what has happened to upset my parents so much.

"We found drugs and a condom in his pocket," Papa says.

"*What?*"

"It was only a joint." Super finally speaks up, defending himself by inadvertently condemning himself.

"How could you be so stupid?" And where is Laila? Did she hear anything?"

"She's asleep. She doesn't know any of this," Papa assures.

"Okay." I sit down next to Papa, not sure what my role is in this situation. Super is fifteen and past the listening age. But he is still my little brother. Have I been so wrapped up in my own little world, in my own life, that I have not noticed the course that my brother's life may be taking?

"There were joints at Ramesh's party. Someone must have stuffed one in my pocket. Everyone smoke joints. It's common."

"It is not common in our household, and it is *illegal*. Do you understand this? Do you understand the health implications?" Papa asks.

Mom is sobbing louder now. "I can't believe you used a condom. You are a child."

"But I have *not* used the condom." Super whines.

"Yes, we can all see it is unused. It is still in its sealed packet. But the question is why do you even have it? Or did someone slip that in your pocket too?" The anger is evident in Papa's controlled voice.

"Really, I've never used one. I mean, I have never gotten there. I mean... look, I just carry one just in case I need it. You know, as a safety precaution."

Before I can stop myself, half a giggle escapes my mouth. Papa glances at me from the corner of his eye, the comical nature of the moment striking him too. I think it might anger him more, but suddenly there is a shift in the tension in the air, and Papa can't resist either. Super visibly relaxes, and I jump in. "Mom, Papa, I will talk to Super. I promise. He'll tell me everything. Let it go right now. Mom, please stop crying. It might seem awful to you, but it is not as bad as it looks."

Super is grateful for my intervention. I am reminded of the time several years ago, when he discovered my sanitary pads in the bathroom. He had gone to Mom and asked her if he could use one. Mom didn't know what to say. I had explained the entire reproduction system to him then, including the menstrual cycle. With a grave expression on his little face, he had said that it sounded painful, he was very sorry I had to bleed every month, and he was very grateful he was a man. I feel a tenderness for my brother and it surprises me. I am still unsure whether I am glad he was ever born, but I *am* sure I love him, regardless.

PART II

Marriages And Mistakes

11

Laila Myna Dutt

The breeze is cool and pleasant and the warmth of the sun feels so good. Meera specially picked Trattoria because of the open-air seating. I feel perfectly content, happy and honestly lucky sitting here with Meera and Super. The three of us are out to celebrate my eleventh birthday. Super is nineteen and Meera is twenty-four. That seems old to me, but I now feel like a big girl too. Papa often says I am the most responsible of us three. I think he may be right. Meera is impulsive and Super simply doesn't care about things that don't affect him. But I do. I know we must care about the world we live in. This evening we will all go out to celebrate – the whole family, like we always do.

My birthday gift from my family is a bicycle. It's real pretty, purple with silver streaks. I love it. Meera said she biked since the age of five or six. I've been using her old bicycle for a few years, but now I have my brand new one. And it's the right size. Meera's was getting small for me.

"Laila, if you could wish for anything at all right now, anything, what would it be? What would you wish for?" asks Meera.

"Hmmm… I don't know."

"Come on, Lai. There's got to be something you want."

Super calls me by his nickname for me. I think he calls me Lai only because he'd rather not be bothered to say the whole name. But I don't mind. I kind of like it.

"I would wish I knew everything before it happened so I could do what I needed to in order to prevent bad things from happening." I was warming up to my idea for a wish. "I could then work with the police and tell them things before they happened."

"You are so practical and good, my sweet little sister," Meera laughs. "I thought you might ask for some*thing* for yourself."

"Yeah, you want to be psychic. What a waste of a wish," Super declares.

I shoot back, smiling, "It's a very good wish, *bhaiya*. I would be playing such an important role in the world if it could come true. So many bad things could be stopped. And I'm not so little anymore."

I love my family. Some of my friends wonder why I am always so happy. They have 'issues' with their families. But I think I lucked out and got the best one.

12

Meera Myna Dutt

Rini and I are out shopping for my wedding. So much has happened over the last few years. We made up after the Raul episode. Rini, unlike Raul, was deeply remorseful. And in spite of everything, I trust her. We met again and talked for hours. We talked about the years we had not talked, and about our feelings for each other. We talked about the meaning of friendship and the impact of mistakes. Rini apologized again for what she had done. I apologized for not understanding her feelings of being unappreciated and sidelined. We cried together and we laughed again. By the end of it, I felt closer to her than I ever had before. My family happily and unquestioningly accepted Rini back in my life. They had missed her too.

Raul tried for a few months to get back with me. I would find cards in my college locker and long messages on my phone. I did not respond. I, surprisingly, had no feelings left for him. From the day I broke it off, it felt like a switch had been turned off. I didn't care to hear his excuses or reasons. I just had no interest left. Though there was hurt — more than that, in fact — I felt relieved that it was over. I think that relationship had not felt right for a long time.

After Raul, there were a few other guys. There was Tony,

who was sweet and melancholic. Tony was still in love with his ex-girlfriend and he spent most of our time together telling me about her, how lovely she was, how much he loved her and how she broke his heart by falling in love with someone else. I often felt like I was his therapist and Tony was my patient rather than my boyfriend. I think the only reason I dated him was because he played the guitar and sang beautifully. I sort of thought that in exchange for the therapy I gave him, he gave me his music. But, of course, that barter could not sustain a relationship.

Then there was Ronak, who could only talk about his desire to join the Indian Army. It was not long before I tired of him referring to me as his commander n' chief, especially during moments of romance. Call me old fashioned, but I prefer 'sweetie'. It's just that Ronak was simply gorgeous. My heart missed a beat each time I saw him. I was content gazing at his beauty. He looked like he belonged in a magazine or a shrine. Each time he opened his mouth to say something though, he ruined it. My infatuation with him shrank shockingly fast. Eventually one evening he tearfully told me he didn't believe I, his commander n' chief, really loved him, and so he was going to move on. Though I felt bad for him, I knew it was best to let him go.

Then there was Sidhu, who swept into my life like a high speed bullet train. That one was a character, he was. He was all personality, larger than life. Sidhu viscerally loved everything and everyone with an overflowing abundance. He went to great lengths to make me feel he cared so much about my every thought and interest. But then I realized that was Sidhu. He went to these lengths for pretty much everyone he encountered, and everyone loved him. The problem, though, was that he had a particular appreciation for beauty, especially that of the female gender. He was endearingly honest and, treating me more like a best buddy than a girlfriend, he shared his appreciation of other women with me. It was cute at first and I thought of myself as progressive and liberal, but it didn't make for a lasting relationship. This time round, the breakup broke my heart. I truly loved Sidhu. I think I will always love Sidhu and his love for all beings. But it felt right at the time to end our supposedly romantic relationship. His spirit was meant to be free, to journey and soar. Perhaps one day his heart would land on one target...or not, but it certainly was not ready yet.

Soon after Sidhu, I met Akash. I was vulnerable and lonely, reeling from the loss of Sidhu from my life. I used to think that all my relationships were doomed and that I'd never find anyone. Akash was charming and dashing. He is Kamla Aunty's neighbor and she introduced him to me at a wedding party we all attended. Younger than me by a year, he was refreshingly honest in a childlike way. And yet it was clear that he could be cold, harsh and manipulative, if needed. There was an unreachable, impenetrable part of him. He himself didn't understand this part of him. Perhaps this complexity was instrumental in the attraction between us.

I must have seen him when I visited Kamla Aunty as a child. He told me he had a crush on me from afar, but was too shy to approach me. We laughed over this like conspirators sharing a secret.

We were so enticed by one another, it felt like live electricity travelled from his eyes to mine and vice-versa. I wanted to touch him, just touch any part of him, all the time. It was not long before we began seeing each other. It began one day when he simply stated, "It's painful to keep this up. We really should kiss." I knew exactly what he meant.

Those were charmed days. We laughed a lot, even when there didn't seem to be anything particularly funny. We talked about everything – from the state of the country to feelings and philosophy. It was cold and hot all at once. Sometimes when we were close, I burned up inside; at other times, I felt chills run down my spine. Finally I was in a deeper, madly passionate relationship, the type that's in the movies. In that regard, I didn't know whether I was entering into a life phase or leaving it. Some of the emotions that came up were new. With Akash near me, it felt like life was constantly moving in some vortex. And I knew he felt it too.

Akash responded to me perfectly. He often got what I was thinking, just by looking at me. At times he answered my thought before I articulated it. And his answers would explain to me who I was. Papa didn't like him. Perhaps Papa didn't like the hold Akash had on me. Though it was still magical, Papa's disapproval dampened it.

Then suddenly one day, several months later, without any explanation, Akash stopped calling me. When I called him, he didn't answer. I was worried and I showed up at Kamla Aunty's house. I could not believe what she told me. He was engaged to be married to someone. My Akash was engaged to be married to someone else. I could not believe it.

To date I don't know how I made it back home that day. All I felt was a heavy grating, crushing sensation endlessly bearing down on me. And then my body was numb. As soon as I was home, I fell into my bed and stayed there for I don't know how long.

There was no explanation or closure. When I could finally feel something other than a deadening numbness, my heart felt like a thousand pieces, each one a shard of glass that hurt with every breath I took. I didn't sleep or eat for days. I was a walking zombie. I wished I didn't exist. I could not understand *why* he did this. I still don't understand. I thought we had something special, something worth keeping alive. But I had been so wrong. How could I have been wrong, when we had so much love, laughter and all that electricity between us? I have never laughed so much in any relationship, before or after Akash. For a long time I didn't want to date, or put my trust in men. And I felt a familiar anger. The anger that still came up those rare moments when something triggered a memory of Monty... or a hazy memory of Ari.

* * *

Rini was with me through the ups and downs of my dating life. Her advice was, as always, stellar. Without her to share everything with, I am not sure how I would have made it through this roller coaster ride. I don't know how girls go through anything without a best girlfriend.

For a long time after Akash, I was not interested in anyone. I was intent and focused on my work. I was working at a dotcom startup in Mumbai. I wrote content for them. It was not exactly where I wanted to end up with my journalism degree, but it was the second job I had ever had and I saw it as a stepping stone.

My first job was with a local magazine close to home, in Delhi. They hired me straight out of college to write about monuments and events. I'd enjoyed my work and remember that entire period of time as tinged with a playful, happy hue, with all my dating escapades, Rini and my family.

But it was time to grow up and when a good out-of-state opportunity came along, I was ready. Even though six months had passed since Akash, I was desperate to get away. It took some convincing to get Papa and Mom to allow me to move to Bombay. They finally relented when Rini got a job offer in Bombay right after I did.

I am glad I liked my job enough to stick around in Bombay; otherwise, I may never have met Neel... again. On the fateful night of my twenty-seventh birthday, Rini and I were sitting at Raja's Pub, enjoying the comfort of being alone after a fun filled evening. Everyone else had left after drinks, dinner and more drinks. I was twirling round on the barstool, high on birthday wishes and cocktails. Suddenly the door opened and in walked a man in a long-sleeved blue t-shirt that hugged his perfect chest and torso. I stopped mid-twirl to stare shamelessly. It was more than a year since Akash; more than a year since I found any man remotely interesting. "Breathe, Meera." Rini whispered.

He had walked right up to us. "May I buy you ladies another round?" He had said it without blinking an eye. I knew Rini would be on guard and cautious, even though he was stunningly irresistible. This is how she always is. I think she wants to explore relationships, but her inner guard comes in the way. Through my dating escapades after Raul, Rini never expressed interest in anyone. On the rare occasions when I tried to give her advice on the subject, she clammed up, assuming, I suppose, that the conversation may steer itself to the painful Raul topic. I wonder if it's because the only guy she claims to have fallen for turned out to be a lying, cheating, player that she's just off men. Sometimes I even wonder if she is actually interested in women rather than men, because she certainly has some strange reactions to male attention.

Rini responded for us, "Um... thank you, but we are okay." Then it was as if Rini took my stool twirling role and started twirling away, ignoring the handsome interloper. I, however, kept smiling at him.

"How are you both?" He was undeterred. "It's been so long."

"Excuse me?" Rini turned around, looking quite shocked.

"Rini, Meera! It's been years." How did this stranger know our names?

"Who are you?" Rini sounded rude.

"Neel. We went to school together." He turned to me, an irresistible smile on his face. "I was the one who had such a massive crush on you, Meera. Remember?"

And the memory had come flooding back. This was Neel; the Neel with the rose poem and the tear in his eye when I turned him down. What a looker he had turned into. I wondered if that old crush of his still lingered. Can't say that would be a bad thing.

We had talked half the night, reminiscing about old times and people from the past. Even Rini had warmed up to him. We updated each other on the courses our lives had taken. Neel was a software guy. I didn't understand the underworld of computer technology too well, so I could not figure out exactly what he did. But he did something that sounded innovative, cool and good for the planet. He worked with 'green technology'. I was impressed that night and it showed. I was hanging on to his every word and he kept looking at me in a more-than-just-casually-interested way too.

Thankfully, he asked for my number. He called the very next day and asked me out. That fateful birthday night was followed by a whirlwind romance. And I hoped with all my heart that this one would have a happily-ever-after ending.

Neel is everything I am looking for. He is charming, sensitive and intelligent. He is popular, successful and deliciously handsome. I have butterflies in my stomach just looking at him. Everyone seems to like him. He is a good guy with all the charm of a bad boy. Even Rini likes him. Rini, with her boundaries and guardedness, is disarmed by my handsome suitor. She is genuinely happy for me. I love being around him. He makes me feel special. He makes me feel like the rose in his poem. Anger is forgotten; Akash is forgotten; and as for Ari, he is a distant memory lost in the history of time. I'm giddy, even though I feel like I have finally landed instead of aimlessly floating.

13

Meera Myna Dutt

It's been one short week since Neel proposed. We'd been dating for about nine months and I didn't expect it. We were out celebrating his cousin's birthday that night. Driving me home, he'd stopped the car mid-route and said that something seemed to be stuck on the wipers. I got out of the car with him to take a look. And around the tip of the wiper blade was a sparkly something. My mind took very long to register that it was a diamond ring, and that this was a proposal.

As I pull the ring off the wiper blade and turn around, Neel is down on his knee, asking me to marry him. But the words don't register in my head, and for a few moments, I don't respond. Neel, thrown off by my silence, looks at me with an awkward, wounded expression, and I realize I am dampening the experience for him. I don't get emotional like women do in movies, but I smile and laugh when I say, "Yes, of course!" It still feels strange this is really happening. Mom and Papa are delighted with the news. Even Super seems uncharacteristically generous with grins and hugs. And dear sweet Laila can't stop smiling. Do I deserve all this?

Very privately, in the depths of my mind, however, are questions. And though I don't let them surface, I can't seem to shake them off. What if marriage ruins things? How come

I've never seen a good marriage in my life, be it Mom and Dad's, Rini's parents', Rita's parents' or any other I know? Nani and Nana had a good marriage, but that was of another time and age. What if marriage changes what Neel and I have between us?

* * *

I am floating in an ether zone. I am so light, I am almost not physical. I am a thought, a moment, a sensation, a realization, a soul. Everything around me is bright and beautiful, but not the kind of bright that hurts the eyes. Perhaps I don't have physical eyes. But I can see more than ever before. This is another realm. What is it? Like a God-kissed touch of heaven, it is a moment in a timeless realm.

Slowly a beautiful, ethereal temple materializes in my vision. Tall columns rise so high that they seem to disappear into the atmosphere. It shines with a blue-indigo light. It is made of something pearly. Its sacred aura beckons me. I am drawn in. Inside this temple are many beings. Yet it is not crowded. There is space for everyone who wants to be here. There is an overwhelming awareness of love. I can tell that all the beings know this too. It feels like being bathed in love. There is something divine about this love. It is more than the everyday human kind. There are many shelves with volumes of knowledge. The beings are looking for their particular volumes, the volumes that will address their hearts' quests.

I am drawn to a table in the back. As I get there, I see four powerful, loving beings. They are spirits. The male beckons me. "Come forth." I realize he is communicating without speaking. I just feel his thought in my head. I look at them. The woman next to him sends love with such intensity that I am moved to tears. But there are no physical tears. It is only a sensation. "Come forth" – I hear again. The other two spirits are sitting back, smiling. The woman spirit has some concern. I feel her thoughts in my head. "Choose always from love, not from fear. Remember this place and remember this love. It is within you. Choose from love, and for love. We are here to love, guide and protect you. We are always with you. Choose from love."

I want to know more. I want her to explain. It is important. "Go forth with love."

I wake up.

* * *

I am disoriented by the dream. It seemed so real. It was not like other dreams. It had a different quality. What did it mean? "Go forth with love" was the parting message. I take this to mean I have made the right choice in Neel. And the woman told me to choose from love and not fear. I want to remember this. I don't know how this applies to me, but I want to remember it.

I don't tell anyone about this dream. Not even Neel. It's too intense to explain.

* * *

I am certain that to attendees the wedding seems like a fairytale. Everyone looks beautiful in their finery, and all the events run smoothly. Being a typical Indian wedding, it is a three-day process. The first evening we have a music and dance program at a fancy hotel poolside, with a troupe of folk dancers from Rajasthan. After the professional performance, Laila performs a dance with Neel's younger sister Asha. The invitees are mingling and having their cocktails, but during the performances, there is silence. The dances are riveting. I wear a yellow and gold *ghagra choli* for this. And for the first time ever, I wear flowers in my hair, which flows in loose curls over my backless *choli*. They are fragrant white *mogra* flowers. I wear pearls in my ears and neck. I feel beautiful and bridal. Neel looks dashing in a dark blue *kurta* and *churidar* embroidered with yellow thread. We are quite the couple. There is a constant loud thumping feeling in my chest that feels like joy. But the pit of my stomach nervously feels like it's going to fall out any moment. I am good at hiding this internal storm behind smiles and laughter and no one seems to notice it as I work the room, talking to people.

"Are you happy, Meera?" Rini whispers, grinning from ear to ear. She herself looks ecstatic. "You look beautiful you know?"

"Yeah, I feel beautiful, but I'm nervous, Rini. I have not mentioned this to anyone, but I don't know. I mean marriage is hard, no?"

"I've never been married, you dodo. Someone told me it's like having a second job, but if you get it right, the companionship is worth it. Don't worry. Neel and I will both make sure you get it right."

"You definitely have a way of reassuring me," I say sarcastically.

"Okay, now smile and look the part."

"I will. And you go get me a drink." Rini dutifully runs off to get me a vodka martini, which she knows is my drink of choice.

As I wait, Neel waves me over from the other side of the room. He is standing with Mom and Papa and his parents. Rini has just returned with my martini and I distractedly grab it and head over to Neel. Everyone looks like they've just discovered a pot of gold in their backyard. I don't understand why weddings bring so much joy. It's not a big achievement. I mean, anyone of legal age can marry. It's not like climbing Mount Everest or getting a Doctorate. Those are *actual* achievements. Marriage, on the other hand, should make people nervous, considering the divorce rates these days. But everyone looks so happy. It's irritating.

"Meera, what do we call each other's parents now on?" Neel winks at our parents and turns to gaze lovingly at me.

We have been calling each other's parents 'Aunty' and 'Uncle'. Tradition dictates we switch over to 'Mom' and 'Dad' after marriage. But no one can compete with *my* Mom and Papa and I don't want to call Neel's parents by those terms. I wish Neel had not put me on the spot like this. Perhaps this is the first time in our relationship that I'm annoyed at him.

"Um… uh…," I stammer. "Yes, what now?"

Neel looks at me funny. But Papa knows what I am thinking. He jumps in, "I think we should give the kids some time to adjust to the idea of marriage. They will figure out what to call us in due time. I would like to make a toast." How I love Papa.

We all raise glasses, and Papa makes the toast. "Here's to hoping your love is modern enough to survive the times, and old fashioned enough to last forever. Here's to the new bride and groom to be." Everyone looks at us. I feel a blush creeping up my face, while Neel looks comfortable and happy. Papa makes it sound so sappy and romantic. I drain my glass. I am supposed to be happy. I think I am happy. I must be. It's just that I am not a sappy person and I haven't seen a single healthy marriage in my life. I know Neel is amazing, our relationship is strong and I want this marriage. I need to hang on to that thought. But I'm uncomfortable and start looking around. I spot my cousin Rita and her husband of one year, Ashish. I smile, tell everyone that I'm going to greet Rita, and turn and walk away.

"Rita, Ash." I call Ashish with the nickname I have fondly used since the time Rita introduced him to me. We all embrace.

"Meera, you look beautiful." Rita says as Ash nods his polite agreement.

"Thank you."

My mind is far away. I think about Rita's journey. If Rita can survive a marriage, so can I. Besides, I think the world of Neel. Why am I so uncomfortable? Why am I nervous and panicky? Maybe I am not cut out for this. The voice in my head drones on and on.

"The dancers were superb." says Ashish.

I smile and nod distractedly.

"Why do you look pale, Meera?" Rita asks, concern in her voice.

Emboldened by my vodka, I whisper urgently, "Is marriage really a good thing?"

"Oh, Meera! Neel is a great guy. I think it's going to be good for you," Rita responds.

"Yeah, I know he's a great guy, but what if things change after marriage? You know? Do things change? I mean, why get married? Why take chances with a good thing? Neel is a happy, positive person. I am more realistic and I just don't want to mess this up. I am nervous."

"Just relax," Rita calms me. "Look at us. Ashish and I are happy. We have both had to make some adjustments but it's worth it. You've found a great guy. There is no reason for it to get messed up."

"You really think so?"

"Yes. Now stop worrying over nothing and listen. We

have something to share with you." Rita looks lovingly up at Ashish. "We are pregnant."

"What?" This is confusing. This conversation is supposed to be about me, not Rita or some pregnancy. I abruptly flash back to my thirteenth birthday, when Papa told us Mom was pregnant.

"Aren't you happy?"

"Yes, yes of course; just really surprised. Sorry." I immediately launch myself at Rita and Ashish and proceed to hug the breath out of them. I don't know why I am misty-eyed. Is it because I am uncharacteristically happy for Rita, or is it because I am deeply sad that the world as I know it seems to be changing forever before my very eyes?

I suddenly want to hold onto my childhood with every ounce of my strength. How do women experience blissful joy, unshaking confidence and intense pleasure at the aspects of marriage and motherhood? Or do they? I have seen bitter disappointment many a times in the eyes of many worldly wise women after they have experienced these life events. And if that is so, then why do women make the same age old mistakes? I don't understand.

And here I am at the threshold of my own wedding, just as instrumental in the changing, shifting sands of time that I am trying so desperately to hold back. I don't like man-made institutions, societal requirements and pressures. I don't like the expectation that every woman must conform and not only embrace, but also *like* the role of wife and mother. And if she shows the slightest deviance, she will be judged. I don't like that Neel does not feel any of these conflicting thoughts. I am envious of his exuberance, his innocence and his untainted love for me. And I wonder if dissatisfaction and confusion are weaved like a thread through my life; and I wonder...

"Stop it." Rini has found me again. She can read my expression. She knows me well. "Here drink up." She hands me a glass of vodka and tonic, an effective, though temporary balm for my angst. And I go stand with Neel and smile as I am expected to. I think I enjoy the evening in spite of my newly emerging trepidations.

* * *

Helped by all the vodka tonics I have drunk, I sleep that night. I feel I am in a cocoon of love, with all my extended family all around for the three-day wedding celebration. Some family members are staying with us at home and others at the nearby Hotel Siddharth. I sorely miss Nani and feel her presence many a time. I miss her more since her death than I did when she was alive. It is sad that we take for granted what we have till it's gone. It's been five years since she passed and in my head I've had a few conversations with her. I believe she hears me.

"Meera, *Beta*, wake up and come join us in the living room. Everyone is sitting together having *chai*."

"Yeah, join the world of the living." Super is awake early today.

"Yes, Mom, I'm awake. I'm coming." I choose to ignore Super's comment.

"Meera, I love you." Laila comes into my room and snuggles comfortably under the covers. We are both in bed, lying side by side. My eyes well up.

"I love you too, Laila."

"Meera, does this mean we won't see as much of each other, once you are married?"

"Of course we will, you silly. I am not going anywhere. We'll be just as we always are." But it feels like there is a

metal hook in my heart tearing it apart, even as I say this.
"Who's in the living room?" I change the subject.

"Everyone. Rita and Ashish are pregnant. They just announced it. They said they told you last night. Are you happy for them?"

"Yeah, whatever makes them happy is good. You know how I feel about such things though. I just don't get excited." I make a face. "Were you excited when Mom was pregnant with me?"

"No. But I loved you the moment I saw you. And that has not changed."

"Meera, are you sure you want to be married?" This seems to come out of nowhere. I wonder what Laila has noted. "No."

"Why don't you tell Papa then? We can wait. Neel will understand."

"No. It's too late. Look at all these arrangements. Everyone is here. Everything has been done. I think I'll always feel unsure, no matter how long I wait, and no matter how amazing the guy is, maybe because I am unsure about marriage itself. I just have to go through with this now."

"Okay," says my wise, beautiful almost-fifteen-year-old sister with a worried look in her eyes.

* * *

That afternoon is the *mehndi* function at home in our back yard, followed by an informal early cocktail terrace party for only our wedding guests. Neel, his family and their guests have their own party today. Mom is going crazy with the preparations, even though everything is catered. I have a whole month off work, and the luxury of being home and being pampered shows on my face. I am not particularly fond of *mehndi*. I love how cool it feels on my hands and feet, and I love how the deep, intricate designs look for the first few days, but then it just starts to fade away. Is this symbolic of marriages, I wonder. Do marriages begin to fade away after the intensity of the first few months or years? Is it typical for one to get as jittery before their wedding, as I am?

Neel texts me that he misses me. I text him back telling him to enjoy his bachelorhood while he has it. I marry him tomorrow.

I wear a deep emerald green *angarkha* for the festivities of the day. My hair is tied up with intentional but annoying wisps escaping all around my face that I try to brush away in futility. My friends surround me as I sit to get the *mehndi* applied. Everyone is laughing and sharing wedding jokes. It does feel festive. Since the *mehndi* is, per tradition, a ladies-only event, we tease Super relentlessly for hanging around. Super has a crush on my friend Roshni's younger sister Kiran. So I know exactly why he is hanging around. And I seize my chance to make him get us drinks and snacks and generally run errands. Since he wants to impress Kiran, he behaves like the cherubic good boy. And it is all very amusing to me. Super and I are closer now than we have ever been. It's almost as if we suddenly appreciate each other, now that I am about to get married. It is a silent fondness, a bond that can exist only between siblings. It is a recognition of the unspoken promise that we have each other's backs.

Before the cocktail party Papa comes up to me, and careful not to mess the still wet *mehndi* on my hands and feet, grabs me in his loving, warm hug. "You are sure you're all right, Meera?" He says astutely. "You know you can tell me whatever your heart desires. You know you can come to me with murder. And I will always be there."

"I know, Papa. Just tell me, will I always be your favorite? Even after tomorrow?"

"You know the answer to that."

"Nothing changes, right?"

"No."

"Then I will be okay." And it's my turn to comfort him. I certainly don't want to plague him with the contradictions in my mind. Instead, I want to push them way to the back, as far as they will go. And maybe they will stay there forever.

* * *

With tears in her eyes, Mom says I look splendid in the traditional red, white and gold. Mom says people will not believe this beautiful bride is her daughter. Why would Mom say that? And do I really look splendid enough to move Mom to tears? I am not quite sure, as I check to see if the colour of my nail polish matches my sari. It does. When I look in the mirror though, I see a stranger; a stranger whose face is decorated with bridal make-up and chunky, stylish *kundan* jewelry. Suddenly I want to tear it all off, wear my jeans and t-shirt and jump into my bed with a good book. But I hug Mom and ask her to stop crying.

"No, Meera, I am not crying. I am very happy. You are my firstborn. You are the one who first made me a mother. You are special to me."

"Really, Mom?"

"Don't you know this?"

I start to tear up too.

14

Neel Kant Duggar

She makes my heart beat faster. She is the sweetest, most beautiful woman I know. She is womanly with her warmth and love, and girlish in her innocence. I am lucky. I can't believe we are getting married. I have loved her since we were in school. Since before I knew what love is. And she loves me back. I never thought... I didn't expect to run into her like that at the bar. And I didn't expect her to love me back. She's been a part of my dreams since I was thirteen. I still have the poem I wrote for her. The only poem I ever wrote. And it turns out it is the song of my life. I won't believe anyone who tells me that dreams don't come true.

Mom and Dad have been asking me to settle down for years. Now they are ecstatic. They love Meera. Can it all work out so well? Does anyone get to be this happy? I love everything about her. I love the way her hair falls down her back in curls. And I love the dimple on her cheek when she smiles. I love the softness in her voice. Most of all I love her eyes... the windows to her soul. I see in them a reflection of the best person I can be. Thank you, whoever it is up there.

"*Neeeeel,* come on, Dude, it's *your* wedding. *You* of all people can't be late."

It is Karan, my best friend.

"Be right there."

I look one last time at the black and white photograph in my hand, Meera and I are at the beach. Laila, bless her heart, took the photo. She is a natural photographer. Meera looks happy. She is looking straight ahead at the camera and smiling, with her hair flying back from her face. I have my face turned to her. The sea, sand and sun glimmer behind us. I put the photo back in my wallet. This marriage is my destiny. And it seems I knew that at thirteen.

15

Meera Myna Dutt

There is a growing, gnawing knot in the pit of my stomach as I walk through the busy Manhattan street. I am meeting Ari yet again for a quick drink at Rene's. I am in tall brown boots – not leather, because I am a vegetarian and don't wear leather – with brown tights under a dark chocolate brown, slightly flared skirt and a grey sweater. My jacket is a deeper grey, with faux fur at the collar.

Neel and I moved to New York six months after we married. It was a tearful, bewildering time for me. Saying goodbye to Papa, Laila, Mom, Super, and Rini was more painful than anything I have ever experienced. I was still reeling from this pain, trying to come to terms with this new phase of my life when, two months after we moved, Papa was in a car accident. A drunk driver rammed into the left back side of our car, and Papa was sitting on the right, at the back. I can't imagine what would have happened if the car had rammed into the side Papa was sitting on, for the left side caved fully and the car had to be totaled. Our driver, Mukund, thankfully had only some minor scratches and scrapes. And though everyone remarked that Papa was really lucky to come out of such a crash relatively unharmed, he did get an injury. A sharp three-inch piece of glass flew from the crash and embedded itself in Papa's left leg. The doctor said it was a good thing that it did not cut into his bone. Papa was rushed to the hospital and had to have sixteen stitches to stem the bleeding and close his wound. Mom told me that his hands shake now.

I wanted to see Papa for myself. I realized that in that moment, that Mom is the one I talk to more on the phone now; Mom and I yearn for and comfort each other, share our daily joys and sorrows. But Papa always has and will remain the one who defines me. My life stems from being my Papa's daughter. And this accident felt like it threatened my very life force.

But Neel didn't want me to go to India unplanned. He said things like thankfully Papa is okay, and that it's so lucky that he didn't get hurt worse than this, and that if he was *really* hurt, then it would make sense for me to go, but because he is okay we should wait till our planned trip. But Papa was *really* hurt, he *did get* sixteen stitches, his hands now *shake*. Neel presented reasons such as how expensive it is to travel, and how it's only been two months since I saw them, and how it doesn't make sense for me to go every time something small happened. But this was not something small, and I explained how I felt till I was hoarse in the throat, but after several arguments that turned into bitter fights, I finally gave up. I couldn't stand up to his logic. I felt controlled and browbeaten, and it was new for me to have to consider a partner's opinion in such a deeply sentimental decision that involved my family. And though I gave up, it left a deep wedge in my heart, perhaps one that could never be filled. How dare Neel come between me and my parents? And though I continued to love Neel, I began to slowly also detest him. At times I hated everything he symbolized – my separation from my loved ones, my yearning, desperate loneliness and most of all my abyss-like, spiraling depression.

I learned to cope, and to push it away to the back of my mind so that I could get through the day. And slowly, I began to get used to it. This pain remains, even though we plan to go back home for three weeks each year, and even though I know that when Neel's project ends, we will move back to Delhi permanently. The facts that it's been less than a year since we moved, and I talk to Mom and Papa every single day, and Skype with Laila, and exchange long emails with Rini, don't stem my sadness.

I push these thoughts and memories away, as far away as I can. The thought of meeting Ari and spending time with him makes me forget my sorrows. I am smiling now and, like my pulse, my pace quickens. I anticipate Ari's warm hug and the whiff of his particular smell that I hold on to, long after his hugs. This old, deep connection that accidentally – by a strange fateful meeting – got revived, makes me happy. It reminds me of who I was before life took over. It reminds me of innocent days. Who knew Ari Hasan Jana was in New York? Who knew I'd find a lost, shimmering piece of my childhood here with him, like an oasis in the middle of a desert?

* * *

When Neel and I moved to America, I think I immediately fell into a semi-depression. I didn't enjoy the pleasures or comparative cleanliness of the 'first world'. Unlike Neel, I was not excited each morning when I woke up. Holding his cup of morning coffee, Neel would look out the bedroom window of our fifth-floor Manhattan apartment, and each morning when he came in to say bye to me before work, and his chest would swell up. He would get a smug, satisfied and excited look on his face. And I would bury myself deeper under the covers. Sometimes I would even pretend to be asleep. He would look at me wistfully and look out the window again. And I don't know why, but the joy evident on his face would anger me.

I longed for the sounds and smells of Delhi and the tropical heat of Bombay. I wanted to eat *pav bhaji, wada pav, bhel puri* and *chaat* at wonderfully unique street corners, not French fries and burgers at standard looking fast food joints. I wanted to chat with street vendors with familiarity and authority in Hindi, not order spice-less food from polite, disinterested servers at clean American restaurants. I wanted to hear the hustle and bustle of busy Indian neighborhoods, not grab the paper from a sterile apartment hallway to read news that didn't interest me. And I certainly wanted aromatic sweet *chai* brewed with love, not bitter American coffee out of a pot. I wanted to turn back the clock, right all the wrongs and to go back to being five years old…or fifteen. I just wanted out. I didn't want to be an adult, or have responsibility, or miss home anymore.

Neel didn't understand this burning, churning, pining, ache within me. I think the ferocity of my emotion frightened him a little. He could not hold me when the tears came pouring relentlessly down my cheeks, or when the heaving sobs left me breathless, or when my panic was evident in my defeated eyes. I was desperate in those early days for Neel's camaraderie, his understanding and his empathy. After all, didn't he also go through a similar separation, a tearing away from his family, his place of birth and residence of twenty eight years? But I was waiting in vain. Neel didn't for a moment experience my plight.

For him, coming to America was an experience and an experiment in success. He felt he had arrived and he faced each day with vigour and delight. His single minded goal was to succeed immeasurably in his work, which would earn him more recognition and yet another promotion with his company. In his mind, his new marriage and his carefully chosen, perfect wife certainly could not, and would not interfere with his success. How could *his* wife be unhappy? That to him would mark his own failure. And he could not fail, because everything he did was good and right, and so he succeeded in all his undertakings. But to me, his failure was blatant in the fact that he refused to see what was happening to us.

When I expressed my angst, he shut down and looked the other way. And though I understood this, I resented not only his expectation of me, but also his inability to acknowledge my experience, let alone to be present for me. This grew like a chasm between us, a silent burden that our relationship began to carry. We both accepted this chasm. Neel accepted it silently, gracefully, fearfully; I accepted it kicking and screaming. And then Papa's accident happened, and gave undeniable definition to this chasm and my resentment for Neel.

* * *

"Meera. Hi, sweetheart."

"Hi." He gives me a hug, holding me ever so gently, ever so close. I avidly take in Ari's special smell. It is like tobacco and spice and musk and sex. I am shocked and embarrassed, and glad that Ari cannot hear my thoughts.

"Your face is flushed." He releases me and peers at me. He pinches my nose as one would a child's.

We walk over to Romano's Grill, which has a bar area – that's our usual place – and we order our beers. Ari is turning me into a beer drinker and it surprises me that Neel doesn't notice these small changes in me. I think I am bolder and more confident, speaking up at times I would have previously remained silent. In that way I feel Ari is good for me. He has historically been present for me at the worst of times and this time around he's distracted me from utter despair.

"Tina is in Las Vegas this week. She's attending a conference there and she wants to take the time to think, so she will spend the week there." Tina is Ari's girlfriend of four years. It seems like Ari always has a girlfriend, because whenever I've known him, he's had one.

"So you are a free man for a week."

"I am always a free man." Ari's eyes twinkle mischievously. My heart flutters.

I am bewildered and flattered that Ari wants to spend so much time with me. He is forty-two years old, wise and kind. So much of life has happened and changed, yet it seems something has remained unchanged between us – the understanding or secret language we seem to have. Perhaps it is the safety of the space between us, a space in which I can express simply anything and be assured of a loving acceptance, just like when I was a young girl. A space in which I can say all those things that I can't share with Neel anymore.

Ari makes life tolerable and I momentarily forget my aching pain. He makes me want to enjoy life and take it as it comes, for he seems to love life himself. He is charmingly warm and so full of welcoming love for everyone, and he wants to hear everything I have to say. Even the difficult things, *especially* the difficult things. This is the third time we have met for a drink in the four weeks since I ran into him. Neel does not mind. He knows Ari as my older neighbour in Jaipur who used to indulge me as a kid, and he is not the least bit threatened by Ari.

* * *

It was at a sidewalk advocacy event that I had run into Ari about a month ago, soon after Papa's accident. It was a Friday evening and Neel was at a work happy hour. I could see from my apartment window the very tail end of the booths and stalls set up on the sidewalk around the bend of our street. Since leaving India, I had not been one to venture out, especially not without Neel to coax me into it. So I don't quite know where my sense of adventure came from, but that day, in my checkered cotton pajama bottoms and a t-shirt, I stepped out into the muggy evening Manhattan air and made my way over to the stalls to see what all the fuss was about. As I rounded the bend, the entire street came into view. There were booths selling ethnic wares, from Native American totems to Mexican sombreros, on one side of the street. Music floated into the air from a booth in the center of the row. The music had a mysterious, sensual rhythm to it and I wondered if it was Middle Eastern.

On the opposite side of the street were three podiums with microphones, and by now my curiosity was piqued enough that I was looking for signs that might tell me what this event was. Suddenly, a smooth, husky voice reverberated through one of the microphones and I turned to look at the speaker. He was tall, lanky and a fit-looking man. Older than me, he looked vaguely familiar, but I brushed this feeling away, assigning my sense of familiarity to him being South Asian in this land of foreigners.

"Friends, I urge you to step up and take a stand. If we, as a collective, don't raise our voices now, a proposition that defies our very constitution will make it to parliament. A proposition that takes away a woman's right to decide about her own sexual health, life and future. A proposition that is preposterous in its very concept. Friends..."

I gathered this speech was about women's rights with regards to the new health bill. Why did his voice sound so mysteriously familiar? Of course I didn't know the speaker, as I didn't know anyone in this country except Neel's colleagues and my distant cousin who lived in the suburbs with her third husband and son. This cousin, Dipika, had a shady history and she kept her distance from the whole family. All I knew was that she had a daughter with her first husband, lost the daughter at a young age to a childhood illness, and left the husband, who then lost his mind and had to be committed to some sort of an institution; her second husband was murdered under unknown circumstances and now it seemed she was finally settled with the third husband and their son.

The speech by the disturbingly familiar man was over and the next speaker was coming up to the same podium.

"Thank you sincerely to my wonderful friend and colleague. He has said it all. This is what we need to fight for, what we need to take a stand for. Ari has described exceptionally well in his trademark powerful way. Let's give it up for Ari Jana."

I tuned out the clapping, I tuned out whatever else was being said. My lucidity in that moment hung on only two singular words "Ari Jana". This was Ari and it was no coincidence that he sounded and looked so familiar. This was my childhood friend and foe; Ari from a long buried innocent time; Ari, my first love after Papa. My hands turned cold and I clutched them into fists, there were butterflies in my stomach, I could barely believe that I was about to meet Ari Jana again.

I didn't hear a word of the rest of the speeches. Time slowed down and sped up all at the same time. Nani and the smell of Jaipur soil flashed in my mind. Was I about to find a piece of my roots? Would Ari want to talk to me? Would he even remember me? Back then he was a glamourous, unattainable, kind teenager, while I was an insignificant slip of a child. My head felt like it would explode with anticipation.

When the speeches were finally over, I walked up to him and tapped him on his back. He had been talking animatedly with one of the other speakers. He had stopped mid-sentence and whirled around. His eyes were searching, wondering, but he had a smile on his face. I had begun to introduce myself, but before I could finish he had pulled me into the warmest embrace and said of course he remembered me and that I was all grown up now. He took my number and gave me his. He had said he would love to catch up.

* * *

The next day he had called me and we'd decided to meet for a drink at Romano's. I had told Neel about it, and Neel seemed happy for me to have found an old contact. Frankly, I think Neel was relieved that finally I showed excitement about something.

Ari surreptitiously told me during our first meeting that he was, 'in a former life', as he put it, involved in corporate espionage and secret operations situations. He worked at the grassroots level for a private protection agency that was contracted for government jobs. He had come to the US as a student almost two decades ago. He first went through the education and training programme, and then climbed up the ranks in the field of corporate espionage. He began working on very sensitive and secret projects. There was a lot of money in the work and an early retirement. It felt risky and exciting. Ari said he felt he owned the world during those days.

However, about two years ago he had a moment of realization that, through his choice of work, he opposed his own beliefs of non-institutionalization. He told me he was horrified at the hypocrisy of the situation, and at his lack of insight until that moment. He, after all, had been facilitating the process of institutionalization, power and control, and promoting government agenda by participating in their espionage systems and secret operations. Over the objections of his ex-wife and some well-wishers, Ari resigned the very next morning. He then devoted his time fully to a New York based women's rights organization, HENNA. He slowly became an instrumental member of the organization, and its biggest public face. Working full time for HENNA, he often participated very vocally in street advocacy and street theatre to showcase their message. He loved every aspect of this work and believed in it with a zeal.

Ari got married twelve years ago, and divorced about five years ago. During the seven years of his marriage he had a daughter and then a son. His daughter, Rumi, was now eleven years old. Six years earlier he lost his three-year-old son Roho in an accident. Roho was playing on the sidewalk by their suburban home and he ran after the ball that rolled onto the street. In the slip of a second, a van that speedily turned the corner rammed into and crushed the child right before Ari's eyes. Though the van screeched to a halt, it was too late. Ari spoke about this in a matter of fact manner and said his marriage never recovered from that incident. His ex-wife, Rumana, fell deeply into an abyss of grief, while Ari devoted his time and energy to parenting Rumi, and to his work. Before they knew it, Ari said, they had become practically strangers.

Ari met Tina at a sidewalk advocacy event a year after his divorce. They had been instantly attracted to one another. Both of them were single and committed to change the world. Tina utilized her MBA from Harvard Business School to manage a big advertising outfit that prided itself on its ethical advertising policy. She devoted her evenings and weekends to advocating for any cause that caught her attention.

I told him about Laila, before whose birth Ari had left India; I told him about Neel, and how we met. He wanted to know about Mom, Papa and Super, of course; and I told him about Rini too, and about the life I had in India. Slowly, intimately, we caught up on each other's life trajectories.

There was something charming about our conversations. They were hushed and had a secretive quality about them. In a sense, he was my oldest friend. I liked Ari a lot. I liked his carefree attitude, his piercing warmth and his passionate love for everything. I admired his solid commitment to his ideals. Besides, how cool was it that Ari could carry off a floral shirt, and stand in front of a crowd, performing and advocating for women's rights! Neel would never even attempt that.

* * *

"We climbed for three straight days, and it was so cold, it took an hour for water to boil. The higher we went, the colder it got. On the third day Mukud realized something was wrong with his feet. He could not feel his toes anymore. When we saw he had frostbite, we started back down as fast as we could. Between the three of us we carried him most of the way down. We rushed him to the closest local hospital in Kathmandu. But they had to amputate nine of his toes."

"Ugh. Why do you tell me such stories? Ari, you love adventure. And you don't care if it is dangerous. In fact, the more the danger, the more the attraction. You are a dangerous man."

"And you have not lost your unique knack of making simple observations sound like profound announcements." Ari laughs.

I love his laugh and the laugh lines that form at the corners of his eyes. I love how he is completely attentive, seemingly enraptured by the conversation, while appearing as if he is pondering some weighty matter and at the same time is amused by some secret joke. Ari has always been a charming person, but now he seems magical, like he holds the key to all the world's secrets. And, over time, he will reveal them to you, if he feels like it.

"Why do you meet up with me?" I ask.

"The heart wants to, and I just follow."

The *heart* wants to? "But why? I mean, I am not, you know... like you." I stumble over what I am trying to convey. I want to say I am so much younger than him, and not as wise, interesting, mature or travelled. Besides, he has a likeminded girlfriend who does all the exciting things he does, and a plethora of friends. Ari understands what I want to express.

"On the contrary, darling. You are a kindred soul."

I fight his magnetic charm and the attraction I seem to have for Ari. He is the exact opposite of my standard-issue husband, Neel. I am suddenly not sure what he wants from this. He seems to be accepting of whatever comes, but is he actually designing it along the way?

Ari pays for our beers and we walk out into the brisk chill. The night is foggy. I miss a step and Ari grabs my arm as I stumble. As I straighten, I look up right into his amused yet patient eyes. Again, the unavoidable is obvious and my attraction is undeniable. But I am a married woman and I married the man of my choice less than two years ago, I remind myself. I look away as quickly as I can, but he does not.

"May I do something, Meera? Just for a moment."

I nod.

"Look here." Ari takes my face, very gently and tentatively, between his hands. He tilts it up in the foggy moonlight. He studies it intently. Then, looking right into my eyes, silently assuring me, he slowly releases my face and brings his hands down by his sides.

I am too stunned to speak.

"I hope that is okay. I just wanted to look at you."

I feel a flush creeping up my neck. He has done a lot without doing anything. Suddenly it is hot and stifling in the chill, and I want to be home with Neel, in our sterile, clean apartment, and wallow in the familiar ache I have had since we moved here. This new ache that I now feel unhinges me.

"Ari, I have to go."

"Okay. We'll talk soon." Suddenly he looks practical.

"Bye." I give him a quick hug and virtually run home.

* * *

"I met Dr. Dugar today. He explained the full application and implication for the medical industry of the product we are developing. This is so exciting. He appreciated the team a lot, and he is the big guy. Meera, did you hear what I said?"

It is both a blessing and a curse that Neel is so obtuse,

because I can't get my mind off the evening with Ari, but I don't need to complicate my life. I am told I have a life that many would envy. Rini, for example, is not married and she worries about meeting the right person. Neel is a good man, so I have to give our marriage a clean chance. Doesn't Ari realize that? Does he know how he affects me? He has a girlfriend. None of this makes much sense and I desperately wish I could talk to Rini about it.

"I am just tired."

"How was your drink with Ari?"

"Oh. Fine. I suppose. He... um... Tina is out of town."

"You should invite them over for dinner when she gets back," Neel says distractedly. He really can't see the angst on my face. I am not sure which one is stronger – my relief or my disappointment that Neel notices nothing.

* * *

I haven't answered Ari's calls for a month and ignored the three messages he left me. I feel a sense of safety in doing this, but it is laced with an anxiety of a different sort. The anxiety of perhaps letting go of something natural and fulfilling and genuine.

"Rini, how are you?" I've dialed Rini's number while mulling over the Ari business. It is ten in the night in India.

"Meera! Oh, I've been thinking about you. I have so much to tell you. First you tell me, how are you? And why have you not emailed in so long?"

"I am okay, Rini. I really want my work permit to come through so I can do something besides sitting in this bloody apartment, going crazy. I miss everyone."

"I wish you both would come back really soon and you would not even have to worry about working there."

"Well, Neel says it would be great to have experience here. And he says it would look good on my resume when we come back. Honestly, if I sit home for two years, I will go crazy. His project will take at least two more years. Maybe longer. It's so fucked up, Rini."

"Hang in there, Meera. I have something to tell you. I can't wait anymore and it might cheer you up. I met someone. His name is Kumar. He is just... hmmm.... He is a scholar and researcher at the TABA research institute. I love him. I've been wanting to tell you for a few weeks now. I know I haven't said anything in my emails, but I didn't know what to write. Phew! Now that I have told, I will write all about it."

"Oh Rini, congratulations! I wish I was there. Can you email me some pictures?" Though I am genuinely happy for my friend, but sad that I'm not there to witness this phase of her life. But it was high time, and I'm glad it's happened for her.

"Now tell me why you called. Anything specific, or just like that?" I can hear the smile and breathiness in Rini's voice. It is good to hear her this happy, this excited. She deserves to experience the heady first stages of a relationship. And knowing Rini, this is the real thing. She has not had anyone serious, ever. She does not flirt. She is a serious kind of girl. I can't tell her about my dilemma anymore. I can't tell her my picture perfect life is brewing with hidden storms of confusion.

"I just missed you. I am happy for you, Rini. Send pictures. I have to run now. Write." And with that, I hang up the phone as fast as I can.

* * *

"Meera, how are you? Where have you been? I've left a few messages you know?" Ari sounds concerned.

"I am sorry I have not called back. I don't have any excuses. I was avoiding you."

"Meera, Meera. You are so you." Ari laughs.

I don't know what he means by that, and I remain silent.

"Oh stop being so serious. I can almost see that stern look on your face. Let's meet at Romano's at six tonight and we can talk."

"Okay."

* * *

"Look darling, you are a very charming young lady. We have an old connection. I like meeting you. I like our friendship. It is simple and doesn't have to be complicated. Our friendship has nothing to do with Tina. I like a lot of people and I like good conversation. And you are special. That's all."

"Ari, this can't be more than a friendship." We are perched on bar stools at Romano's. Ari can sense my discomfort with what is between us.

"Of course. I respect your boundaries. But can you lighten up? I love when you smile." He looks very amused. There is nothing more to say about this. I find I don't want to give up this bond with Ari due to the fear of what may happen.

"Rini found someone," I blurt out, blinking back unbidden tears.

Ari looks concerned and attentive.

"I know, I know, that's good for her. It's supposed to happen and she deserves happiness and romance. But I don't know why I just could not talk to her," I add.

"You miss her. And you miss sharing this part of her life."

I sigh. I tell Ari then about the whole Rini-Raul episode.

He is so attentive, so understanding. In the end he takes my hand in both of his and says, "You are going to be just fine, my love." After a pause he adds, his eyes twinkling, "And that is from one *friend* to another."

* * *

Neel is excited about the latest breakthrough in his green technology project. He's been talking about it for the last forty-five minutes and I am finding it exceedingly difficult to follow what he is saying. I am making *aloo tikki's* in the kitchen and Neel is perched on the bar stool by the counter, busy peering into his laptop. He looks up at me periodically, but I don't think he would have even noticed had I been cooking naked. Neel's cheeks are flushed and his eyes glow as they did the night of our wedding. He wears his happiness on his face, and I almost can't bear to look at it. And yet, he remains my good hearted, good natured, loving, committed, handsome husband. It would be easier if he were obviously flawed.

"Rini has found someone."

"Oh, that is wonderful! We can meet him on our next trip. You must be happy."

"I am…"

"I know, I know. September is not too far and you will get some time with her. This new development is going to be radical in energy conservation. Did you follow what I explained, Meera? I mean, I can't believe we are at this stage so soon! It's better than expected."

"Um… Do you want to eat soon?"

"Yes, lets. You know Meer, I know you get bored here. I know you miss Delhi and Bombay and Laila and everyone. *I know.* I am trying to finish this project at turbo speed, sweetie. I know you want to go back. But can you enjoy our time here a little bit? And can you not be mad at me for enjoying life here?"

I am stunned he knows all this. I've stopped what I was doing, and I am staring at him with my jaw hanging open. "How do you know?"

"Don't you think I see the look in your eyes every day? I try to get you excited about my work, and about other things here. Our neighbour in the apartment next door, Myrah, she's approached us several times because she wants to be friendly and hang out with you. But you don't show much interest. Why don't you invite her over one day? You have to make an effort, you know. I am glad you've found a friend in Ari, though. At least that makes you happy. I want you to be happy, baby."

"I didn't think you knew all this." Silent tears flow down my cheeks. Neel comes quietly over to me, and wraps his arms around me. I sink into his chest, not caring that the mashed potato and spices from my hands are getting on his shirt. These moments of understanding seem far and few, and I savour his love. And I vow to myself that I won't let any distractions deter the course of this marriage.

* * *

"I am comfortable thinking of you as a friend." Emboldened by the beer, I tell Ari this at our weekly happy hour.

"And I am comfortable flirting with my special friend," Ari says, winking at me.

"You have to stop with that, Ari. You know, I never talk about Neel with you, or my marriage, but Neel is just such a good person, and I've quite a straightforward life."

"I know, darling, I have not met many people as straight

as you. You call your mother every day." Ari is very amused by now. "And even your back is always ramrod straight. You don't hunch at all. Let loose a little. Are you coming to our street theatre on Saturday?" Ari is performing again.

"I am not sure. Is Tina going to be there?"

"Yes."

* * *

"Neel, I want you to come with me for Ari's street theatre tomorrow. It's called *Rama Rama*. It's about the ideal of sacrifice in the South Asian communities, and I want you to meet all those people. They are an eclectic, umm... humble group. You will like them. You are always busy when I go to their events. Will you come this time?" We are snuggling in bed, in the aftermath of lazy, gentle lovemaking. He is wrapped around me, his head buried in my neck. His tousled hair tickles my chin when I talk. I shift slightly. Neel grunts sleepily. I want him to wake up and talk to me. I miss the long conversations we used to have, when I had all his attention. "Will you come?" I ask again.

"Yeah... of course." He mumbles and falls asleep.

I am wide awake and my mind wanders. I wonder if Ari falls asleep after lovemaking. Or does he sit up, hold his partner, look into her eyes, and hear every word she says in his rapt, attentive manner.

16

Ari Hasan Jana

Meera has not talked to me for a month now... again. Oh well! Another one bites the dust, I suppose. Though this was a strange one. It was so organic and basic with her, but Meera could not handle it. Well, I hope she is well. I am glad she didn't meet Tina beyond the cursory pleasantries. Tina may have picked up on something and that would not be a good scene.

Meera is young, wrapped up in some mysterious melancholy, unaware of her appeal. I like the way her hair curls down her back. I like the way her cheeks still have a hint of baby fat from how I remember her as a child. I like how she simply says things the way she sees them. I like her full plump lips and how they move when she talks. I like when she thinks she's said something rude or silly and tries to hide her embarrassment, bites her lip and falls silent. I like her. I would love to bite that lip she bites, but she is tricky. The way to get to her is through her mind. I think I already hold a special place in her heart. Ah... we have a strange history. I miss the girl, and in her peculiar way she's made a place for herself in my heart too. Oh wait, I don't have a heart.

"Ari, what's up?" Tina says as I guffaw out loud at my amusing, mindless, indulgences of thought.

"Nothing baby, go to sleep. Here… mmmmm." I snake my arm under her head and hold her. Tina is stretched out on my bed. I am lounging next to her, trying to read my book. But my wandering thoughts seems to have their own plan. I hope I am able to break the silence between Meera and me. I want to get to her mind… and I don't mind getting to her body too. In fact, I've wanted to do that since I met her six months back. Pleasantly surprising, the conversations between us have been fabulous. She is a good conversationalist and she doesn't even know it. She is an irresistible combination for me, and I need to smoke some dope, and get this shit under control.

Tina is a freaking maniac when it comes to my love for other matters of attraction. But I too am a master of camouflage, and good at not letting her get a whiff of my designs. I don't conceal my beliefs from her at all, though. She knows I believe polygamy is not a natural circumstance. What more is there to say?

"Baby, I am just going to pull my arm out. I have to roll a joint. You want one?"

17

Meera Myna Dutt

Maybe I should not, but I do answer Ari's call. I have, once again, not spoken to him in a month. The only way to resist him is to avoid him. The last time we'd met about a month ago, we had stopped under a tree by the sidewalk after coming out of Romano's, to finish our conversation about something – I think about Ari's last street performance that had got a mention in the local papers. I'd missed that one. I remember the warm summer night and the abandon in the air. Suddenly Ari had stooped down, and looked at my feet intently. He had asked if I could pull off my left sandal. I had thought perhaps something was stuck in the sandal, or perhaps he wanted to look at the design. The strangeness of the request had not struck me at that moment, and I had compliantly pulled off my sandal and handed it to him. He had put the sandal delicately on the sidewalk, bent down on one knee, and then he had gingerly taken my bare foot in both his hands and examined it, turning it this way and that. It was an inexplicably delicious feeling, to have his hands cupped around my foot. Almost in worship. I was frozen in place by the intensity of the moment, as well as the shock of feeling something so unexpected. Since I met him again, this was the second time that Ari had touched me intentionally, the first time being when he had held my face in both his hands, quite like how he held my foot. After the face experience I'd stopped talking to him for a month, and navigated our friendship back to safer grounds, but he just crossed that boundary again.

I'd momentarily closed my eyes, to savour the intensity and sacredness of his gesture. I had let myself be swept away for a moment, and then something had jostled me out of my reverie. I had snatched away my foot. "Ari, let's go," I'd almost yelled in panic. I had to get away from him.

At home I'd stood shivering and crying in the shower for a long time, but Neel hadn't noticed anything unusual when I'd come out red-eyed and scrubbed raw. He was more interested in telling me about his office politics. I had to let go of Ari. I had to stop talking to him. We were on a risky precipice, dangerously close to letting boundaries fall away. What about all my promises to Neel, my marriage vows, my commitment? I couldn't destroy all that, right?

* * *

"Meera, finally you answer my call. Thank goodness. How are you, darling? I've missed you."

"Hello, Ari." He does not ask me why I have been avoiding him, probably because it is so obvious. All this feels wrong. Does it feel wrong to him?

"Hello, hello. When is a good day for you? I want to tell you about a lot of developments in the movement. Are you around anytime next week?"

Neel is out of town for a conference for his company for three days next week. His entire team is going to Atlanta and Neel is excited about this. He gets to see the latest technological gadgets, of which I know little.

"Do you want to come to my home for dinner on Thursday next week?"

There is silence. "Your place?" Ari sounds just as surprised as I feel about this sudden invitation.

"Yes. Neel is away on a conference. I can cook something. It will be vegetarian, though."

"I can do vegetarian." In his voice is his trademark smile. And despite myself I am excited.

* * *

"Laila, what is that cut on your lip from?" Laila and I are skyping and I am peering at her face in the screen. Something about it looks different. There is something harder and suddenly mature in the line of her jaw. And something about her eyes that doesn't seem that innocent anymore. She's fidgety, looking everywhere but the screen. I want to reach across the distance and hold her shoulders and look at her. Sometimes I don't know if it helps or hurts to be able to Skype.

"Laila, where are you lost?"

"I have exams going on. Been studying a lot."

"Okay, but what happened to your lip?"

"I cut it on a chipped glass at college while drinking chai. They need to use better glasses there. I didn't ice it and it got a bit swollen. That's all." Laila is in her first year in junior college. I remember the time she was born. How have all these years slipped by? I don't know why, but I don't believe she cut her lip on a glass. But I have no reason to doubt what she is saying, so I shake off the feeling.

"How's Supe?"

"Oh, the usual. Busy doing he-alone-knows-what. When are you coming?"

"Now probably December. It got postponed because of Neel's work."

Laila gets quiet on hearing it will be another few months before I visit. "Cheer up. December will be here before you know it."

* * *

Nothing can dampen my spirits today. Not even the vague anxious guilt hovering somewhere in the pit of my stomach. Neel left yesterday for his conference. I was teary-eyed when he left. But today is another day. It is the day Ari comes over for dinner. I know my limits and I have been clear with him, but even then it promises to be an evening full of delicious moments. I am humming along with the CD... *Jab ghungruo si, bajti hai boonde, armaan hamare, palkein na moonde...* as I clean the apartment, water the plants, chop up some fruit and cheese. I have a vegetarian *biriyani* in the oven. And I have cucumber *raita* cooling in the fridge. It doesn't strike me that this is one of Neel's favorite meals, and that he loves the way I make it.

My hair is in a loose braid down my back, with liberated wisps curling this way and that in the humid New York air. I am wearing an ankle length purple soft jersey skirt that clings to frame my shape, and a simple black t-shirt.

Neel knows Ari is coming over for dinner, and trusting, busy, preoccupied Neel does not mind. He is glad I have company for an evening and it makes him feel less guilty for going on his trip and for being so excited about it. What harm can come from a dinner?

* * *

I have butterflies in my stomach when the doorbell rings. Ari stands in the door frame, tall and athletic looking in jeans and a black t-shirt that fits his runner's body like a glove. He looks freshly showered, and as he hugs me, as always, I take in his scent. It is a heady feeling to have him here with me, in the privacy of an enclosed space for the first time. I can't believe this is the same Ari of my childhood, for he had seemed so old then. And now he feels like the perfect date. But this is not a date, I remind myself sternly.

I clear my head and turn on my charming hostess self. I bring out the fruit and cheese and pour the wine that Ari has brought. Ari is peering at the pictures we have up. There is one with Mom, Papa and us three siblings, and then a wedding picture of Neel and me, and pictures of Neel's family.

"It is delightful to see Noorie Aunty and Varun Uncle. It takes me back to those years, Meera. And this must be Laila. She looks a bit like you. Oh my, Sagar was a baby when I last saw him. He is a strapping, handsome young man now."

"Don't call him Sagar. Call him Super."

"Why?" He turns towards me with a half grin and a raised eyebrow, his hands at his waist. He looks very, very attractive at that moment.

"Because after he came and you left, life changed."

"Well, I am back. If you allow me back."

"Here you go." I hand him a glass of wine, ignoring his suggestive comment. I wonder if time with Ari would be just as much fun without the flirting.

We talk for hours. I am lounging on the couch and Ari is sitting on the floor with his back resting against the other couch and his legs stretched out in front of him, one ankle lazily crossed over the other. We go through the bottle of wine and open another one, but I am careful to take it slow and not match Ari's speed. We talk about Ari's experiences in the corporate espionage system, and his decision to leave. He tells me about his distaste when his ex-wife fights this decision as she doesn't want anything to affect her alimony amount. Ari then tells me about his divorce and how he tried his best to keep it friendly. Ari's relationship with his daughter is interesting. They travel together during her summer breaks and they share common interests such as basketball, reading and dancing. Ari and Rumi's time together is filled with such activity, but when it comes to regular life stuff, he leaves it to her mother. He says she has always been good at discipline and nurturing. I tell Ari about my journalism studies, about my two jobs, and my dream to someday write a book. I tell him about what kind of positions I plan to apply for after I get my work permit. And about how I would give all this up in a moment if I could go back to India right now. I tell him about Akash and my heartbreak, about Sidhu and the deep love I felt, and I tell him amusing tidbits from my other dating experiences. Ari and I conspicuously avoid talking about our respective current relationships.

At some point during the evening we drift to the dining table. We are discussing our love for reading. Ari is animatedly telling me about his interpretation of Rushdie's work and I am enraptured. Ari praises the *biriyani*.

After dinner, Ari is on one end of the long couch, with his legs stretched out towards the other end. I am propped up against cushions on the floor. I want time to stop and the night to not end. We are now talking about the life of the prophet Mohammed, and Ari's knowledge of history and religion and their interplay with politics is impressive. Other than the hug when Ari arrived, we have not touched at all, and that makes me comfortable and safe. But I am to soon find out that the feeling of safety is just an illusion.

It is midnight now. Ari looks at his watch and then back at me. "I should leave, right?" He is looking meaningfully into my eyes. I understand his question well.

"Yes," I say. And he gets up, holds me in a bear hug for a long moment, and leaves, leaving behind the almost tangible, magical, surreal quality of the evening.

18

Laila Myna Dutt

He hits me. I am ashamed to tell anyone. He loves me too, though. And Mom and Papa don't even know about him. I can't tell anyone. Not even Sunaina, my best friend, who knows almost everything about me. Not Meera, who does know everything about me except for this. Not Super; he would intervene. Meera will be here in December. If Meera and Super find out, there will be chaos. If Sunaina finds out, she will likely tell Meera. I can't tell anyone.

I remember the first time we met at my school funfair. He was so very sweet and boyishly charming then, his hair flopping over his forehead. He bought me candy-floss from the stand, and stayed right next to me the whole evening, so attentive. He looks like a lost school boy though he is twenty now – four years older than me. He loves me too much. That is why he sometimes loses control of himself, but then he always apologizes and cries with me and for me. Who would do that if they didn't love the person? He can't stand to see me in pain. But then why does he hit me?

It is confusing sometimes. It has only happened twice in the four months I've known him. The first time it was a slap because I challenged him in the conversation we were having about poverty in India. I should not have challenged his views with our group of friends present. Maybe that was my fault, so maybe I should not blame him for that one. The second time he hit me and bruised my lip because we were kissing in the car and I told him about Sunaina's younger brother having a crush on me since we were kids. Maybe that was my fault too. I should not have ruined our romantic moment by talking about another guy. Even though it's only Sunaina's *younger* brother who is a kid, a year younger than us, and his crush is sweet and funny.

Meera saw the cut on my lip during our Skype talk, but I gave her the same excuse that I gave Mom and Papa. Super didn't even ask me about the cut. Maybe he didn't notice. Well, I have to deal with this myself. I have to grow up some day. I have to keep Ravi happy so he does not get so angry and lose control. He suffers when he does that.

There are so many good things about Ravi, like his bubbly personality and his wit. He can charm anybody. And he knows so much more about life than me, because he has gone through a lot – losing his mom at age nine to a senseless car accident, and then having to deal with a step-mom who beat him. I can't even imagine that. He cried when he told me about it. I can't cause him any pain on my account. Maybe the hitting will never happen again.

19

Meera Myna Dutt

So much has happened in the last few weeks, and life is finally a shade brighter than it was. I received my desperately awaited work permit. Neel brought home a bottle of champagne that day and we celebrated by getting ragingly drunk. We had a great conversation that evening, after a long time. Neel's mind was, for once, not on his work. He even honoured my request of putting away his phone and laptop in the other room.

I began to apply for journalism jobs the very next day, as soon as I recovered from my hangover. A position that became available with a women's magazine – TRENDS – appealed to me the most. Their office is a convenient ten-minute walk from our apartment and the publication covers everything from gardening and recipes to events, innovation and entrepreneurship, linking the topics to the larger landscape of women's movements historically. They have a liberal outlook and I typically enjoy their articles. I was thrilled to get an interview call from TRENDS and within three weeks of receiving my work permit, I landed a job.

Mom and Papa are happy. And Neel is so proud and excited, he cannot wipe off his grin. It is cute to see him like this. It feels like a lighter phase has descended on my gloom-and-doom outlook. Since I got the work permit, I have been waking up early and making *chai* in the morning for Neel and me. I feel a sense of companionship sharing this chai-time with him; surely some of the old magic is back between us.

It's Friday and I am due to start work on Monday, which makes me both nervous and excited. Neel is at his monthly happy hour meet this evening with his work buddies, and Ari has convinced me to go out and celebrate. It is Friday night after all, and I cannot spend it home alone.

I get ready for the evening, humming some tune that I can't fully recall. I stop and make a face at myself in the mirror. I look bold and happy in blue jeans and a black t-shirt and sweater. Satisfied, I take off for the brisk walk to Romano's, my hands deep in the pockets of my coat, the chilly breeze lifting my hair. Nothing can go wrong now, and everything seems to be falling into place.

I have not seen Ari in the last three weeks, since our dinner at the apartment, and I spot him almost as soon as I enter, sitting on the barstool. I see something subtly different in his face, as though he is perturbed beneath his loving, cool Ari exterior, but maybe I am imagining this. He gets up and encloses me in his warm hug, allowing me to enjoy the familiarity of his touch and scent, yet again.

"Is something the matter?" I ask as I settle on the barstool next to him.

"Why do you ask?" He turns to me with a raised eyebrow.

"I don't know. I just sense it."

"My sister Zubaida*jaan* – you remember her, right? She is going through a divorce again. This is her second one. She has two boys. They live in Pakistan."

"Oh, no! I am sorry to hear that. Is it her choice to divorce?"
"There is more to it. The divorce doesn't bother me. She can marry and divorce to her heart's content. Sometimes I don't understand why people don't learn and just date instead of signing a contract called marriage. But anyway, that is another conversation entirely. What makes me really angry is that he used to beat her. I didn't know this. I could have been more involved, or more available for her. But I didn't know she needed that. The neighbours took her to the hospital with a bleeding ear that he tried to rip off. Bloody barbarian. How can humans behave like that, Meera? I mean what causes a person to violate another person like that! She is alright now. My middle sister Zohra*jaan* and her husband are there now. Zubaida*jaan* and the kids are with them. They are filing a case against him. But what's going to come out of it? Nothing!"

"Oh Ari, I am so sorry." I lean forward on my barstool, and wrap my arms around him. I have never before seen him angry. He rests his head against me for a moment and draws in a deep, luxurious breath. Suddenly I am embarrassed to hold him like that, and I pull back. The moment passes and he looks down at his hands.

"So helpless, Meera. I am so freaking helpless. I advocate for women's rights here, and my own sister is being abused back there. The joke's on me."

"You didn't even know, Ari. You can't blame yourself for something you didn't even know. The important thing right now is not to spend your energy criticizing and blaming yourself, but instead thinking about what you need to do to ensure Zubaida*jaan*'s and the children's safety, and help them."

Ari is staring at me, his jaw slightly open. His eyes have a hint of mirth and suddenly he starts laughing. I don't understand this and wait patiently for him to stop, because I have no idea what to say.

"Meera*jaan*," he says, when he finally stops laughing. "Meera*jaan*, you certainly set me straight. Where did you get such wisdom from? The last time I looked, you were a tiny tot." He is still grinning.

This is the first time he has called me Meera*jaan*. 'Jaan' means life in Urdu, and it is a term of endearment, and I like the sound of Meera*jaan* – it feels intimate. Like family. By now I am grinning too, and it is astonishing how in the face of such a crisis, there is also this small human moment of laughter.

"Well, self-criticism is an indulgence," I say.

"It is, it certainly is."

"A complete waste of time, a distraction from action, a victim position, a learned helplessness, a cop-out..."

"Okay, okay, I get your point. And I agree."

"Cheers to that."

"Oh, darling, it is your big day. We were going to celebrate, and here I am offloading my burdens on you. Sorry. I just got the call half an hour ago."

"Ari, we are friends, and of course I want to be there for you. I care about what happens with your family. Thank you for sharing with me. Do you want to leave? We don't have to stay here."

"Thanks for being so understanding. Let's finish our beers and leave. Let's go for a walk, if that's okay with you. I am waiting to hear back from Zohra*jaan*. If the legalities get difficult, I will go to Pakistan in the next week, but at least they are all safe right now. My sisters are very close with each other, and I know that Zubaida*jaan* has the emotional support she needs right now."

We walk that evening, perhaps for an hour, talking about our respective childhoods. The cold makes us hungry, and Ari asks if I want to try a kebab cart he knows on the corner of 55th and Lexington. They have vegetarian kebabs and falafels too, he assures. We walk there and stand under the awning eating the most delicious hot kebabs, and I am content and happy, momentarily forgetting what a burden life in America is to me. Standing here with Ari, in the dusky evening light, sharing life and kebabs, is just exactly how life is supposed to be. As Ari exchanges pleasantries with the cart owner, I take an after-mint from the bowl that is kept on the cart for customers. Ari and I begin our twenty-minute walk back to my apartment, after which Ari will take the subway to head to his suburban pad. I am grateful for the night air, the moon above and Ari's friendship.

We walk in companionable silence, and the crackle of the mint wrapper is loud as I unwrap it and start to put it in my mouth.

"Do you have another mint?"

My hand stops where it is and I hold the mint between my teeth, turning to face Ari, shaking my head to indicate I do not. I am about to offer him half my mint, when I see his head bending down towards mine, and I feel his lips barely and fleetingly touching mine as he gently bites off the part of the mint sticking out from between my teeth. It is only after this entire surreal incident is over that I realize we are stationary on the sidewalk. He looks at me, assessing my reaction, I think. I don't say anything.

"That was delicious. Thank you." He sounds tender, unsure.

Then he takes my hand and pulls me along, and we

continue our walk in silence. I have pulled my hand back and stuck it deep in my pocket.

* * *

I am grateful to be back in the security of the apartment. I can still feel the softness, the tenderness of the fleeting touch of Ari's lips. I touch my lips with my fingers, right where Ari's lips touched them not fifteen minutes ago. Did that really happen? It was over before I could even blink. It was magical with the moon behind Ari's bent head. Yet I brush my teeth and wash my face with vigour, trying to wipe off any trace of that touch. It is hazardous to leave his touch on my lips. What is next? My mind keeps fleeting back to the memory of that moment. Where do I file this one away? In the most secret, most hidden compartment in my head? How do I ensure that it can remain locked forever? Do I want it to remain locked?

* * *

It's a mellow evening and after a long time I am alone at home, curled up under a throw on the couch. I have a book I am trying to read, but I am not getting anywhere with it. It has been three months since the fake kiss with Ari (I refer to the touching of our lips as the 'fake kiss'). I have settled into a pseudo-comfort, pseudo-happy place. I enjoy my work at TRENDS and, most importantly, it keeps me busy. It keeps my mind occupied so that I don't think about forbidden matters such as Ari and the fake kiss. It has also helped ease my ache for India, though I am still unable to keep my thoughts at bay when I am alone. It's best when I am at work and writing. Neel and I are okay right now too. I think he is glad that I am working, because it makes it easier for him to ignore the issues. It certainly makes it easier for me to pretend that life is absolutely fine. Neel and I have settled into this pseudo-happy understanding, and as long as I don't upset it, we appear to be a perfectly normal, happy young couple.

I have Rupa now, my friend and colleague, the only other South Asian at TRENDS. That's not why, but for some instinctive reason she and I gravitated towards each another from the very first day that I started my job. Rupa, with her long skirts, vivid colours, wild curls and sexy nose ring is thirty years old, single and crazy. She is the opposite of me in her outspoken and bold ways. She dates but does not commit. She says she is bisexual and does not know any other way to be.

Born and brought up on Long Island, Rupa now lives alone in a tiny one-bedroom on 4ᵗʰ and Atlantic in Brooklyn. She is close with her family and goes back to her parents' home in Long Island at least one weekend of the month. The rest of her weekends, she says, are for 'adventures of all kinds'. Rupa loves her life and her lifestyle, and I think I could have been her if I were not me. I envy her and vicariously enjoy her pleasures, and slowly I grow to admire and love her. She seems to have taken me as her confidante too. The phone rings, shaking me out of my reverie.

"Meera, *beta....* Is everything okay?"

"Yes, Mom. How are you?"

"Nothing, *beta.*" Mom begins to sob.

"What's wrong, Mom?"

"I am sorry, Meera."

"Why? What? What's wrong?" I start feeling a mad panic and my stomach knots. Why is Mom crying? "Mom, say something! You are scaring me. What is the matter?"

"Laila."

"Laila? What happened to Laila?" I am not quite sure why, but I am sobbing now too. I don't know what it is but what I know is that something is not right with my baby sister. "MOM, SAY SOMETHING."

"Laila is in the hospital. *Beta*, can you prepone your trip? She wants you here."

"Hospital? Why? WHAT HAPPENED?"

"*Beta*, she was… she got… she was involved with some boy. He hit her. Badly. *Raja beta*, just come. Can you come?"

"Okay Mom, slow down. Where is Papa? Where is Super? And how badly is Laila hurt?"

"Papa and Super are at the police station. Papa asked me not to tell you. He said you would panic. I'm at the hospital. Laila is asleep right now. She will recover, Meera, but she has a broken arm and… and her face is hurt. And she is in shock."

"Mom, I am coming. Ask Super to call when he gets back."

* * *

I can't stand it. My skin crawls and my jaw hurts, but I can't seem to loosen it. I am pacing in our apartment, and Neel's phone repeatedly is unreachable. He is on a yacht for a company poker party. His yacht will dock only at eleven pm and it is seven in the evening right now. I get on the computer and look at flights and tickets. The best I can find is a flight out on Tuesday. I will have to inform work and I hope they understand my taking time off within three months of starting my job. I don't really care. My family needs me. I'm undecided whether I should wait for Neel to search for a flight out sooner than Tuesday, or if I should go ahead and book this one. I have to do something. I have to take some action. I realize I am clutching the edge of the table so hard that my fingers hurt.

I call Rupa, even though I know she was planning to go out on a date tonight, but as expected, I reach her voicemail and I don't leave any message. I try Neel's phone again, in vain. I drink some water and it tastes like melted iron going down my throat, so I throw it away. I am pacing again. I think about calling Mom back, but I don't. I pick up the phone and dial Ari's number, and he answers on the first ring.

"Meera?"

"Can you meet me?"

"Romano's in thirty."

And we hang up.

* * *

After one beer each at Romano's I want to leave. We wander out and make our way over to Battery Park. We are sitting on a bench near Battery Park looking out at the Statue of Liberty looming up, reaching towards the sky, well lit and yet full of shadows. Why does it have shadows? Why does life have shadows? At Romano's I told Ari all about Mom's call, and about gentle, precious Laila with a broken arm and a hurt face. I told Ari about how she could not stand even getting a scrape when she was little. About how the sight of blood makes her nauseous. I told him about how when Laila was very little she had stepped on a snail that had ventured out after the monsoon, and she had jumped back on hearing the crunch under her shoe. She had been inconsolable then. Ari is perhaps the best listener I know.

There are young lovers sitting on the steps diagonally to the left, in front of our bench. I observe them kissing passionately, and Ari follows my gaze.

"Today they love each other, tomorrow they may hate each other."

"Why do you say that?"

"They don't even know what love is, and they place their lover on a pedestal, expecting that one person to make their life beautiful. When that doesn't happen, the entire illusion collapses, and it can get very ugly. That's why lust is so much purer than the illusion called love."

"But lust dies, no?"

"It gives no false promises, no illusions, and it does not demand monogamy either. Lust in its pure form recognizes polygamy as the natural state of being."

"Have you ever been in love?"

"Once."

"Tina?"

"Rumana." Ari names his ex-wife.

"What about Tina?"

"Yeah, that comes pretty close too." His answer is vague and I am surprised, for I have never thought of his relationship with Tina as anything but spectacular. I turn to look at his face and see something intense, very different from what I expect, in his large luminous eyes. It looks like sadness tinged with pure, warm love. I turn my head upwards, while he bends down towards me, and ever so slowly our lips find each other's; ever so gently he begins to kiss me, and me, him. The river of emotion flowing through me is touching every cell of my body, igniting something almost spiritual.

There are decades captured in this one kiss, and yet it feels brand new, an expected evolution of our relationship. Something about our intimacy is very natural and I notice that I am not surprised, that I knew this would happen tonight. We kiss for what feels like an eternity packed into a minute, and afterwards we part, out of breath. Ari puts his arms around me, embracing me firmly, still sitting on the bench, and though I am stiff against him, he does not loosen his grip. We don't speak, and I finally let my head rest against his chest, and melt into him. He runs one hand through my hair, brushing it back, smoothing down the curls. His fingers burn through my scalp, leaving their undeniable scorch lines.

"Let's go," I say. "I have to go home." I refer to Delhi as home. I now feel a serenity and a strength that I didn't before. Ari releases me, sits back, and encloses both my hands in his, as though it is unbearable for him to completely untangle from me. He peers into my eyes, looking, searching, and seemingly satisfied with what he sees there. Finally he lets go.

"Let's get you home," he says.

This magical evening with Ari is a one-time oasis in the desert of my life, and so I must not let guilt enter my mind. This is not an affair, for this cannot be something as ordinary as an affair. This is a one-time only expression of a spiritual bond, and nothing more. Or is it?

20

Meera Myna Dutt

I land in a few minutes. Super will probably be at the airport and Mom and Papa will be home with Laila. I can't wait to see her. I feel I am late, but nonetheless I am here, and I want to hold my sister and reassure her that the fairytale life she believed in is still possible. But is it? And is it fair of me to encourage a fairytale? There are no fairytales. Am I responsible for sheltering her so much that she was too gullible, too naïve to prevent what happened? Too trusting to read the signs? Too gentle to establish her boundaries? Can I reverse the harm I have caused?

I am on the ground and I have made my way through Immigration. The smells, sounds and sights of Delhi's Indira Gandhi International Airport seize me with such familiarity as though I never left India, and I melt into the hustle-bustle, immediately feeling at home. Neel was worried about me. He knows how protective I am about Laila. He offered to come, but I feel I have to do this alone. And right now Neel seems to be far, far away. Untouched by the mess in my head, he remains the successful golden boy who does no wrong, who does not kiss old childhood friends, nor melt into their arms. But thoughts of Neel and Ari are buried somewhere deep; the overwhelming need to be with my family shadows everything else.

* * *

"His name is Ravi. He met Laila seven or eight months ago at her school fair, and has been pursuing her since. He's hit her before, she says, but never this bad. The police have confronted the guy, but his parents are rich and they bribed their way out of any charges. Papa doesn't care so much what they do or don't do, nor does he care to pursue anything legally. As you know, nothing happens here – the whole system is corrupt. And even if we are able to do anything legally, it would take years, and Papa doesn't want Lai to be dragged through that. He says instead we have to focus on her getting better, and we all need to recover as a family. He says anger is pointless, but if that dude were to come in front of me, I swear, Meer, I would bash his fucking face in."

Super and I are driving back home. I am choked up hearing all this, but I am unable to cry. I don't want to cry in front of Super, I don't know why. I think, perhaps, I want to protect Super from all this too. I am the oldest of the three, after all. And I was, unfairly, far away when this was happening. It is my responsibility to make it all right, isn't it? I have an urge to console him, to take away his pain and restore the magic in his life too, but I can't find the words.

"How did you all find out? Did she come home with the bruises?"

"No. You don't know? Mom didn't tell you?" Super looks surprised, and then with his jaw set tight, proceeds to tell me the details, "They had a fight. After school hours, at the back of the grounds, the bastard was hitting her in the parking lot. Sunaina had stayed back at school too. She says she doesn't know why, but she felt nervous about things, afraid for Laila. Ravi had been angry at Lai for a few days and Sunaina felt something was brewing, and something was going to happen. But to give them privacy to talk, she was waiting in a classroom. As soon as she heard Laila scream, she called her older brother. Thank goodness they live so close to the school! He reached the front entrance within five minutes, and Sunaina got into the back seat of the car when he pulled up. Then they both drove around the school building to the back where the bastard had her pinned against the wall, and Sunaina opened the back door, yelling for Ravi to let her go or else they would call the police, and for Laila to bloody get her ass in the car. She said she was not sure if Lai would comply, because Lai was so much under the fucking Ravi spell. So she was very forceful. Apparently Sunaina had been working on Laila, trying to get her to break up with this character right from the beginning.

"Anyway, thank goodness Laila listened, and in that moment that Ravi loosened his grip in the shock that someone had caught him, Laila wriggled out, ran and jumped in the car. But by then she had a broken arm and the left side of her face was covered in bruises. She has some on her left leg too. The bastard had smashed her against the wall and then held her head, rubbing it hard into the concrete, while twisting her arm behind her. That's the fucking story."

By now I am even more determined not to cry. I put my arms around Super as he drives the car, and kiss his cheek. "We will get through this. Papa is right. Let's focus on getting Laila better. I want to know why she got into this mess with this guy to begin with."

"She says he was charming in the beginning. And apparently he has only hit her three times before this, and those were apparently small incidents. She says she can see her fault too. What is she talking about? The idiot doesn't know that any guy who raises a hand on a woman, is a bloody f-ing ball-less coward! I should have spent more time with Laila. Then I would have been able to teach her to read the signs and protect herself."

"Oh Super, I should have been here for her. But we can't blame ourselves, okay?"

We all seem to be going through our own personal hell.

* * *

Her left eye and the left side of her lip are still swollen, and she has scrape marks and bruises on the left side of her face. Her right arm is in a cast. There are various bruises on her body. Her eyes are either closed or tearful when they are open. She keeps apologizing to all of us, as though she is the culprit and she has harmed us.

Papa has a solemn expression most of the time now, Mom cries a lot when she thinks no one can hear her, and Super is clearly very angry. I can't add to this with my own sorrow and guilt. So I don't. I have to fix something that seems so broken, or else I will go crazy. I dress Laila's bruises and gently hold her hand, stroking it, reassuring her that we don't have to talk about things, that we don't have to talk at all until her lip is better and her face doesn't ache as much. I tell her over and over that it is not her fault, while she whispers 'sorry', looking at me with her large sorrowful eyes.

I go for walks with Papa, because that's what we always do together. We talk about nothing and everything and at times we are silent, side by side, with a matching pace, stamping down our demons. I ask him what he needs, and he says it is enough that I have come. He says I am the strong one, and he doesn't need anything more. He says to give this whole thing some time, to be patient. This is the first calamity we are facing as a family, and hopefully the last.

When Laila is asleep and Papa is gone to work, I spend hours listening to Mom share her fears, suspicions and concerns. I listen while she vents and blames and fans her own personal hell, believing that this fire is going to burn itself out at some point. I let her repeat herself and exhaust her worries until they are out of her body, and I console her and reassure her repeatedly, day after day.

With Super I am more affectionate than I usually am. I pay more attention to him and sit with him when he is home. Super and I sit together in Laila's room, watching her sleep sometimes. When it gets unbearable for him, he stomps out. I watch him come to terms with what has happened. I watch him, and he knows I am watching. He knows I am there for him.

There is no room in this household for my agony. What I must do is collect this live, throbbing ache from my family and flush it out. And therein lies my own healing too. So when I go to shower, I pretend the water pouring over me is washing away all the pain I have collected that day.

* * *

Mom and Papa have a swing in the back porch of the house now. Laila and I are sitting on the swing, wrapped together in a blanket, under the moonlight. I am swinging the swing slightly, pushing against the ground with my feet. She is curled up next to me, leaning against the backrest. Super is sitting on a deck chair. Two weeks have flown by and tonight is my last night before I go back.

The desperate, deep sadness in every pore of my body threatens to overflow and I bite down against the lump in my throat. There is a hollow churning in the pit of my stomach, a fear, an anxiety, and it feels like it will never go. We three sit in silence.

Finally I speak. "Laila, will you do something for me?"

"I know you want me to take care of myself. I will," she says, without moving from her curled-up position.

"No, it's something else."

"What?"

"I want you to let this go. It was never supposed to happen. It was not right. I want you to learn from this and then throw it out. Just let it go. Don't hold on to it. Forget it."

"She can't. None of us can." Super is still very angry.

"I am sorry, Sagar." Laila uses his real name.

"I don't want an apology, Lai. That's not why I am saying this. I want a promise that you will keep away from him."

"I know. I will."

"Look, none of us want you to feel guilty. In fact, we all feel guilty towards you, that we didn't detect something. Super is angry because he could not protect you. I feel upset when I imagine what you must have gone through, and I was not there for you. I want you to know, Laila, that we all love you so much, and you deserve the best. So the job now is not to forget = because as Super says maybe that is not possible − but to just let it go and not let it interfere with your life anymore."

"I know."

"What kept you in it, Lai? We didn't even know that you were seeing someone." I have decided not to bring this up, but Super finally asks the question we have all been wondering about.

"I know. I don't know. I mean… he kept asking me out. He really loves… I mean he said he loved me. I don't know."

"People don't hit someone they love. In fact, guys that hit girls are cowards." Super can't hide his anger.

"I know." Laila sounds so sad.

"I don't think we need to know the reasons why this happened." I chime in. "We need to all put this behind us."

"You keep saying that, Meera. It is not so simple. I want to know why this happened. Doesn't Lai know better?"

"Laila knows better now. And this will not happen again. Right, Laila?"

Laila nods mutely and automatically in answer to my question. Tears glisten in her eyes. I wrap my arms around her and put my cheek against hers. I feel the wetness of her tears. I want to squeeze out her misery. We remain like that for what feels like a long time, rocking back and forth.

* * *

I will be back in Delhi in six months for Sharda's wedding, but that seems too far away. The tears still have not come, and after saying excruciating goodbyes and making many promises, I am on my way back to my bright and shiny, successful, almost-newly-wed life in New York. No one knew about this visit, because we don't want to tell anyone about Laila's bad experience. Not even Rini knew I was visiting. Other than the fake kiss and the real kiss with Ari, this is the first time I have kept something this big from Rini. I have not thought about Ari in a long time. I wonder what it's going to be like between us now. He is a good kisser.

And Neel? Neel will be at the airport to pick me up. I have not thought about him in a long time either. Hardworking, handsome Neel. The man I married, my husband by my own choosing. Why does it feel at times that I am living a fake life? That I am living someone else's life? That my place is back home with my family, and Neel and the life that comes along with him are fake, like a mirage, shiny and perhaps tempting, but not real. It is exceptionally difficult to be a good Indian woman, a good Indian wife. It would be so much easier to go back to being a child and not having to think about all this. But I can never ever have the existence I am looking for – for I don't know myself what exactly that is.

* * *

"I've missed you, baby. How is Laila?"

"It was horrible seeing her like that, and it was very difficult to leave." My voice chokes and the tears finally threaten to come. I don't hold back. I want Neel to know, to understand how much it hurts. "I hate what this has done to the family, Neel. Super is so angry, he is seething all the time. Papa is silent, swallowing his own feelings. I think he is grappling with the same questions, the same guilt. What could we have done different? What did we do wrong, that this happened? Mom is overwhelmed and can't stop talking or crying. And Laila is carrying the burden of everyone's pain, the guilt of having hurt the family like this, the confusion of how this relationship turned out, and I don't even know what else. She doesn't talk much."

I am sobbing by now. Neel reaches out and holds me gently. He doesn't say anything.

"I would give all this up in a heartbeat, Neel. I need to be back with my family."

"I know baby. We will be back soon. Trust me. It's going to be alright."

But how? I need to be back there now. I need to be with

them today. But Neel does not have an answer to that, and so I let him enjoy his reassurance to me.

* * *

I am in Ari's arms now, in his home, in Montclair, NJ, an anticipatory twenty-nine-minute train ride from Penn Station. He holds me for a moment longer than necessary, before letting go. It is the Sunday after my return from India and Ari has invited me over for dinner. Neel flew out this morning to Minneapolis for a training course, and he will be gone for four days. Not knowing what he is encouraging, Neel wanted me to accept Ari's dinner invitation. He said I have been sad since I returned from India, and I need good food and good conversation. He was sorry he has to go for his training and he felt better knowing I had company this evening.

Ari often boasted about his cooking abilities, and today he spent the afternoon cooking. He looks freshly showered and has a beer open. His hair is still damp. This is my first time in his home. It is a '70s, three bed, two bath home, double story, with old wood floors. There are windows all through the house, bringing in the streaming sun. Ari's walls are bare and his décor, minimalistic. The only indulgence is his bookcase. Ari has shelves lining one entire wall from floor to ceiling, filled to overflowing with books and music. There is an energy, an excitement in his home that is very much like him, something simple yet numinous, warm and welcoming. An emanating love seems to have touched part of his home until it's well-worn, its sharp edges rubbed off with endless adoration. I can almost smell the energy, and almost touch it. It is Ari's energy. The energy that tells of a life well experienced. It excites me.

I am admiring his collection of books when he walks back over and his arm appears from behind me, holding a beer out. He is standing, it seems, directly behind, so that if I were to take one step back, my back would be against his chest. I can feel and hear his breath and his heartbeat. I take the beer, turn around and step sideways, breathing through this moment. I don't ask him where Tina is today, because I don't want to know. But I am determined to not overstep the boundary of friendship, preferring to think of the real kiss as a moment out of time, perhaps to be followed up on in another lifetime.

"Thanks for cooking."

"My pleasure, darling. Let's turn on some music, and you tell me all about your trip."

* * *

"Meera, I'm going to have to work on you. You know the difference between selfishness and self-preservation? Sometimes we can't think of these very painful matters. It just doesn't get us anywhere. We have to learn to live in the present, and do the best we can. And we have to be patient and trust in the ability of others too. She will heal and learn from this."

"But she is my little sister and I *know* I need to be there. I don't do enough, I *can't* do enough from here. I wish I knew I would feel this way, then perhaps I would never have married. You know, you might find this strange, but sometimes I almost wish I had an abusive marriage, because then it would have been easier to just leave. Neel is a good person, but sometimes that makes me sick. I know I can't leave him or hurt him." This is a day of firsts. It is the first time I have voiced, even remotely, these abysmal feelings for Neel and my marriage.

"I'm grateful Neel is not abusive. You don't want that, darling. Don't ever wish it. You don't need that to leave him, if you truly want to. Look, there is a lot of beauty around. And a lot of misery too. That's the way of the world. If you can do a little bit to change the misery part, it's good. And if you can do that without losing sight of the beauty part, that's exceptional. You *have* changed the misery part. You *have* done your bit. I am sure it makes all the difference that you went, and you were there for all of them. They don't want you to disrupt your life either. That would not help."

"But what I have realized is that my life without them is just bleak."

"Your life is not without them, darling. Don't be so melancholic." Ari shakes his head as though he does not know what to do with me.

"Forget it, Ari. This is an endless, conclusion-less topic."

"Here, come here. Let me give you a hug." And while he is holding me, Ari whispers "Share a shot of vodka with me?"

"I have to get back home."

"It's not even six in the evening. I will get you on the subway by eight."

"Okay."

* * *

We have had two shots of vodka between the two of us. I think Ari probably had seventy percent of it, but I am feeling significantly better and less inhibited. So when Ari asks me to sing a popular Indian duet with him, I break into song. Ari has a melodious, full bodied voice. I sound too soft and slightly drunk. After our duet is done, Ari sings a folk song, with his eyes closed and his head nodding slightly to the tune. The evening sun picks up the silver highlights in his hair as I admire the straight line of his nose, his closed heavily lashed eyelids, his full lips and the geography of his chin and jaw. My scrutiny goes unobserved because his eyes are closed, and it feels like I am secretly, reverently paying homage to this beautiful, multifaceted man in front of me. His warm, earthy presence takes over the whole room and changes its hue. I must keep vary of him and not let this take me over. I must keep him at arm's length. I must be so vigilant, because I am treading on dangerous ground.

"You are watching me, darling. What are you thinking?"

"That was a beautiful song," I answer, looking away abruptly.

"It *is* a beautiful song traditionally sung by young women at the advent of the monsoon, asking the rain Gods for a faithful man."

"It's a haunting, catchy melody."

"Kind of like you."

"Huh?"

"Haunting and catchy." Ari says, reaching across the couch and taking both my hands in his. What follows is entirely outside of my control, and any illusion I have that I can keep Ari at arm's length is completely shattered as I am rooted to my spot. As an observer I see Ari bending towards me, kissing me fully on my lips, slowly prying open and examining every part of my mouth, and it seems, with that, my heart. I see him looking at me with love and the same old sadness, and then, finally, ending the kiss to peer into my eyes, seemingly to see if he has overstepped the delicate boundary between us. My hands are still in his, that being the only part of us that is touching. I pull my hands out and grab the back of his head, pulling it towards me once more, and then I kiss him like I have never kissed before. There is nothing gentle about my kiss. It explodes like a cannon finally let loose. And Ari kisses me back with equal ferocity, until my lips burn like they are on fire.

We teeter on the edge of this crossroad for a moment.

"I deserve this, don't I?" I mutter.

"Yes, darling." He whispers back as he pulls off my sweater, resuming kissing me. I will myself to forget everything else and remain in this moment, savoring it with all I have. I want its sweetness to refuel my senses, and release my anger. I want to feel carefree and young, reckless and desirable. I want to rebel against the unfairness of pain and separation, of violence and power, of wealth and fame, of institutions and chains. I want to corrupt the incorruptible and show the world I too am affected by its horrors. Most of all I want to corrupt myself, before the world does it. And some impulse says I can resolve all this through this unthinkable liaison with Ari. There is no way I can know how wrong I am, because I don't understand any of this as yet. All I feel is the lust and desire.

He leads me by the hand into his bedroom. It is cool and dark. We stand facing one another by his bed.

"I want to love you, Meera. Completely. In a way that I am meant to love. In a way that I know."

"I know. I feel it."

And he resumes kissing me all over, till I cannot distinguish where his kisses land. I cannot distinguish where I end, and he begins. I cannot distinguish if I am a participant or an observer. Plummeting me to nothing but sensation, he quivers, and I am surprised to see I have this effect on him. It excites me, provokes me, and I want to be dominant now, holding him, loving him, reducing him to nothing but an extension of my own desire. We dance this dance with exquisite tenderness alternating with extreme urgency. It feels like I am being touched for the first time and we are traversing virgin territory, igniting fires as we go. I don't recall when exactly he picked me up and put me on his bed, when we shed the rest of our clothes, or when he began making tender love to me. But we are finally spent. I lie limp, with my head resting on his extended arm. He holds me close.

"I've known you before," I say.

"Yes, since you were five, baby."

"No, before that."

"Before that?"

"In some other lifetime."

"Sweetheart. You've known me in your dreams."

"Your scent is so familiar. It's always felt that way. Every time we hug it is like deja vu. And it was like that when I was a kid too. This crazy, weird familiarity."

"Who knew we'd end up lovers. Did you?" He chuckles.

"No. But I think I had a crush on you even back then. I didn't like that you had a girlfriend then. Renu, right? I was so jealous of her. Though I didn't really know the meaning of jealousy. You used to leave to meet her. I never wanted you to go."

"Ah, Renu. You have a good memory."

"Ari, I don't think you know what you meant to me. Everything changed after you left."

"Ah, I was twenty-one when we moved. I didn't know much of anything then, Meera. All I wanted was good food, fun, and damn good sex."

"What?"

"Honesty, baby."

"But you were so good with me."

"You were a delightful, angry little bundle, Meera."

"You saw that?"

"Yes."

"So you had sex at twenty-one?"

"Ha! No, no. I was indoctrinated at the tender age of fifteen, at the back of the school yard by a gorgeous Indian beauty who, at the time, I thought was an Amazonian goddess."

I chuckle now. It excites me to know this man, lying next to me, has been well loved through many experiences. Vicariously, I live a little.

"Was she fifteen too?" I ask.

"Oh no. She was older. In her late twenties. She was a teacher."

"Really? That is considered child abuse here."

"Yes, but it was delightful, and educational for me, and not at all abusive." Ari is grinning now. "You are a strange one. Most women don't want to know about my war-crimes. But you, you enjoy hearing about them, don't you?"

"Oh yes." I grin back.

"If I may be presumptuous enough to assume you are drawn to me... Tell me, what is the draw?"

"You are an incredibly unique combination of vulgarity and sophistication."

Ari bursts out laughing. "Hah!" He says, "Only you can come up with such a well packed statement that I don't know whether to take as a compliment or insult." And we are both laughing now. "Listen, my incredible curry is calling our names. Let's go eat."

* * *

I am home now. Careful not to touch anything, I step into

the shower right away. My clothes lie in a heap on the floor. I wash my hair and scrub myself. I can't think about what I have done, what line I have crossed. I can't think about this relationship with Ari as a transgression. Rather, it is, in my subconscious world, a natural evolution of something that began when I was five years old. Still, this need to wash away every last vestige of the past six hours is an urgent, albeit mechanical task. And the need to keep Neel far from my thoughts at this time is critical to my being able to breathe.

When I am finally in bed, I dare to peek at the terrain I am traversing now. It is dangerous, but like a moth to fire, I am inexplicably drawn to it.

* * *

Rupa takes one look at me and asks "What's wrong? You look like wild dogs have been chasing you all night."

"Yeah. Didn't sleep much. Can we go out for lunch today?" I decide in that moment that I can't hold it in. Rupa will understand this whole situation.

I get through the morning with some effort. It is difficult to focus on what I am writing and I don't produce much even after three hours of being holed up in my cubby and looking into my computer screen. Finally, there is a tap on my shoulder. "Dude, do you want to go or what? I am starving."

We go to the deli by the corner and order our sandwiches.

"Ari – you remember Ari?"

"Yeah, your childhood neighbour you ran into here. What about him?"

"I met him yesterday. He invited me for dinner. Neel wanted me to go too."

"That's cool. I like men who can cook. Damn, they need to have some skill to compensate for being male." Rupa guffaws. "Why are you deadly pale though? Was the food that bad?"

"No. We kissed. The food was fantastic. The kiss too."

"What? Are you pulling my leg?"

"No. We kissed."

"Like as in real, full on?"

"Yes."

"Anything more?"

"Yes."

"Dude, you are in trouble. You need to backtrack and wipe last evening off the surface of your history."

"I can't. I am so drawn to him. I've tried to keep away."

"What about Neel?"

"I can't leave him. He is a good guy."

"Meera, please think about this very carefully. You are playing with fire here. There is no way out without extreme pain, and you can still prevent that. Just step away and forget about last night. Repent, and focus on your marriage and your future, and don't get drawn into a life of secrets. Trust me, I have been there, and it is faulty by its very definition."

"It feels out of my control. I have tried in the past to break it with Ari. It's crazy. Last night just felt so natural."

"Yeah, but natural does not mean healthy or good for you. An affair always feels good and heady when it begins, but it's really bad news."

"It's not like an affair, it's… it's a spiritual connection or something. What am I going to do, Rupa? When I die, I don't want to regret not having experienced this. I would rather carry the regret that I did this. It's magnetic and sensory and I just *can't* walk away. I've tried. In the past I tried to break it up a few times."

"I see desperation in your eyes. I don't think you know what you are doing. I don't think you understand there is no turning back. You know one thing that I love about you? Your 'fuck-you' attitude that is apparent in your own quiet way. You have this transparent innocence that indicates you have nothing to hide. You say it like you see it, fearlessly. Do you know you are forgoing that part of you by going down this road?"

* * *

I don't know what to do. I know what Rupa says is true. I will lose a part of myself in this fire, but the fire's got to me and I can't get away from it.

The phone rings.

"Baby, how are you? I miss you. Do you miss me?" It's Neel.

"Yes."

"You sound dull. Are you okay? Sorry I am gone. Two more days. That's all. How was your dinner with Ari?"

"Good. Um... fine. He is a talker, you know? He was just very talkative." I am rambling, but Neel doesn't notice.

"The training is exceptional. I wish you could have come with me. But it is very busy here too. We just broke out of the evening session, and now I'll meet up with the group for dinner. It's crazy, this American way of packing so much into one day. I love it, Meera. And I love you. Love me?"

"Love you."

"Bye."

"Bye."

I am trapped. I am the good wife and I am supposed to play nice. But I am a fraud, because I can't adhere to these imposed doctrines and nor do I have the strength to tell the truth. But I willingly got married. Though when I signed the marriage certificate, I didn't sign away my right to be happy too. I didn't promise that I would follow him to the ends of the earth so that he may fulfill his dreams. What about my dreams? What are my dreams? Whatever they are, there is no space in my marriage for them, because I have to fit into his ideal life. That's the unspoken expectation.

The phone rings again. It's Ari.

"Darling, come over tomorrow?"

"Tomorrow? No, I can't... I...I'm not sure about things, Ari. I need time to figure things out."

"Of course. Let's meet and just talk. Okay?"

"Just talk. Okay. Romano's at six tomorrow."

"Yes."

* * *

"Neel returns tomorrow." We are sitting at Romano's and I find it essential to mention Neel in our conversation.

"I know. How are you feeling?"

"I am not sure at all. Can we be just friends again?"

"If that's what you want. But it's not what I want." His eyes are wide, and he looks very serious. "Is that what you want, Meera?"

I look away. "Yes."

"Are you happy?"

"As much as I know how to be. Are you? Why are you even interested in me?"

"I feel a kinship with you. It is very comforting to be around you. There are so many *desi* aspects of you – like your attachment to your family. I don't know anyone who talks to their parents every single day. There's something about you that's sweet and innocent, that I don't get to see often. And I've known you since your diaper days." He winks. "And now I have revealed more than I am used to... So I hope you are satisfied and you stop wondering why I am interested in you. I just am."

I can't help smiling and feeling lighter in my heart. Suddenly I get up from my barstool, wrap my arms around him and plant a kiss on his cheek. He doesn't lose a moment to draw me closer and hold me firmly in his arms. He is sitting and I am standing so very tightly held, that I can't move. His cheek is next to mine, and he whispers in my hair, "Let's get out of here, darling."

* * *

We are lying in his bed, our legs intertwined, my horror and guilt pangs at what I am doing gone. The time is too precious, too relished, to feel anything other than delight and excitement. Everything about this is exciting, Ari's smell, his body, his understanding and maturity, his persuasion, his skill at love-making, the secrecy, the history, the sense that I finally have my retribution... It's surprising I feel a need for retribution, but I do. It is retribution with Neel, for promising me the world and refusing to even acknowledge his non-delivery; with Akash for his betrayal; with Rini for stepping away from our friendship even though for a short time; with Rita for breaking my trust and our bond; with Monty for violating me; with Mom for loving Super more; with Ari for breaking my heart and leaving me... at the world for being a corrupt place.

"You are lost somewhere."

"Just surprised by strange thoughts."

"Like?"

"Like using you to avenge myself against you for leaving India when I was seven."

"That's what I like about you. No bullshit! And that's actually very smart, darling. Use me, please use me." Ari makes large innocent eyes at me and I laugh with abandon.

* * *

"Rupa, Neel will be back tonight. I don't know how to face him."

"You have two options. Either tell him the truth, or keep silent and behave normal, keep your demons to yourself, and keep yourself as far away from that charming conman Ari as possible."

"What makes you say he's a conman?"

"Don't you see, Meera? He is ruining your straightforward life. You both are cheating his girlfriend and Neel. And you would not be in this predicament without his persuasion. He picked up on your weak pulse and he went for it. Neel is a good guy, Meera." She softens her voice, trying to reason with me. "You may feel he doesn't understand you or doesn't care enough for your sentiments, but I see him as someone really trying to make it. I see him as a committed, happy, accepting husband. Look, tell me who doesn't have problems. Show me one couple that is fully satisfied. You can work through the kinks, you have a lifetime for that. It is hard to build a relationship and very easy to break it. Don't give up on yours; work on it."

"What am I going to do, Rupa?" As she talks, a churning discomfort is building up inside me. It is now a full-fledged throbbing from the pit of my stomach to my throat. I am finding it hard to breathe.

"Don't tell Neel, recommit to your marriage, work hard to

make it good for you. You can do it, my friend. Don't think about what is already done, and forgive yourself."

I stare at her hard. I don't know if I can do all that. I don't know if I want to.

21

Ari Hasan Jana

I have it all with Tina and her ferocity, and Meera and her softness, and then the occasional flavors all around. I am loving my life. It's happenin'... oh happenin'... happenin'... oh happenin'... I wish I had a travel machine and I could zip around from one lovely situation to another. Or if I could clone myself like the Hindu God Krishna. Didn't Meera tell me he had many loves and was with them all at the same time?

Time for a joint now, and then I must jump in the shower and get my swanky self all cleaned up and ready for the gala dinner tonight for Tina's ad launch. Got to love this life – it's fun and play. I am lucky that it all comes easy to me. The wit, the charm, I can turn it on at will. It's easy, I'm easy and life is easy. There is no fathomable reason to get serious about anything, anything at all... except work. I don't quite know why the women in my life are so serious. Tina could fight a war all on her own. She never backs down on anything. And Meera could write poetry when she gets into her melancholy mode. But it sure works out to be a heady combination for me. I am grateful I was able to break through Meera's hesitations. Undeniably, the attraction is there, and also it allows me to enjoy Tina more too.

Oh, I thank the forces that are that created me. Thank you. I love me! I'm gonna dance a jig in the shower. Oh, oh, oh... And tonight it's time to turn on the charm full blast. Besides the usual suspects, there's going to be many interesting people at the gala.

"Hi Tina, I didn't hear you walk in." Oops, she caught me dancing my jig. I have to be careful around her; she can never catch me with Meera. That would be the end of both Meera and myself.

"You are too self-absorbed to notice small sounds, Ari." Tina laughs at her own statement. Well, there is an element of truth in it. I am self-absorbed, but then why shouldn't I be? I am the most important being in my life.

"You look nice, baby." I admire her compact and curvaceous figure as she strips down, ready to jump in the shower. Still under the water, I stick my head out and kiss her full on the lips, devouring her tangy city-air breath, loving the softness of her skin, and dripping water all over her face. I feel myself harden, but I know Tina wants to be on time to the gala and will not entertain any delaying activity. So I step out of the shower.

"Thanks."

22

Meera Myna Dutt

I finally relented and invited Myrah, our neighbour, over for tea when I met her in the elevator yesterday. I am regretting my social generosity, as I have no interest in making small talk or entertaining anyone. But Neel really wants me to have more friends, and when I was stuck in that elevator for forty-five seconds with just Myrah, I just grit my teeth and invited her. I imagined that Myrah knew I was avoiding her and I had to prove that wrong. Besides, I had to do as Neel wanted, because I've wronged him so gravely.

So now I have a pot of *chai* brewing and salty crackers out on a tray. I rub my hands and look around. The apartment, unlike me, looks warm and inviting.

Thirty minutes have passed since three, the time Myrah was supposed to come over, so she may not show up after all. I am comfortably reading my book with my feet propped up on the couch, drinking the flavorful *chai*, grateful for this Saturday afternoon alone as Neel is out golfing with his boss, when the bell rings.

"I am so sorry, Meera, I have been running late. I am sorry. May I come in? Here, let me take my shoes off. Oh, what a day this has been! I work on Saturdays, you know?

I see some clients, and sometimes clients are so needy, you know?"

"Hi Myrah, please come in, make yourself comfortable. I made *chai* for us." I pour her some. Shucks! She seems like a very high energy person.

"Oh, thank you, I *love* Indian tea. It has *so* much... *flavour*. Okay, come sit with me. I got my tarot cards and I can do a reading for you if you like. It is a great ice-breaker, but more than that, I am a psychic. You probably didn't know that about me, huh? I don't tell a lot of people, because then either they want a reading, or they look at me like I am a quack. You know what I mean? But you are special and I will do a reading for you if you like."

The afternoon may not turn out so bad after all. I am pleasantly surprised by her forthrightness and her offer to do a reading for me. "Sure Myrah, I would love to get a reading, if you don't mind. Thank you so much."

"Okay, I was hoping you would say yes. I have been feeling that you need this reading. It is important for you. Come, sit."

Why do I *need* this reading? Suddenly the peace I felt earlier has evaporated, and the knot in my stomach is painful.

Myrah holds out the cards for me to choose from, "Close your eyes, rub your hands together and pick a card. Let's see. Very good." She proceeds to lay down my card face up on the coffee table, followed by a whole array of cards laid face up in a strange symmetrical arrangement. Some of them look pleasant, with pictures of the sun and an entangled couple, and some of them look scary, with pictures of daggers and dragons spitting fire. Myrah is nodding at the cards thoughtfully.

She closes her eyes for a moment and begins to tell me what she sees. "I see a woman close in age to you. She has anger, jealousy and hostility within her. She is toxic for you. She will bring you unhappiness. You will have some wounds that will take three years to heal. The wounding has already begun, but still has to manifest; after that, you will heal in about three years. You have some sort of a relationship that is unhealthy. That will end. This woman is connected to all of this. There is cruelty and violence involved. The cruelty is directed at your marriage. You will not be physically hurt, though. I see another woman. This woman will help you in the future. This woman is very bright and strong, full of sunlight. She will bring sunlight to your life. She will help save you and help you heal from your wounds. She will help you escape. After you heal sufficiently, you will become more spiritual, and more active. Peace will return to your mind. This is what your cards say."

My face must be white, for she continues. "Meera, don't worry, dear. Isn't it better to know so you can change what you can, and be prepared?"

I am not convinced I can change my destiny and I don't even know if tarot cards are a real thing, or if Myrah is indeed a skilled psychic, but I feel chills run down my spine, and my hands are icy cold.

"Are you okay? I am sorry dear, if this reading has frightened you."

"I am… I am okay. But I don't want these bad things to happen."

"Yes, of course, my dear. There are ways of fighting things off. The wounding has already begun, but you can lessen the intensity."

"How? How do I do that?"

"Let me see." She closes her eyes and appears to go into a trance. "Tell your mother. Tell your mother about this reading, and some secret you bear. She will know what to do. Your mother is a pure lady. She has a pure heart. Tell her."

Myrah opens her eyes and for a moment we sit staring at each other in silence. "It's okay, Meera. Our cards and our destiny change every moment. Some things can't be averted, but everything can be helped with the good forces and with the power of positive thought."

"Okay."

* * *

"Mom, all this is such weird stuff, and I was freaked out by it when she was doing the reading, but I am okay now. So don't be scared. She asked me to tell you, so I told you, otherwise I would not have."

"Okay, *Raja beta*, but it worries me. And with you so far away, I don't even know what to do. If something happens to you, it will take us a day to even reach you. I don't like you being so far, *beta*. Come home."

"I know Mom. Soon. Please don't tell Papa all this. He will worry."

"No, no, not Papa. He will just ask you to stay away from that girl. But I think I will tell Roshni *tai*. She will know what to do."

"Okay."

Roshni *tai* is a mystical, vibrant lady who lives in the neighbourhood with her family, three houses down from us in Delhi. She is said to have divine powers, and she says her purpose in life is to serve people. She does astrological readings, palm readings, spirit communications, and special *pujas* to remove curses. She discovered she had powers at age nine, when she predicted her neighbour would have an accident the following day, and he did. From then on people began consulting her, and her fame grew. Now people from all over Delhi and beyond come to her for advice and readings. *Roshni* means light in Hindi, and like her name, she seems to be full of light. I have seen her three times in all in the neighbourhood, and each time I saw her, I felt there was brightness and sparkle that seemed to emanate from her face and flow around her. Now that Mom mentioned her, consulting her seems like the obvious course of action.

* * *

"Meera, did you tell Neel all this?" Mom has called me back after speaking with Roshni *tai*.

"No, why?"

"Roshni *tai* said Neel and you have some differences, but you both will never separate. She said your neighbor's tarot reading is accurate, *beta*, but she said everything will eventually be okay. She said you will go through a rough time and will be targeted by someone, but she will do some *pujas* to protect you. I think you must tell Neel."

"I will. We just haven't had a chance to sit down and talk, you know. But now I don't want you to worry about this reading, Mom. I got scared initially too, but there is no way to know if it is genuine."

"But Roshni *tai* verified it. I just told you."

"I understand. But even so we can't live in constant fear that something will happen. Don't worry, Mom. I will tell Neel, and I will be careful. I promise."

"What differences do you have?"

"Nothing to worry about. Nothing big. Just small everyday things… like you and Papa have."

"Okay *beta*. I wish you both would just come home now."

* * *

"Really, Meera. She sounds very strange to me. I would not get worried over a tarot reading. Anyway, your Mom is getting this *puja* done, so it's fine. And nothing is going to happen to us. We are good, baby."

Neel and I are sitting on the couch and having *chai* together on Sunday morning and I have just told him about Myrah's reading. I'm instantly irritated that he insists on believing that our relationship is strong. He is unable or unwilling to see how far I have drifted from him. It irritates me too that I am so uncomfortable, because inadvertently, Ari comes to mind, along with pangs of guilt. How can Neel be so blind?

"What if we are not good, Neel? How will you even know how good or not our relationship is if you don't even ask me how I feel about it?"

"I know you want to go back to India. You think I don't know? And I know you blame me for being here. But this is a temporary situation, and I think as you grow to enjoy life here, your anger about this will lessen. But everything else about us is fine. I am doing this for us, baby. My experience here will make me very marketable in India, and succeeding in this project is huge for my career. You know, it is trailblazer technology. It will forever change the way the technological world functions. This is very big, Meera, and we will reap the benefits. Trust me."

Too late, Neel. It is already too late. The history of our relationship now irrevocably has my secret. I am not innocent anymore. I am not the same person who used to hold on to your every word adoringly.

"You look so sad. I promise you we will go back."

"It's more than just that. Our relationship has changed for me."

"What do you mean it's changed? Nothing has changed. You just feel that way because you are angry about being here. That's all."

"You don't know me as well as you think you do, Neel. And you don't want to hear anything that makes you uncomfortable."

"What are you talking about? We are young, successful and we love each other. Life is good. Why be morose? Stop being sad and let's go to the farmers' market. That's always fun. And I think no tarot readings anymore."

"You never want to talk about the real stuff."

"Meera." Neel sighs, "What is the real stuff? Isn't spending good time together and enjoying each other's company real? Isn't that what really makes a relationship better and brings us closer? I love it when you are goofy and happy and I don't like it when you get morose and try to pick a fight. Listen, trust me, you will feel better once we get out. Come on, I know you love the fresh fruit at the market."

* * *

"Ari, I have to stop. I am sorry but we have to end this. It's all a big mistake. I can't stand when you touch me, but I love it and I can't stop. I can't stand when I am with Neel, because I am constantly concealing something so big and it's eating me up. I don't know what to do."

"Darling, relax. We are first and foremost friends. I want you to be comfortable. Nothing is more important than that. And you know these are adult, complex relationships. You don't have to be completely transparent about your choices. It's your life and no one needs to know how you run it."

"But I am lying and that's not fair."

"Then do you want to stop?"

"No... I mean, yes. I have to."

"Relax. You are not hurting anybody."

"Are you okay with this secret, Ari? Does it bother you that you are hiding something?"

"No. I am okay with it. I am open about my views and beliefs and I don't think what I do with my life is anybody else's business."

* * *

"Rupa, I am so confused."

"You are getting over the top of your head, girl. You need to stop this affair ASAP."

"Don't call it an affair."

"Well, that's what it is. A secret affair with a cheap sleaze ball."

"I know you don't like him, but don't call him names. Tell me, do you believe in tarot readings?" I've just told Rupa about Myrah's reading.

"We are the biggest egotistical fools if we believe science explains everything. But there are too many charlatans out there too. If your neighbour is not one, you need to be careful and protect yourself and your marriage. Meera, you have a good thing with Neel. Why are you jeopardizing everything?"

* * *

"Hi Laila, how are you now?"

"I am well. See."

It hurts somewhere in my heart to see Laila on Skype, and I feel my throat choke up. I yearn for the old, carefree, young days and for India even more; for the days without men, and without complications. Laila is now sixteen and it's been four months since the Ravi episode. It feels like we almost have the old Laila back, the Laila who ignites joy in everyone she comes across. It is my thirtieth birthday and my family and Rini all wanted to wish me on Skype today. It is so good to see them all, but also so painful, because it only reminds me of the vast distance between us, and the poor compromise of seeing my loved ones on a screen.

"How are you celebrating today?"

"Neel and I are going out for dinner."

"Meera, you look different. Are you okay? Are you happy?" My perceptive little sister is peering into the screen and I can feel her scrutiny. Her eyes are probing and wondering what it is that they cannot see.

"Yes, Laila. It's just that I miss you all so much."

"And we miss you. Can't wait for you to move back. But everything's okay with Neel, right? You guys are good, right?"

"Yes. Sometimes I blame him for us being out here. But I am working on it." I am working on it by running away and hiding in Ari's arms, but I don't tell her that.

"You are not telling me something, Meera."

"You are too suspicious for your own good, Ms. Sweet-sixteen."

"Okay, I'll stop." She laughs, "You have to enjoy your day. We cut a cake for you here today. Mom told you, right?"

"Yes."

* * *

"Neel, thank you for a lovely birthday dinner."

"Baby, thank you for being you, for being born, and for being in my life."

"Why do you love me so much?"

"I wish you could see yourself through my eyes. You are perfect and exactly what I want and need."

"That doesn't tell me anything. Why do you love me?"

"Meera, I've loved you since you were thirteen and I was twelve."

"But my question is, why? Why do you love me? Why did you love me then? What did you see in me?"

"You were kind of quiet and shy then. No one knew much about you. Rini mostly spoke for the both of you. I was drawn to you then, I don't know why. But then when I saw you and Rini at Raja's pub three years ago, it was that same magical, mystical feeling again. I am just drawn to you."

"So you can't tell me why you love me?"

"Oh, Meera," Neel laughs, "No wonder you are a journalist. If a question gets stuck in your head, you will get to the bottom of it. I love you, my love, because you are bold and sensitive and there is something mysterious about you, and you are kind and you love your family with a fierce loyalty. I could go on. But just accept it, I love you. Tell me why you love me."

"Because you love me so much."

It doesn't bother Neel, but I am horrified with my own answer that day.

* * *

I am at Ari's and he has stepped out to pick up dinner we ordered on the phone. I am content with a few beers and shot of vodka. If guilt shows its ugly face, I push it back to the deeper recesses of my mind, and the more I do this, the easier it becomes to catch the guilt and push it away. Ari and I have settled into a semi-routine. I see him weekly now.

Sometimes we meet at his home and the inevitable always happens. He is irresistible, and I don't try to fight it any more. What is the point? In fact, my rendezvous with Ari are precisely what allow me to continue on in my life with Neel. I think of it as refueling for the soul. The conversations with Ari are deep and meaningful, and the physical relationship we have is merely a byproduct of our mental and spiritual connection. That's what it is − a spiritual connection.

"Darling, you're deep in thought. What's going on?"

"Nothing. Just trying to rationalize 'us'."

"And what is the rationale?"

"That I need this for my soul."

"Aw, darling! And now let's eat, we need this for our bellies. I am starving."

After dinner Ari is propped up against some cushions on the carpet and is tapping his hand on the wooden floor to the beat of the rhythmic background music.

"I love you."

"Excuse me?"

"I love you."

Suddenly he sits up grinning from ear to ear, "Yeah, me too."

"You love you too?"

"No, I mean you." He pauses. "Meera, I love you."

* * *

It is done, the dye is cast, and the matter is sealed. Gradually Ari has become a big important secret, and though I still have pangs of horror at what I am doing, for the most part I am able to bury them and not deal with the duplicity of my life. I try not to think about where this is leading and what the possible eventualities are. I try not to think about leaving

Ari when I ultimately move back to India with Neel. I still desperately want to move back, but the pain of being away from my family has been replaced by a sort of anxiety and nervousness that is soothed only when I am with Ari. Neel does not look at what he does not want to know and I am getting better at pretending for him that everything is fine. In my gut I feel though that the day will come when Neel will know the truth. It is not fathomable that the truth can remain hidden forever, and yet I am drawn inescapably to Ari and this burdensome secret, like a moth to a flame.

23

Laila Myna Dutt

It's been a year since the Ravi episode and I feel normal now. I am lucky and blessed and I have never been more aware of that. My face in the mirror looks happy again. I am excited about going to the fair with Sunaina today. Thank goodness the past is in the past now and I am ready for my new life.

"Laila, *beta*, be careful, okay? I just want you to be very careful."

"Mom, don't worry. We are in a crowd, Sunaina is with me, and honestly, I learned my lesson. I will not ever put any of us through that again."

I know Mom is worried about me, and Pappa too, though he tries not to show it. Today is the first time I am going out without any of them, since the Ravi episode. It is strange how we all refer to it as 'the Ravi episode', but it has become a marker in our lives. I am determined to not get involved with anyone at all, ever again. Maybe I will opt for an arranged marriage. I am so grateful that Meera found such a good person as Neel. It's easy to get duped, because they always pretend so well to be what they are not, and I could not bear it if Meera was unhappy. Life is good and back to normal.

"Hmmm, hmm, hmm…, love you, Mom, love you Pappa.

Bye! See you by nine. And I forbid you to worry, okay? I am fine and Sunaina is with me all the time."

"Bye, *beta*."

* * *

It's really lovely and freeing to be out here in the fair, with just Sunaina. I squeeze her shoulders with my arm and side hug her. "Thank you, Sunaina, for everything, for being my friend, for saving me, for everything. You are the best friend one could ever have."

"And so are you, Laila. I love you like a sister. I don't want anything bad to ever happen to you again. But why are we talking like this? Nothing bad is going to happen anymore."

"I had such a good time today. Thank goodness Mom and Papa are finally okay with me going out without any of them. They are comfortable knowing I'm with you."

"Yep! You needed to get out on your own." She grabs my arm suddenly, "Listen, I can't hold it anymore. Finally there's the restroom, and I am sure it's nasty, but I have to go real bad. Just wait here by the candy floss stall, okay?"

"Okay, okay, go."

Candy-floss brings back memories for me. Ravi had bought me candy-floss at my school fair the first time I met him. I used to love candy-floss then, and now I will never eat it again. I can't stand the sight of the pink coloured sugar being swirled onto the sticks, and being handed to excited kids. That's what I was back then, just a kid. I have grown up a lot over this last year and a half. I will never allow any man to treat me like that again.

"Hello, Laila."

I freeze. His voice sounds so familiar. Am I imagining

this, or is Ravi really standing right behind me? I won't turn around; maybe it was nothing.

"Laila, I just want to say I am sorry."

It is him. If I still don't turn around, he will go away. Where is Sunaina, and why is she taking so long? Should I just run? But my legs feel heavy and they are not cooperating. I can't move. And what if he starts chasing me?

"Laila, please let me just say how sorry I am." He comes into the line of my vision slowly, as he walks around. "Not a single day has gone by when I have not thought about you, and regretted my actions so badly. I hate myself for doing what I did. I need your forgiveness to go on."

He looks handsome and more mature, with a new sadness in his eyes. His hair still flops over his forehead, making him look like a boy. He is wearing a brown t-shirt over jeans. The t-shirt clings to him, framing his chest. It is broader too.

"Laila, please say something."

"Sunaina, will be back any moment. You better go."

He pulls out a scrap of paper and a pen from his pocket, scribbles something, and holds it out to me. When I don't even move, he slips it into my open handbag hanging from my shoulder. "That's my number Laila, call me." And then with a sad half-smile he is gone.

As if right on cue, Sunaina is back.

"The bathrooms are filthy, and the lines are a mile long. Ugh! Be glad you don't need to pee. Gosh, I want to go home and shower. Where are you lost, missy? You look like you've seen a ghost."

"Oh, nothing," I say, clutching my handbag. "Let's go home."

* * *

I stare at the scrap of paper with Ravi's number in the privacy of my bedroom. I know I can't call him. Maybe I should tell Meera about this. How would that help, though? Meera would only worry from so far away. If she were here, then I would tell her. I can't tell Sunaina or Super, because they both hate Ravi so much, they would be angry. And if I tell Mom and Dad, it would be pandemonium, and perhaps they would not let me go out alone. I hope I just never see him again.

I crumble the paper in my hand, then straighten it out, rip it up, and throw it in the trash. But his number is embedded in my mind and I can't get rid of it from there.

24

Meera Myna Dutt

It's been almost two years that I've been secretly meeting Ari. We are comfortable in our secrecy and routine. We usually meet at Romano's on a weekday evening when Neel is either working late, or is at a work happy hour. Neel encourages me to hang out with Ari, because he thinks our friendship is a healthy outlet for me. Usually from Romano's we go over to Ari's place for an hour or so. We rarely vary from this routine, but every once in a while we skip Romano's. We seldom skip going to his place, though. When my secret is not killing me, it thrills me. I don't know if it's the fact that it is the forbidden, or the fact that I've loved Ari since forever, or the feeling that I am 'getting back' at Neel for trapping me in this life I don't love, but whatever the reason, I count on my weekly meetings with Ari. They feel like the fuel for my soul. I am still reluctant to call it an affair, because that word has a cheap ring to it, and what exists between Ari and me is very special. I believe completely that this was meant to be.

At some point during these last two years, Neel's touch began feeling alien to me, and very quickly I learned to pretend. Neel is content that I don't bring up old sore subjects with him anymore. I am content that I have found a way to survive, an outlet, a love that adds a deeper meaning to my life.

There is a chasm between Neel and me now that may not ever fill. I've thought of divorce from time to time, but then I realize I don't have the courage or energy to face our families. I daydream about what it would be like to be married to Ari, to not have to hide but rather openly express our love, and to be able to share my relationship with my family. But when I return to reality, I realize I can never have any of that, for castles cannot be built on corpses, and Neel would surely be the casualty of my betrayal. Besides, I have a kind of intimacy with Ari that can only come with sharing such a secret as we do. And that intimacy gives me power over Tina, and over any of his other more legitimate relationships and friendships.

And then I wonder what Ari wants out of this. He loves me, but he continues his relationship with Tina as well. I realize that in his world, Tina is the perfect girlfriend for his public image and I like to believe this is the only reason he still sees her. I like to believe that I am his great love, but our story, like any inordinate tragedy, is entrenched in pain.

Neel and I continue our routine of morning coffee together, goodbye kisses, asking each other how our day has been each evening, and making love weekly. But I have shut down to him, and I live for that day of the week when I can get away from my pretentious life and be real. I like to believe this is Ari's experience as well. But deep within I know that his reality may be very different from mine, for he is very different from me. While I worry about how all this (our affair) is going to end up, he lives in the moment and seems to enjoy every aspect of his life.

Deep within I believe that the truth about us can't be

hidden forever and someday, somehow, something will be known by someone. Every so often I revert to my childhood habit of chanting Lord Krishna's name, hoping that it never happens.

Rupa only knows about the first kiss and then I didn't tell her any more after those few initial conversations. My relationship with Ari is now entirely his secret and mine. I have grown in my position with TRENDS, and while I still write and report for them, now I also supervise interns. I find a sense of belonging and security in my work. I don't love it, but I enjoy it enough for it to distract me from all the other areas of my life. Rupa and I have grown closer in our friendship and I share everything with her except the taboo subject of Ari. Rupa is my only friend in this country whom I trust and can count on, but she is strongly opinionated about the whole Ari affair. Her sense of fairness is offended by my choice, and I just can't explain to her how I feel, how inescapably I am drawn to Ari, or how I need him for my very survival.

The time I came closest to telling her everything was one evening when, after a rendezvous with Ari, I returned home with my shirt worn inside out. I realized that only when I went to shower, a few minutes after returning, and somehow it struck me hard. Why hadn't Neel even noticed the shirt when I walked in? And what if he had noticed and caught me? What could I say? Surely I couldn't say I spent the whole day at work with my shirt inside out. I was on the shower floor trembling and crying for a long time. I was afraid of what I was doing, but I felt unable to stop. I felt trapped and I wanted the simple, innocent times of my life to return. Those times when I wasn't a fraud living a dual life. That night in the shower I decided I needed help, and I would confess to Rupa and ask her to help me find a way out, but by the next morning my resolve was gone, and I knew with surety that I could not let go of Ari.

* * *

We've been back to Delhi twice since the Laila episode. Once was for Sharda's wedding and that was a lot of fun, because all the cousins were together at the same place and I actually enjoyed having Neel there. The second time I went alone and just spent time with my family and Rini. I go to Jaipur each time I am in India. Jaipur is home to me, my paradise city that holds my most beloved magical memories and some of my most beloved people. I miss Ari when I go to India, but it still feels like home, and like a purer me exists when I am there. It feels like I never even left.

Rini is now married to her Kumar. I didn't go for her wedding and I feel guilty whenever I think about that, but Neel says I should not. Neel says it would be foolish to live in the US and not learn the practicality of American attitude. He says we would certainly have gone if we could have, but he had a high profile deadline at work, and I was unfortunately given a special project which could potentially lead to a promotion, and so we both had pressing reasons to stay. Besides, Rini got married in Kumar's village, a four-hour journey by road from Delhi. It would have been exhausting to travel to India for a quick week and then go to the village for her ceremony. But deep within I know these are all excuses. I know that I value my sentimentality above practicality and that I would have, could have, and should have dropped everything to be at my oldest friend's wedding. I know that I don't want to be practical, or American, and live as someone

I am not. I resent the fact that Neel is pleased I didn't insist on going to Rini's wedding. Rini, my ever-practical friend, completely understands, and for her it is not a big deal, but for me it is. And it seems to me Ari is the only person who understands the complexities of how I really feel. He had once, many years ago, called me a kindred soul, and that is just what he is for me. He gets me.

Perhaps I am destined to live this dual life. I certainly am used to it by now, with my loyalties quite confused.

* * *

It is a cold Sunday morning and I must be dreaming, for I scream out "No!" when the shrill relentless ring of the phone brings me into consciousness. Neel, propped up on one elbow and looking as bewildered as I feel, reaches for the phone on his night table, while turning his head to see if I am okay. The digital clock on my night table indicates it's not even four AM yet.

"What?" Neel's voice is shrill after listening to the caller for a minute.

"Who is it, Neel?"

"Shhh! I will tell you in a minute." Neel whispers from the corner of his mouth, one finger on his lip, indicating to me to hush.

"Okay... okay. I see. Okay." Neel is saying a lot of okays on the phone.

"Yes." Though sleepy, I'm very curious now.

"No." I strain to hear the voice on the other end. Neel's yeses, no's and okays don't tell me anything, and I can't hear much from the other end of the phone. I sink into the bed and begin to drift off again. Neel's body feels warm next to me. He puts his arm over me, pulling me closer. It feels protective and I enjoy the warmth of his embrace, and this momentary, unspoken, sleepy intimacy.

I slowly become aware of Neel's hand on my arm, gently shaking me awake – I must have fallen asleep. He is off the phone now. "What is it? Who was that?"

"It's Laila, Meera."

"Laila? Why did she call at this time? Is it about Mom or Dad? Are they okay?"

"No, it was Super calling about Laila."

"What?" I am fully awake now. "What about Laila? Tell me, Neel."

"She's in the hospital. Super said she will be okay. She has a concussion, two broken ribs, a broken arm and injuries all over. I am sorry, Meera."

"What... What happened? Was she in an accident?" My stomach is starting to tighten up and hurt.

"Baby, I am so sorry. It was that guy, Ravi, again. He hurt her. The police found her in a hotel room where he had left her like that. Beaten and bruised." Neel's voice sounds tight and controlled. I can tell he is angry.

"But, Ravi? How did he get to her? What was she doing in a hotel room? And where are Mom and Dad? Do they know? Oh my goodness, I have to go to her."

"Yes, I know you have to go to her. Mom and Dad know and they are at the hospital with her. She was in contact with Ravi and was secretly seeing him for some time. Super didn't know how long."

The pieces didn't fit. I remember the trip right after the first Ravi episode like it happened yesterday. Laila herself had felt so guilty and sorry and she'd wanted nothing to do with Ravi anymore. She'd promised me she would take care of herself. How could this happen? Is this a bad dream?

"Meera, baby, are you okay?" Neel looks concerned as he gently pulls my hand away from my eyes – I have been rubbing them frantically, so much that they are starting to burn.

* * *

The last few days are a blur in my mind as I disembark at the Delhi airport and go through the immigration line. There is a strong sensation of déjà vu and I am certain that I will find Super outside to pick me up, just the last time I was here for Laila after the last Ravi episode.

Sure enough, Super is outside and we silently get into the car.

"What happened?"

"About a year ago the bastard approached Lai at some fair she had gone to with Sunaina. Sunaina didn't know about this, as she was in the restroom when he found Lai. He gave her his number. She threw it away, but says the number was embedded in her head, and she wanted to ask him 'Why'. Why? Because he is a sick bastard that's why." He lowers his voice and continues, "Anyway, she resisted for six months and then, one day, she just called him. The bastard apparently told Laila he could not stop thinking about what he had done to her and was very sorry. He wanted to meet her and it took some convincing, but the little fool believed him and secretly went to see him. He was all apologetic, even shed some f-ing tears to reel her in. A month later, it seems after some phone conversations she met him again and they began to see each other. It was all wonderful in the beginning and then he began to lose his temper about small things, but always apologized after. He didn't hit her during those incidents and so she believed him, and thought he is working on himself.

He had a difficult childhood or something, it seems, so she says she gave him more leeway. Leeway, my ass. She should have known better. He obviously worked on her psyche and gullible as she is, she agreed to go to meet him in this hotel room so they 'could be alone', as he told her. She had lost some bet with him and apparently the deal was whoever lost would do as the other wished for one whole day. She told me she had decided that if she won, she would make him go and see a psychologist. In my opinion, he does not need a psychologist – he needs a jail cell. Anyway, she met him in the hotel room at noon, as per his demand. I don't know what happened between them – she refuses to tell anyone, but around two in the afternoon he began beating her. The bastard..."

Super's voice chokes, and I turn to see the tear at the corner of his eye. It matches my own tears which are, by now, silently streaming down my cheeks. Super swallows and continues, "He broke two ribs, her left arm and her left toe. Her head was bleeding too, and she has bruises all over. Someone heard her screams and called the hotel staff, who called the police. When they forced the door open, she was sitting in a pool of her own blood, and just staring blankly, they said. She was in shock and couldn't answer their questions, or say anything for a good two hours. But they took her straight to the hospital in an ambulance. We got a call from the officer, and reached to hospital too. The bastard was arrested and it seems his family is trying to buy peace. I don't know the status on that front, but I won't let him get off scot free this time. I can tell you that."

All I can say is, "Neel didn't tell me about the broken toe."

* * *

"Laila, why did you get back into this relationship?" In spite of my resolve to not question her, I ask.

"I am sorry. I didn't know better."

"You promised us." I know I need to stop making her feel worse than she already does, but I am angry. My sister, wrapped in bandages and casts, lies motionless in her hospital bed, staring out the window, tears rolling down her cheeks. This time it seems as though we each must bear our burdens alone. I am unable to console her or myself, and I silently walk out of the room to find Super in the corridor, on the phone with the lawyer we have retained. Mom and Papa are sitting in the visitors waiting area, talking in hushed voices. I go over to them and sit as close to Mom as I can on the couch, sinking into her and laying my head on her shoulder. She cradles my head with her other hand and continues talking to Papa about the logistics of moving Laila home and the care she will need. I am tired, so tired, of nothing working the way it was supposed to. If I had been an only child, none of this would have happened, and I would never have moved away from my parents. If Super had not come along, I would have got all the attention from my parents, I would not have got close to Ari, and maybe things could have been different. If Laila would not have come along, then she would not have to suffer through these horrors.

"I am sorry I am not doing more," I say to no one in particular.

"You being here means more than you realize," Papa responds.

* * *

I am on a flight back to the US in one short week, because a week is all the time I could take off work. I didn't spend much time with Laila, because I could not bear to see her in pain, and because I was angry at her. And I still am. I don't understand why my beautiful, wise sister knowingly went back to the same sick man to get herself beaten up. Laila will be seeing a psychologist and a physical therapist now. During my week there Super was wrapped up in the case that seems inevitable. His friend Rohit is a lawyer now, and is helping. Super was constantly on calls with Rohit, or meeting with Laila's actual lawyer along with Papa, in-between running his start-up pharma business. Mom cleaned and cooked up a storm while I was there. Everyone was busy and dealing with this in their own way, and Laila was quiet.

I am mostly relieved to leave it all behind, except I also feel, as always, such a mix of remorse, guilt and sadness.

25

Rumana Hasan Jana

It's been a busy summer with a lot to do for our move to Long Island. Rumi will now be further away from her dad, but I think the move is good for her. I love our new condo with its bright and roomy interior. Besides, it's right in the city too. It's a lucky find, and decorating is very exciting.

It's been so long since Roho's death, and with the grace of God I finally feel free. God knows I would do anything, give up everything in a moment, to get Roho back, if only that was possible. But I'm finally able to accept he is gone and I feel gratitude for learning to be happy again, learning to live again. I like this feel of fresh air in my lungs. It feels like I'm letting air and light into a musty, dusty room that has been locked up for a long time.

It feels good to be a mother to Rumi. I had forgotten how to do that for a while. My therapist Dorothy often reminds me that I have the rest of my life in front of me. It is my choice to either carry a weight in my heart, or to release the sadness and grief and enjoy this life filled with so many precious moments. Letting the sadness go does not mean I'm betraying Roho. Roho would want me to live again. He was such a bright and positive child, always laughing, always ready to play. And now, letting go of my grief is a way of honouring his memory. My precious son will always live on in my heart, and so I must make my heart a happy place for him to live.

Rumi and I will make this condo our home. My daughter deserves my attention and love. She was so patient with me in the years after Roho's accident, waiting, always believing that I will one day be able to smile again. She is my pillar, my shining beacon of light.

Ari will just have to do the long drive and we will work it out so she can get enough time with each of us. That's another blessing I am so grateful for. Unlike other divorced couples, we have a friendship. Ari has supported and loved me, and to an extent understood my grief. And who else but he would? For the loss is equally his as it is mine. In the early years I used to feel angry that he appeared to not suffer, while I was completely torn and lost in my loss. But now I understand better that he just experienced and expressed it differently than me. And thank goodness for him, for he took on Rumi's responsibility while I was barely able to lift my head from the bed on many days.

It's been a difficult journey, but we have come far, and the dark days are behind us. On a whim I buy a lottery ticket as I check out at the grocery store with milk and other supplies. With my optimism these days, who knows, I might even win.

26

Meera Myna Dutt

"So what are you going to do?" I ask Rupa, in shock. Darryl, whom she had been dating exclusively for four months now, had failed to tell her one small detail about his life. He is a married man. Rupa found out only by chance when she ran into him at the farmers' market on Sunday. He could not possibly run away as they abruptly came face to face. She said his face had turned scarlet when she'd said 'Hello' to him, as he was forced to introduce her to the woman by his side: his wife. Then he had hurried away as fast as he could, while Rupa stood rooted to the spot in shock.

"I don't know. I mean, what a bastard. How could he do this to someone? I can't believe I've been such a fool. We actually discussed moving in together. Can you believe that? What was he thinking? That he would just reel me along? Just continue to fool me? To what end, though? He lied about this; he can lie about anything. What if he's a psychopath killer?"

Her phone rings. "It's him." She answers the phone with, "I am not going to waste time by asking how you could, and why you did what you did. I will just get to the bottom line – I am going to be informing your wife about your deception, and your affair with me. Oh, and don't ever bother to call my number again."

Rupa is silent for some time while she listens to I assume whatever arguments and pleas Darryl is presenting on the other end. I'm perched on her office desk, and she is leaning back in her chair. I can't hear anything of what Darryl might be saying. Then she says, "Don't bother," and hangs up the phone. "Let's get out of here," she says to me.

We take the liberty of leaving a bit early. God knows we've worked late on many days. We head downtown and inadvertently, I lead Rupa to Romano's. It's just really the familiarity that takes my footsteps there, and though it feels strange to be there with someone other than Ari, we settle in a corner booth and order a bottle of wine.

"Meera, I feel so stupid, so damn stupid for believing him, and liking him. I thought I was a worldly wise woman. How could I get fooled like this? And I really care… cared I mean. I really cared for this bastard. Turns out I didn't even really know him." Unshed tears glisten in Rupa's eyes. I think this is how Tina would probably feel if she found out about Ari and me. This is how Neel would feel, for that matter. My head starts to hurt and I take a sip of my wine.

"I mean, seriously. I never thought something like this would happen to me. I thought I was too smart when it came to cheating, lying, bastard-men. I thought I would be able to detect one of those from a mile away."

"What did he say on the phone?" I ask.

"That he is sorry, he didn't have the courage to tell me, he really loves me and intends to leave his wife, he planned to tell me at the right time, didn't want to lose me, yada, yada, yada. Bullshit!" She is almost yelling.

"Are you going to tell his wife?

"Heck, yes!"

I sink lower in the couch as she continues. Almost as though she is admonishing me for my wrongdoings.

"So I've wasted four months of my life. So the question is, can I live with that? Okay, I can live with having wasted four months of my life. But the achy part is that I began to really care about him. He is the closest it's finally come to 'The Thing'. You know? That's what sucks. The bastard really got to me. And then the other thing – the guilt I feel towards his wife. Though it's not my guilt to carry. But still. I was sleeping with another woman's man. They are freaking married, for goodness's sake. I need to tell her. Most definitely."

"What do you think will happen?"

"I don't know. It's not that I want to hurt the woman, or break their marriage. It's just that she deserves to know the truth. She deserves to make a real choice."

Rupa's eyes glisten again. I can't tell if they are tears of pain or anger. Probably both. The churning in my stomach is even more intense.

"Rupa, is it going to help you, though? I mean, telling her. Will telling her help *you*?"

"It will make me feel better that he's not getting away with this. And that I've told her the truth."

"I understand. Okay."

"Really Meera, I can't get over how anyone can do this."

"Either he is a manipulative pervert, or he is genuinely unhappy in his marriage, just fell for you, got himself in this mess, and didn't have the balls to be honest."

"He's a sleaze ball, Meera. Come on! Could you intentionally lie to your lover, your partner for even a day, let alone months, about your fidelity and faithfulness? Could you? I couldn't do that. And that too with a straight face and full confidence. I mean, to be able to do that, you've got to be a certain kind of low level scum. And for what? For sex? Variety? Maybe he developed some fondness for me along the way (if he is capable of genuine feeling), but very clearly he intentionally lied for his own pleasure and amusement, let's make no mistake about that."

I feel chastised and I feel like a fraud. Can Rupa hear my accelerated heartbeat? If she knew about me and Ari, she would probably never talk to me again. She feels so hurt and wronged by Darryl, she would never understand how I can do the same to Neel. Am I doing the same to Neel?

"I think I will stick to lesbianism for a while." Rupa continues. "Girls are much more trustworthy."

"They aren't, Rupa. A woman could have done this too. Take your time, but don't let this experience colour you. And you know what? Stop blaming yourself for not realizing he was cheating. You were just being trusting and you didn't expect him to lie. Don't blame yourself for that."

Rupa is quiet. Her eyes are lowered to the table and she is contemplating something in her drink. When she looks up, two small tears have slid out the corners of her eyes. "It's just that no one came this close, this fast."

"There will be others, my friend. There will be others who are genuine, not frauds."

"You are right. Do you think I should inform his wife?"

"You should do whatever makes you feel good and helps you leave this behind. If you want to inform her, do it. If you want to just walk away from it all, do that. The person I am concerned about here is you, not them."

"I know. As a woman who has slept with another woman's man – unknowingly, but still – I feel owe it to his wife to tell her, so that she can have a fair choice."

I don't owe Tina anything, do I? Though it's hard to ignore the throbbing that's started at my temples, I try to shake my mind off my own story and focus on what Rupa is going through.

* * *

Two days later Rupa meets Darryl's wife Sherry for coffee, and tells her everything. Apparently Sherry and Darryl were married last July, which means they are not even one year into their marriage. Sherry had no inkling of Darryl's deceit and she is completely devastated. Rupa and Sherry cry together, and they want to confront Darryl together. I tell Rupa it's more dignified to just walk away. I'm worried that my advice really comes from a place of fear that this kind of confrontation could happen in my life too. I feel an unsettled, uncomfortable knot in the pit of my stomach constantly. Irrationally it feels like whatever Rupa decides to do in this situation will determine my destiny too.

Neel is so wrapped up in his work now, he is unaware of my internal chaos. And I am persistently awaiting Rupa's updates. I have not slept well in a week.

* * *

"What's wrong, darling?"

I tell Ari Rupa's story. We are at a coffee shop today, and not the usual Romano's. I am not sure why Ari wanted to detour from our typical plan, but I don't question it. We are in a corner booth. He's sipping his coffee, while I am nursing a glass of triple filtered hot water with lemon, to help my scratchy throat. It's probably the weather change that's given me a scratchy throat and achiness in my body.

"Don't look so worried. That is not going to happen to us. Meera, seriously, I wanted to talk to you about something too."

He never calls me Meera, unless it's something very serious, and that's rare. I search his face for a clue.

"Meera, I…" He looks away, and then down into his mug for a long moment.

"What is it? You are making me anxious."

"We will have to be careful."

"Of course. But why say that now?"

"Well, there is some level of suspicion."

"Tina?" After our initial conversations, and pseudo-explanations about our respective legitimate relationships, we've rarely talked about Tina or Neel.

"Yeah! She has a lot of anger about other stuff."

"What happened? Tell me."

"Well, it's not easy to talk about this stuff, darling. I want you to know I love you, and everything I've said and done has been real and genuine."

"Ari, this sounds like a breakup conversation." I am stunned. I didn't see this coming.

"Don't think of it like that. We'll see when and how we can meet. I have to be especially careful. If she catches us, she is likely to do anything."

"Like what?"

"Attack me or worse, attack you. Try to destroy your marriage."

"What triggered the suspicion?"

"I've disappointed her in different ways and she's carried anger about all that. Call it a woman's sixth sense – she's been questioning things a lot lately."

"What do you mean by 'disappointed her in different ways'?"

"Let it go, Meera. It's not important. Let's just say she doesn't trust me."

"Ari, why are you with her?"

Ari chuckles nervously, "Always the direct questions, darling."

"Seriously, why? Do you love her? The few times you've talked about your relationship, it's sounded like an arrangement and a burden. You don't seem like the kind of person to settle for something, so why? I ask as a friend, not as a lover."

Something hardens in his eyes, and he looks away. His jaw is tight. I reach across the table and touch his hand. But he doesn't take my hand in his like he usually does, and so I pull away. I am numb, not feeling anything. Maybe it's because the thought of breaking up with Ari seems so unreal to me. He turns back.

"Meera, I can't explain certain things. It's complicated. Tina is a lovely person, but she has some quirks. She doesn't know about us at all, but she suspects something is going on. We are going to have to cool it. If she finds out, it will be disastrous for the both of us."

"You still didn't answer my question." I say softly. I realize my teeth are clenched and it surprises me that I am angry with Ari. The anger is familiar. I need to know what exactly he is trying to say.

"What exactly do you mean by 'cool it'?"

"We can't meet at Romano's anymore. She found some Romano's receipts in my car. We can't go back to my place either. In case she shows up."

"Has she hired someone to watch you? Like a detective?"

"No I think she just might do random checks herself. I've seen her car outside my place in the middle of the night. I think she's trying to catch me in the act. Meera, I don't want to hurt you or your marriage in the process, I think we need to hold off for a while."

"Like not meet at all?"

"Yes."

I am silent. His reasons are valid, but how can we not see each other? "Ari, is there no way around this?"

"You tell me. I can't think of any."

"Why don't you take a stand with her and ask her to stop harassing you."

He looks down again. I've not known Ari to bow down to anyone's demands, and it is difficult to understand why he is scared of Tina.

"Meera, listen, you have to trust me about this. It will get ugly if she finds out. And the best way to protect ourselves is to not give her anything to find out."

"Okay... So do you want me to not even call you?"

"Don't call me from your number. If you need to get in touch with me, call me from a blocked number. Don't say hello until you hear my voice on the other end. And if I say 'wrong number', and hang up, just understand that I am unable to talk, and don't call back. I will call you back when I can."

"That's a lot of instructions." While I am numb, I also feel what he is asking will surely kill me. But I don't want him to see that.

"Look darling, we'll get through this, okay?" He turns on his charm.

I nod.

Ari leaves money on the table and after a few minutes of heavy silence, we get up. There is a sad look in his eye, but he smiles and gives me a tight hug. After a moment, he leaves. I feel very little, and very alone. The unsaid words hanging unsaid on my lips are *I hate you Ari, I hate you again for doing this...*

27

Tina Sylvia Amanar

The fucking bastard. I want to kill him. How could I let this happen to me... again? Deep inside, I knew he was fucking around. I've known for a while now. I should have listened to my instinct. I thought the asshole would never do this to me. Never. I just can't believe he is going back to Rumana. He's been messing around for years. We've been together five years and as far as I know, he's cheated for four out of those five. First it was Nicole, then Roshni, and now he is going back to Rumana? His ex-wife? After eight years of being divorced? Really! Got to give it to the bastard.

I pour myself another drink. There is nothing I can do. My friends who know tell me I have to move on and not even look back, that he's bad news, and that the best thing that could happen to me is this break-up. But gosh, I can't love like that ever again. All I wanted was a normal married life with him. Perhaps a kid or two and a dog. We are compatible in so many ways. He is stupid to give all this up. I don't understand at all.

I call Justin. "Hello."

"Tina, have you been drinking?"

"He's done it again, Justin. The bastard Ari has done it again. He's left me for good this time. It's the big break. I know you'll say that's good for me. But it hurts, Just. It hurts real bad and deep."

"Tina, I am coming over."

28

Meera Myna Dutt

I don't know the time of day, or the day of the month, or really even what month it is. All I know is that my daily calls and my weekly meetings with Ari have come to an abrupt, rude halt. It's painful to get through the days now, and the nights are even worse. The scale says I've lost four pounds in the last month. Buried as usual in his work and his fulfilling life, Neel notices nothing unusual. I write a lot sometimes in a journal, sometimes on my laptop. I don't know what I write, but there is some relief in just blindly, cathartically penning down thoughts that pass through my mind.

At first I waited for his call. Then I called him twice from blocked numbers and both times it went to voicemail. I didn't leave a message; instead, I just waited some more. And then I began to lose hope, and accept that Ari may not want any contact. For if he wanted to contact me, he would have found a way to do it.

About a week ago, I could not hold it in anymore, and over tears and beers, I told Rupa everything.

"Meera, two pieces of very interesting news!" Rupa bursts into my office. "One: Sherry – you know, Darryl's wife – filed for divorce (good for her!), and two: Your precious Ari is dating his ex-wife again."

"What?"

"Ask me how I found out."

"What? Tell me everything!"

"Okay, okay. So remember Justin? My artist / journalist / photographer friend. You met him at one of our Galas. Anyway, apparently Justin was covering HENNA's street theatre this past weekend and he interviewed Ari as part of it. He said there was this gorgeous, long haired, middle aged, ethnic beauty hanging around there and he approached her because he thought she might be part of the organization too. So, and this is priceless – Ari walks over to them right away and puts his arm around her and tells Justin 'this is my ex-wife, soon to be my wife again', or something of that sort. They have a weird story, Meera, did you know?"

I just shake my head.

"They invited Justin to get some beers with them and they ended up hanging out for a few hours. Justin did say Ari is very charming… so I will give you that. He said they seemed in sync and well suited to one another… Oh dear, are you okay?"

I nod. "Go on."

"So they got divorced almost a decade ago, but remained friends. You know they lost a son in a car accident and that broke them apart. They said they mourned in very different ways and could not understand each other at the time. But they said they always loved one another, and now it seems they have found each other again and plan to get married again. Goodness, Meera, I have not trusted this Ari character from day one, but even then, this is a shocker. He told you that Tina was getting suspicious, but here he is with his ex-wife. I wonder whatever happened with Tina, and whether it was all lies that he fed you."

* * *

I finally pick up the phone and call Tina's work number, which I got off her company website.

"Hello, may I speak to Tina Amanar?"

"Hold on, please."

My knuckles hurt from clutching the edge of my desk, but I can't let it go.

"Hello?"

"Hello, Tina. My name is Meera. I would like to meet you in regards to Ari. Would you be available to meet for a cup of coffee?"

"In regards to Ari?"

"Yes."

"Okaay... I don't know who you are, and I don't know how you know me. I need to know something."

"I am someone he was dating for the last two plus years. He told me you found receipts from Romano's in his car. Romano's was where he used to meet me." I don't know where this courage is coming from.

"I'll be at Coffee Corner in Downtown at 6PM. Do you know where that is?"

"Yes."

* * *

"Tina?" My legs are trembling, and I clench them together.

"Hello."

"Thank you for agreeing to meet me." I slide into the booth opposite her.

"How could I not? You are Meera, I assume. Would you mind showing me some ID?"

"Um... yeah, sure." Surprised by her request, I rummage in my bag and pull out my driver's license and my business card. She examines both, gives me back my ID and keeps my business card.

"Okay, thanks. Now please tell me exactly what has been going on." She says so softly, that I almost don't catch the words.

"I am so sorry. I really am. Let me first just say that to you." Suddenly I am reminded of a similar conversation Rini had with me about Raul, a lifetime ago. That situation was so much simpler and easier compared to this. We are in seated in a corner booth and she has coffee, while I get hot tea. I shift in my seat trying to find a more comfortable position, but there is none. "I really am sorry." I say again.

"Okay. Now I need to know everything."

"Yes, and I need to tell you. It's just that it's so difficult."

She crosses her arms and stares intensely at me. I notice the bags under her eyes. This woman, like me, has been suffering. I take a deep breath and force out the words.

"Ari and I had an affair that lasted over two years. He broke it off with me a month ago. I knew all along that you are his girlfriend, and believed that he was somewhat unhappy in the relationship with you, based on what little he told me. I... I'm sorry. I didn't realize..."

Tina doesn't say a word. After a moment, I continue.

"It was not planned. I knew him from before, from India, from when I was a kid. I ran into him during one of his street performances. Then we began to hang out, and I don't mean to just put the entire blame on him, but initially he pursued me. Finally we started seeing each other."

"When was the first time?"

"In his home. A little over two years ago."

"Bastard."

"I can't tell you how sorry and ashamed I am. I wish I had never run into him. I… I'm sorry."

"You should be. If only you could know how it feels. Why are you telling me all this now anyway?"

"I… I thought you need to know, and I want to come clean. I heard that Ari is back with his ex-wife, and it suddenly became apparent to me that he's… he's not who I thought he was. I don't know what to believe now, and I don't know if your relationship was sort of bad, like he made it out to be for my benefit. It's not like he discussed it much, but he just implied that it was not great, you know? I am sorry I didn't question anything."

"How frequently did you both meet?"

"About once a week."

"And what did you do?"

"We… we usually had a drink at Romano's and then went to his place." My face feels hot.

"And then?"

"Um…"

"How was he in bed?"

"Excuse me?"

"No, you know what? I don't excuse you." Her voice rises an octave and her face is red. "I will never excuse you. Whatever your story is, you are not excused for sleeping with my man. As a woman you didn't realize what this would mean to another woman? You didn't realize what you are doing is immoral, and downright rotten? And whatever pathetic excuses you want to give yourself, about my relationship not being great and thus your illicit affair – just remember that's all they are. Fucking pathetic excuses!"

With that she gets up and walks out of the coffee shop. No one has ever spoken to me like this before, and I am trembling. Unannounced, I feel the warm, wet tears on my cheeks. My next task is even more difficult. I must now come clean with Neel.

* * *

"Hi Mom, how's Papa?"

"Fine, *beta*, why do you sound tired?"

"I am not tired. I just miss everyone so much."

"Come soon. We miss you too."

"Mom, has there ever been a divorce in our family? You know? Before your and Papa's parents' time?"

"Where did that question come from?"

"Just tell me."

"Well, actually, yes. Nana's father married three times because his first wife died in childbirth, his second wife left him for another man, and then he married his third wife, who was Nana's mother. The second wife and he got formally divorced, but at that time in India it took many years for it to be done. Apparently it was not easy, especially for the wife. She moved away to another state."

"Is it always harder for the woman?"

"*Beta*, why are you asking me this now? Are things okay with you and Neel?

"Yes. I was just wondering. How come you never told us this story?"

"It didn't come up. I remembered all this now only because you asked. Are you sure everything is okay."

"Yes. How's Laila, Mom?"

"Better. Slowly she's getting healthier and her injuries are healing. She is starting to look a little bit like her old self. I think all that therapy is doing her good too."

"Do you guys go for therapy too?" I wonder if Laila's treatment involves family therapy.

"Us? No. Why would we?"

"Nothing. Just asking."

"Meera, should I be worried about you?"

"Nope."

"How are things with you and Neel?"

"Good. He's good. You know him. He loves his work and he loves life."

"And you?"

"Yeah. Everything is fine, Mom."

* * *

I am surprised to get a call from Tina. She calls my work number and wants to meet again. I am hesitant, but I can't say no. If she wants to tell me off some more, I don't want to deny her that. So we meet at Gyu-Han, a Korean barbeque restaurant with very few vegetarian options for me. I don't mind, as I don't have any appetite anyway.

"Hello, Tina."

"Have a seat." She says. After a moment of awkward silence, she continues, "Well, what's done is done. By no means am I saying that what you did is forgivable, but I intend to move past it. I have some more questions, and some information for you."

"Yes, of course... um... thanks." My stomach is knotting up. I didn't expect her to speak to me with civility, but then I don't know what I expected. I suppose she would not have asked to meet for Korean barbeque if she just wanted to tell me off.

"When we met before, you told me he pursued you. Tell me, how did he pursue you?"

"I tried to keep it at a friendship. He... he was very clear that he wanted more than just a friendship. Um... he was flirtatious and initially I stopped speaking with him a few times because of that."

"So times when you stopped speaking with him, he would call you and you would start up again?"

"Yes, he called, left messages, and eventually I would call him back."

"What did he tell you about me?"

"Oh, he didn't say much. He was always very respectful, and made it clear that he cared a lot for you, but it was just sort of implied that he was not happy in the relationship. I can't put my finger on how."

"So he didn't tell you anything specific?"

"No. Only that you were suspicious when you found the receipts from Romano's. Oh, and once, a long time back, he said you'd gone to Las Vegas and that you were thinking about your relationship."

"So didn't he tell you anything else about me? Or my life?"

"No. I knew where you work, and he said you are very good at what you do, but that's it."

"How did you know him in India?"

"He was my grandparents' neighbor in Jaipur. That's how."

"How old are you?"

"Thirty-two." This is how one must feel when they are put in a witness box. But I owe her these answers.

"So you must have been very young when he lived in India."

"Yes, he moved when I was seven and I didn't have any contact with him after that, till I saw him here a few years ago."

"Does anyone else know about your affair?"

"Um… a friend of mine."

"Are you married or seeing anyone else?"

"I… I am. I am married I mean."

"Does your husband know?"

"No."

"So you are doing this to him too?"

"Tina, I am sorry. I know how wrong all this is. I told you about this because you deserved to know the truth. I will tell my husband. I don't know what it will do to my marriage, but I *will* tell him. I am so sorry for everything. I could give you, and my husband too, a hundred reasons why this happened, but none of them matter. It should never have happened. I understand that. And I understand that I will face the consequences of what I have done."

"Okay. Look, thanks for the transparency. It must have been difficult to approach me about the affair, and you didn't have to. I would never have known if you hadn't told me. You and I can never be friends, but I do want to give you some information in return. Ari has cheated on me before. We don't need to go into details, but I want to tell you this so that you realize what kind of a person he is."

I didn't think it was possible to feel worse about the whole Ari affair than I already did, but I was wrong.

"Now he is back with his ex-wife, Rumana. Do you have any idea why?"

I shake my head.

"She won a lottery ticket. It was a million point four dollar lottery. It was in the papers. The next thing I know Ari is re-kindling his relationship with her."

"What? Money?" Is all I manage to say.

"Yes. Money! I had the same initial reaction. But yes, money is the reason behind his sudden reunion with his dear beloved. And it's hard to believe with all the lofty ideals he talks about. He is a hypocrite. A very intelligent hypocrite. A self-centered, pleasure-seeking person with double standards, and no care about who he hurts along the way. One of his favorite lines to say to me was, 'There will always be incidentals'."

"But are you sure this is the reason? The lottery ticket, I mean?"

"Yes." She looks me squarely in the eye.

"Oh, my goodness. Does his ex-wife understand this?"

"I think they are cut of the same cloth. Don't waste your energy anymore on this. Go tell your husband, do what you need to and live an honest life."

I look down and examine my hands. My nails need to be cut and filed, and it would help to use lotion on my hands more regularly.

"Now I don't owe you anything. I've repaid your debt," Tina says, and then gets up to leave.

"Tina, wait." She lowers herself back down, and raises her eyebrows at me. I can feel the tears in my eyes and I blink rapidly, but am unable to stop them. "Thank you." She waits silently. "Thank you for telling me all this. You didn't have to. And you didn't owe me anything. In fact, I owe you, but I still have one favour to ask of you."

"What?" Her voice sounds softer now. Almost resigned.

"Will you think about forgiving me? And if ever you do, will you let me know?"

She nods, gets up and leaves.

* * *

I type a letter to Ari and read it many times.

Dear Ari,

I came apart at the seams. I feel lost and small and crazy and insignificant. I lost my sense of self. Nothing makes sense. I feel I am underwater – I am drowning, falling down, down a deep abyss. I don't know what it is that sharply keeps pulling me up and refuses to let me go. Perhaps it is the stories of courage, the kindness of strangers, the absolute, resolute and steadfast love of a few individuals. But on this ledge between sanity and insanity, I have a precarious balance.

I don't know how to be distant with someone I was so emotionally intimate with for so long. I don't know how to cut and sever and seal and function. So in some ways there remains a gaping wound and this is an unedited letter.

I naively thought there would be a grand reason for your distance that would explain certain things and then I would find peace. And it is difficult to accept this grand, mysterious reason really is money. But then I realize this is YOU – you, with your immense sense of self preservation. You did what you needed to do to remain intact. And so my words may profoundly touch you and remain with you at some level, and at some other level you will pause and sigh and blink and move on, because the world needs you and there's things to be done that are much bigger (and perhaps better) than you and me – and besides, if it ain't broke, why fix it? And as one must epitomize pleasure, you are only but following God's design.

I have a high pain tolerance. I can tolerate all this – but it is not pleasant and I want it to end.

The thing is, you were so loving, tender, understanding, and interested all the time I've known you, that I didn't foresee this. If I had, perhaps I would have held on to stronger boundaries. But I let myself get lost... really lost in you. So much, now I am lost without you. I trusted with all my heart. Now I feel like a joke. The one person who had begun to feel so safe, fooled me.

And still yet I miss your whispers of love, our luxurious conversations; the smell of your skin, your eyes, the circle of safety your arms created... even if it was all untrue. I was a well-kept secret in your life of many secrets. Maybe you feel everything silent is unreal and you don't have to commit to what you don't proclaim.

This past month I was yearning for some indication from you, some understanding, some semblance of what I thought we had... for I thought what we had was very real. In response, I got complete silence. The silence felt cruel, rude, bewildering and very painful... I lost you from my life. And more sorrowfully, along with that I lost faith in faith, in kindness and compassion and respect... I lost a huge part of who I used to be. You possibly made a practical choice for yourself. It's just that my whole heart was in your hands, and I stampeded myself for us. I risked everything. And I would have gone to bat for it. We were happy when we spent time together – no? I thought you felt happy too... and free. And now...

can you tell me how you made it all wrong? Tell me now why it reeks of guilt and filth and steaming hot silence? I was never meant to be in your life? I was never meant to be a part of your story and so I was easily disposable. You were never meant to be in mine either... I hope you find what you are looking for. I am trying to find myself again.

I thank you so very much for getting out of my life forever.

Meera

Someday I may give it to him.

29

Meera Myna Dutt

I am so afraid, but I know I must do this. It's my only option – if I don't tell Neel, my secret will eventually poison my soul. Last night I spoke to Rini after a long time. I told her how she felt like home to me, and how much I missed her and our single days together. I told her how special our friendship is to me. It is my only friendship that has sustained since the time I was about four feet tall. With no one else have I had the history of our shared times.

She asked why I was being sentimental and I told her maybe because I was about to do something very scary, but that's all I said to her. She persuaded me to tell her more, but I just didn't. Eventually she made me promise I would not 'endanger' myself and I would call her after the scary thing was over. She and Kumar were doing well and were 'family planning', she said. It all sounded so foreign to me. The only thing Neel and I seem to plan is his next career move. But then, considering the shenanigans I've been up to, how can I 'family-plan'? Besides, I can't imagine having a child right now. It would be so much more difficult if we had a child in this marriage; this marriage which may not even exist after I tell Neel what I plan to tell him today.

I hear the door handle turn and know that Neel is back.

I'm sick to my stomach, and when I swallow, my throat feels like sandpaper.

"Neel, hi. Can you wash up and come sit with me? I need to talk to you."

"What's up, babe? Yeah hold on. I got to get these three emails out and I'll be with you. Is it about the season passes you wanted to the theatre? You know I can't commit to specific dates."

"NEEL." I shriek in a strange hoarse voice. He comes running out of the bedroom.

"Can you come sit with me and do your emails later, please? This is important."

"Are you pregnant?" On his way back to the bedroom, Neel stops suddenly, a questioning look on his face.

"NO. Just go wash up and come sit down. Is that too much to ask for?"

"Okay, okay. Boy, you are wound up today. Go for a massage this weekend, babe. There is a new place that's opened on the corner... next to Bakers, you know? I think it will do you good."

I am sitting at the edge of the couch and I feel like screaming. I intensely hate small talk. And sometimes I wonder how Neel can be so obtuse. I try to focus on my breathing. For a moment the room spins and I feel nauseous.

"Okay, I am here. Tell me, what's your big news?"

"I've had an affair, Neel."

"You are funny."

"NO, I am serious."

"Next you will tell me you are really a lesbian and your affair was with a woman. Myrah?" Neel laughs. What makes him so confident that I am joking about this? His confidence, his blind faith and trust in this relationship, his taking for granted that nothing could go wrong between us is not only annoying, but almost insulting. I silently reprimand myself for my annoyance, don't say anything in response, and finally Neel stops laughing and is peering into my face.

"What do you mean?" He finally asks in a small voice.

"Neel, I've had an affair. It's over now, but it went on for a few years. I am very sorry." Suddenly I find it hard to breathe. "Say something, Neel."

"Who was it?"

"A... Ari."

"WHAT? He is so much older than you? Are you playing some sick joke?"

"No. And yes, he is older. And I am sorry."

"WHY?" Neel is shouting now. "What? Are you... you are... how long has this gone on?"

"Little over two years."

Neel leans forward with his elbows on his knees. He holds his head in his hands for a long time. I feel sour bile rise in my throat and wonder where it comes from, as all I've had today is one cup of *chai* and an apple.

Just as I am getting used to this pregnant, silent discomfort, Neel looks up right at me and I almost jump. His face has shrunk within itself and his eyes are red and teary. I marvel at how quickly facial expressions can change, and how people can look completely different in a matter of minutes. I wonder what my face reflects. It feels as though my angst has subsided into a numbness. And this numbness is allowing me to breathe normally.

"Why did you do it?"

"What can I tell you? I don't fully know. I was unhappy. He was available, and interested, and very attentive. And it just happened."

"It just happened? IT JUST HAPPENED? WE ARE NOT ANIMALS FOR 'IT' TO *JUST HAPPEN*. WE HAVE CONTROL OVER WHAT WE CHOOSE TO DO. WHY DID YOU CHOOSE TO HAVE A *FUCKING AFFAIR*?"

"Neel, I... I'm sorry. I..."

Neel shakes his head from side to side rapidly and holds up his hands as though he is blocking my words. "I am sorry. I don't want to shout... but I need to understand. I need to know." He's pacing the room now and breathing deep, the way he does to calm himself down. Finally he sits down again. "Tell me everything."

And I do. I tell him everything. More than I thought I could or would. His face changes from time to time. At times he looks angry, at times sad or anxious, but his voice is calm. It's a data-collection voice. As long as he is collecting data, he is focused on just that task. I can see his mind filing away the pieces of data for future use. I don't know what he will do after he has all the information. I focus more on his face than on the content of what I am telling him. I feel sorry; his face reflects the damage I'm inflicting. Strangely there is a sense of being removed from the emotionally charged energy in the room, and of watching it – like a movie.

He wants to know when it started and how, whether I felt guilty, whether anyone else knows, what Ari and I talked about, was it just about the sex, is Ari better that him in bed, did we ever make out in our apartment, who made the first move, did Ari believe it was okay to do this, what about his girlfriend, why did we break up, why am I telling him everything now, and most importantly, do I love Ari. I answer what he asks as honestly as I can, and I volunteer what he doesn't ask. I go through the history of my relationship with Ari in a dispassionate manner.

Finally, Neel asks me whether I love him. I silently nod. I wait, as though for a judgment. One that will determine my fate. What is going to happen now?

"It is past three in the morning, Meera. Let's sleep."

"But don't you want to say anything? I mean, now what? What about us?"

"We will talk in the morning."

"Neel, please... say something."

"I am going to bed, Meera. You may come if you wish to."

* * *

The next morning we go about our morning activities in complete silence and I wait for Neel to say something. I've managed to sleep only about two hours, but I am not tired or sleepy. I feel like someone with a tumour waiting to find out if it is malignant. I want to ask him if he is going to leave me, but I don't. I realize in those moments that I want this marriage, that the only redemption for me is to repair the damage I have caused, that Neel so far has been acting surprisingly reasonable.

"Can we talk?" His voice breaks my reverie, and I sit down on the couch facing him.

"I don't know what path our marriage, our relationship will take." He says, "But I know we need help. *You* need help, and *we* need help. I want you to see a counsellor... um, a shrink, whatever-they-are-called person, and figure out what has happened. And I want us to see a shrink together and decide what we want out of this relationship."

I am stunned. This is not a response I expected. The only words that I manage to say are: "Aren't you angry?"

"Yes I am. I am very angry and hurt. But what's the point of that. I want an action plan. I knew you were unhappy when we moved here, and I believed that it would go away, that you were going through the adjustment, and that we were still rock solid. I think that was a big mistake on my part. But I had no idea it would lead to this. It was hard for me too, Meera, but I tried very hard to put all my energies into work and into making it, so that I could make you happy and get us back to India after achieving something substantial. I had no idea that this path would lead to so much destruction. But I have not given up just yet. The way I see it, if I choose to give up on this marriage right now, I might be shortchanging myself.

"I know, Meera, that life is not a bed of roses. Not that I expected what you have done. Affairs don't solve anything and never end well. They never lead to happiness. I don't take responsibility for what you have done, but I could have heard to you more, I know that. And for that, I do take responsibility. I thought by not listening I was discouraging your sadness. And because you showed an affinity for him, I pushed you to spend time with Ari, just as I pushed you to work and focus on your career, and make other friends because I thought these things would help you out of the slump. But maybe I should have listened more. I realize this now."

I am even more stunned, for I had no idea Neel knew all this. My cheeks are wet from the tears that have been seeping out of my eyes. I feel I've lost the right to hug him, but I tentatively go to him anyway. He lets me put my arms around him and cry into his chest. I am unable to say anything, but over and over in my mind rings a silent 'Thank you'.

PART III

Reasons And Realities

30

Neel Kant Duggar

I don't want to give up, but I am so close. It is difficult to remain calm, to sustain the civility. It hurts. I want to smash something up and scream. I want to shake her. It's hard to believe this is actually happening to me. *Me!* I had it all. My career, my wife, my life were all set and wonderful... or so I thought.

I am blindly, briskly walking down some side alley near Central Park. My watch says it's been over two hours since I left the apartment. The walking makes the insides of my head somewhat tolerable. The repetitive motion is like a trance and it dulls some of the anger, but still my life feels suddenly like an endless abyss. My previous calm has long gone. I don't want to return to the apartment like this. I know anger will cloud my reasonability and I have to handle this situation with care, or else I will lose what I have worked so hard for. Actually, I don't know what I want anymore. I want everything to go back to the way it was. But that will never happen. Things can't EVER go back to being the way they were. She's ruined it all with her damn irresponsible behavior. Who am I kidding? Irresponsible, my ass! She had a FUCKING affair and its best I face it and accept it. It's the only way to move on from here. How will we get past this?

How do people recover from affairs? I believed that nothing is impossible if you set your mind to it… but this task seems momentous. I don't know how I feel about her anymore. I've adored and loved her forever, but right now I hate her too. I want to throw a punch somewhere.

* * *

"I've found a shrink, Neel. I've made us an appointment at Orange County Health Psychologists, in Bronx, for Thursday 4pm. You will have to leave work a bit early, and I will too. I'll give you the address and we can meet there. She's a doctor – a psychologist – and she has very good recommendations. Her specialty is infidelity and couples. Neel?"

"Yes, yes, I heard."

"What's wrong?"

"Everything." I mutter.

"What do you mean?"

"Every fucking thing is wrong. Why are we going to a fucking *infidelity* expert? Don't you think something is wrong with that scene? Does it sound to you like everything is fine?" I am surprised by the contrast between what I say, and how I say it. The controlled calm in my soft voice belies my fury and sounds eerily threatening even to me. Meera's staring at me, unblinking. I make no attempt to reassure her. I just turn and walk away, feeling her stare on my back. *Feeling her sink to the floor on her knees, sitting still beside the king size bed, resting her forehead on the polished wood of the end table; feeling her dread like it is red-hot lava seeping into the space between us. The thirty-two years of my life feel full of the pain of thirty-two lifetimes.* She won't say anything to me. There isn't much she can say. But I don't like who I'm becoming.

* * *

I watch the dancing dust in the muted sunlight seeping in through a thin white curtain covering the large window to my left. We are in a plush office, sitting across from a kind but stern looking woman, seemingly in her early-forties. She wears chic looking glasses, and has thick wavy black hair. She is attractive in an upper New York way. She is the therapist Meera found for us. I'm trying hard to avoid looking at her. Instead, I play a game of fixing my gaze on a single dust particle and seeing how long I can follow it before it inevitably settles on the pastel rug in front of us, or deceives my gaze and disappears. Meera is next to me on the red three-cushioned couch. She doesn't seem nervous... though she should be. Therapy was my idea, but I am not so sure about it anymore. I mean what can a stranger tell us that will help change all that has happened?

"I can't say or do anything to change what has happened," says Dr. Mona, and I almost jump up. Can she read my thoughts? I stare at her, pleading with my eyes. *Help us!* I say in my mind. *Is there any hope for us?*

"But we can work together, to help you both understand the whys and the whats of the affair, to understand your relationship and each other better, to heal together and individually, and to make a choice about where to go from here." She looks from Meera to me, and back to Meera. I am careful to keep my expression as polite and blank as possible. I don't want her to know anything more than she needs to.

"Thank you, Dr. Mona. We want to work through this, and we need your help," Meera responds.

"If we *can* work through this," I blurt out.

Meera turns to stare at me, but Dr. Mona responds kindly, "Neel, I can understand your apprehension. I don't know what the outcome will be for you both, but what I can tell you is that over the years I have seen many couples go through different relationship struggles, the most common one being infidelity, and heal from it. Affairs sometimes happen in healthy relationships too. Sometimes for couples an affair is a wakeup call to look at and make changes to their own relationship. Sometimes this leads to a new and deeper understanding between the couple; a new intimacy, a new appreciation, and though it may sound impossible to you both right now, a deeper level of trust."

"Neel?" Meera speaks and I realize they both are waiting for me to say something.

"Um... Yes. I... we do really appreciate it. It's just that it's difficult," is all I manage.

"As it is meant to be, Neel. This is not easy. It is exceptionally difficult and there will be good days and bad."

And so we began therapy. Something I never expected would happen to our marriage. And reluctant though I was, I knew I had to see it through and put in all my effort. If I still felt this way at the end of six months, then perhaps I would have to start imagining a life without Meera.

31

Meera Myna Dutt

We are in Dr. Mona's office for our session again. It's been about two months and we've seen her six times already. We haven't made it every week because of Neel's job demands, but we've made it most weeks. I haven't seen or heard of Ari since my last meeting with Tina. I still have the letter I wrote him, but I don't have the burning need to give it to him anymore. I have not told Neel or Dr. Mona about the letter.

We are on shaky ground. In the last two months we've had numerous conversations, great looming moments of silence, a spontaneous email exchange expressing anger and sadness on Neels part, and regret on my part, and we've had sex once just a week ago. It feels like the sex was a desperate attempt to strengthen our relationship. It happened the evening Neel came back early from work and opened a bottle of wine. By the time I got back from work, he was already two glasses in. "Why are you drinking alone, Neel?" I'd asked', worried. And he'd poured another glass and handed it to me with a wistful, desperate look in his eye. "I want things to go back to how they were when we married," he'd said. And when we kissed, sitting on the couch, I felt the pure, untainted love of before swell in my heart. I'd held his head to my chest and stroked his thick black hair. Our love-making that night was beautiful and gentle. It was healing. We haven't had such a night since then. It's almost like neither one of us wants to ruin the memory of that night, in case the next one isn't as magical. We need to hold on to whatever we can, so we don't drift apart.

Dr. Mona says it takes time. I didn't realize how much I hurt Neel until our second session with Dr. Mona, when he cried more than I've ever seen any man cry in my life. He'd sat on the floor, on her rug, with his face in his hands. It was a two-hour session, and though it was difficult to see him like that, it was also a bit of a turning point, a realization that I don't want to hurt anyone in that way ever again. It seemed like he let the poison in his body out in his tears, like he needed to cry. His voice still rings in my ears. In-between sobs he'd said *'I'm crushed, I'm crushed'*. I'd cried too. I'd cried tears of guilt, shame, shock, regret... of horror at what I had done.

Neel is a gentle person by nature, but he's been angry and moody since I told him about the affair. And though I understand his moodiness, I wish we could just get past this. But as Neel often says, every action has an equal and opposite reaction. So my overwhelming horror and Neel's anger are my punishment. My personal hell. "What did the affair mean to you? Why did it happen, Meera?" Both Neel and Dr. Mona are looking at me, waiting for me to answer the question, and I am brought back to this present moment by Dr. Mona's voice. "I think it meant that I didn't have to face the reality of my painful, lonely life here. It meant that I could go back to being who I was in India... you know? It even gave me the feeling... the feeling I felt with Neel back then. I felt like Neel was perfect. But then the other part... that he's too good for me. I don't deserve him, so how did I get him?" I hear my voice choking up.

"You don't deserve him?"

"No," I whisper.

"Why?" When I don't answer, Dr. Mona asks again. "Why don't you deserve Neel, Meera? What happened to make you undeserving?"

"Because... I am impure, okay?" I am angry. "Because I was molested when I was seven years old. I was innocent then. I didn't know what Monty was doing to me. I told Mom after it all happened but she didn't believe me. I thought he... he did a magic trick on me and gave me some disease, okay? So I hid it from everyone. I never told anyone else. Even years later, when I understood what the bastard had done. It's not like I can ever erase it, right? So why bother. With Ari I could go back to the time before the molestation. When I was still pure. You know? Before Monty. You see, Neel is untouched by all this filth. I... I can't corrupt him."

* * *

The space between Neel and I has changed. It has a new maturity and intimacy, and best of all, a new gentleness. It is a relief to shed the illusion of perfection, and to be seen. Perhaps that is the reason behind finding a mate to begin with.... to be seen. Perhaps that's the unspoken agreement between couples – you witness my life, my joys and sorrow, my idiosyncrasies; you take the time to see me, to really see me. And I will do the same for you. You allow me to shed my shield and my armour, and you help me see myself. And I will do the same for you.

We still aren't in a happy, connected place, though we do have moments. We certainly aren't in an in-love place.

I think we are in a place of understanding, shared grief, compassion and hurt. I still don't know if Neel can forgive me, but sometimes it feels like he really wants to. I don't know if I can forgive myself, though Dr. Mona has helped me understand why I did the things I did. She says I should treat myself with compassion, as I would a best friend who has gone through her share of childhood horror. She also says she sees in us a deep appreciation for each other and all the signs of survival. Neel doesn't say much about the survival part yet. He knows I want the reassurance that we are going to be okay, but he still needs time to assess whether that reassurance is his to give.

On that note, it is somewhat surprising to me how badly I want this marriage to survive and revive when just a few months ago, I wanted it to un-exist. Having Ari out of my head in this way, perhaps for the first time, is refreshing. Ari was closely tied to the abuse, and now I have a distance from both Ari and the abuse, I see things differently. For example, I don't see Neel as the villain who pulled me away from my family; I see him as a man who gave me his love and trust, and is trying to build a life for us. There are differences in our personalities, priorities and views. But isn't that the case in most relationships? Would I have had it better in some other relationship? And would that other relationship have been as loving or forgiving?

* * *

"WHAT??"

"Rini, I am not like you. I'm just not the good girl, okay? You know that about me. I don't know… Dr. Mona drew the connection with the childhood stuff." I've just told Rini about the affair, and then about my childhood abuse incidents. She is sniffling on the phone.

"Why didn't you tell me when we were kids?"

"I couldn't." I am strangely numb, and I don't want to play the role of consoling her or explaining why I didn't tell her sooner. "Rini, please, just deal with it. I don't know why I didn't tell you, but I need to focus on what to do now. I don't know what's going to happen between Neel and me."

"Did you explain? Did you say sorry? I don't know though... if Kumar did this to me, I would leave."

* * *

It is true that blood is thicker than water. The only other person I shared all this with is Laila. I found my sister non-judgmental, and so very loving. My baby sister is more mature than I expected.

"Don't you think I've done something so unforgivably wrong?"

"Who am I to judge? None of us have that right. Only you know what you went through. It's never good to hurt anyone, and I know Neel is hurt. But I also know, Meera, you didn't do this with the intention of hurting him. And I think what's important here is forgiveness. And figuring out what you both want now."

"You are so wise. But I don't know what to do now. I don't know if Neel will ever forgive me."

"Can you forgive yourself? Meera, you didn't have to tell him... but you did. Can you appreciate that? He is still in the marriage because he wants to be in it. He is trying. Wouldn't it be better for you to focus on nourishing what you and Neel have, instead of wallowing in this in-between stagnant stage?

Meera, you need to forgive and recommit... if that's what you want. Step away from this stuck, I-don't-know place. You do know what you need to do next. And that is to have the patience for Neel to go through the stages he will go through, however long that takes."

"I miss you so much. I wish we could just sit together and have *chai*."

"So come."

"But the therapy?"

"Ask."

* * *

"Go to India if you like, Meera. I need time. I don't know how long. I couldn't tell you. I know you want answers, but I just don't know... I... I've to get there. You go if you feel like, take a break from everything. We both have a lot to figure out."

There's no anger left between us. Just a resigned sadness. Will we ever be normal again? This is the same Neel who used to be so excited about our life together and didn't want to spend even a day apart. And now it seems like he actually wants me to go, or even worse, is indifferent to my absence. I turn my head away to hide the tears. I've done this to us. If Dr. Mona gives the green signal, then I will go.

* * *

My heart heavy with all the insecurity of the impending doom of my marriage. I have to constantly remind myself that it is not over yet. True that he hasn't touched me since our one beautiful night of lovemaking, but I haven't touched him either. Dr. Mona says healing evolves. She says just as you can't take a jackhammer and force a bud to flower, it is not realistic to expect the relationship to heal on demand. That our job is to nurture ourselves, be patient, nurture the relationship, and be honest. The problem is that Neel doesn't yet know what he wants... and for once I do.

I try to brush these thoughts aside as I hear the announcement that we are now descending into Delhi, India. I buckle my seatbelt and sink further in my seat. Along with the relief of soon being in my family home is the anxiety of having to face their questions and worry. Mom and Papa are wondering why I planned this sudden trip, but I didn't give them much explanation. Just that I miss home too much, and Neel has a busy month ahead. Only Laila knows all that's happened, and Rini. I've taken a three-month unpaid leave of absence at TRENDS. Rupa and I had a long lunch together the day before I left. She thinks I have taken the right steps by going for therapy and giving Neel his space and time. She reminds me that she's never doubted Ari is an 'asshole'. In fact she refers to him as the Asshole, when we talk. She will miss me, but she supports my three-month sabbatical and says that I owe it to Neel to give him the time he is asking for. I've always known Rupa to be fair in her judgment and much as I don't want to, I know I must give Neel his space. So here I am, in Delhi, and for the first time not entirely happy about being here.

* * *

"I am sorry it's come to this." Rini, Laila and I are sitting at *Doko Dhaba*, a week after I arrive in Delhi. A week after I've given all the explanations that I can for my long, unexpected visit, and shed tears in secret. We've been here for an hour and a half and had endless cups of *chai*. Everything is beautiful, but for the predicament I'm in. I hear the cuckoo – the *kala papeeha* – cooing somewhere above, and the hustle bustle of the street some distance away. We are seated outdoors on *muddhas*, the little stools made of hay and twine, immeasurably comfortable in their simplicity. The rickety wood table between us has eight empty small *chai* glasses. It's only nine in the morning on a Sunday. But we came out at six-thirty, bundled up in our jackets and scarves to brave the Delhi winter, and headed over to the *dhaba*. Rini and Laila, my only two confidantes in India, had decided that I needed their conjoint input to deal with the quandary of my marriage, and that it was time to convene.

"Well, we can talk about this as much as we like, but in reality there is nothing to be done except to wait until Neel is ready to say something."

"And you still don't want to clue Mom and Papa in?" Laila asks.

"And say what? I cheated on Neel? And now I'm here, waiting for him to tell me whether he even wants this marriage?" I am angry now. "Laila, there is nothing to be done right now, except wait. I will tell them if and when something happens."

* * *

Sujet is an old family friend and Super, Laila and I are at his party. I look and feel vibrant after a long time. I want to forget my worries and just enjoy the moment. The party is at a new trendy club not far from Cannaught Place. Mom and Papa seem worried about me, so I came partly just to reassure them, but I am glad I am here. I've spoken to Neel twice in the two weeks I've been here. Our conversations were short, clipped and awkward. But in my heart the emotions have been overwhelming. I miss him, I miss his love, and I hate this new awkwardness between us.

"Meera, let's get the fuck out of here." Super's voice cuts into my thoughts. I hurriedly turn around to see him with an arm around Laila's shoulders, urgency and anger in his face.

"What happened? What?"

Laila jerks her head back indicating the reason for this hurried exit. As I look over her shoulder I see Ravi struggling to walk towards us, held back by some guy in a red beret that makes him look quite comical. He appears to be trying to pull off a French painter look, but his heavy set features don't cooperate. We start walking towards the door and suddenly Super whirls around midway. Ravi has escaped the French painter and has a hand on Super's shoulder trying to stop him.

"I just want to talk, man. Please. Give me one minute."

All three of us stop in our tracks. No one says anything for a long moment. Some guests glance at us, but then turn back to their own conversations and drinks, as the music, crowd and dark lighting make it impossible to tell if our little group is worth observing.

"Sagar, I want to say I am sorry." Super's face is a stone mask and his fists are clenched. Ravi then turns to Laila, who is standing right next to Super, while I am a step behind them. "Laila, I am so sorry. You don't know how sorry I am. If there's any way I can make it up to you and your family, I want to."

"Don't touch me ever again, unless you want your face rearranged," Super says between clenched teeth, referring to Ravi's hand on his shoulder to stop us from leaving.

Ravi pulls his hand away looks down at the ground, but still not giving up he says, "Can we sit down somewhere and talk. I am in therapy. And I can't tell you how grateful I am that your family dropped the case. I am sorry. Truly."

I sense in my gut that Laila is already melting a tiny bit, though she doesn't say anything. "My therapist says one day I will be ready for a relationship again," Ravi continues. "It... I... I now..."

"Please." I move up next to Laila and cut Ravi off in his effort to explain and absolve himself. My voice is calm and even toned. "That's really enough. It's wonderful if you have realized what a heinous *crime* you committed, but we are really not interested in hearing about your *therapy* or what your therapist says. We are the hurt party, not really your fan club. The only reason the case was dropped was because your parents bribed everyone concerned, and our parents didn't want my sister to be subject to court. Don't be under the illusion that we have forgiven, even for a second, the way you hurt Laila. And don't even think of approaching any of us again. Though the case was dropped, all those legal records still exist and if you *ever* cross the line again, they will be pulled up, and next time around we will pursue it no matter what. Because societal burdens like you need consequences. Now kindly leave our line of vision, Asshole."

Tempted to land him a punch myself, it takes all effort to turn back around, grab Laila's arm and begin walking out. I feel good about the speech I just made, and as I am gloating over my sense of victory, I hear a *phooof...* ugh... crash.

Before I register what is happening, there is a barstool flying in the air in Laila and my general direction. Laila pushes me to the right, and lands right on top of me. We've completely avoided the barstool. I look up to see five or six men landing punches at each other. Super is right in the midst of the fight. Someone's pulling Ravi back, but not before Super gives him what looks like a very hard punch on his jaw, sending his face flying at an unnatural angle. Thankfully, Ravi's head seems to snap back on and he's held back by two of his buddies. I've never been in a party fight before, and I'm mesmerized, not even realizing that I should be concerned about Super's safety. Laila is scrambling to her feet, so I follow suit. By then Sujet has arrived at the scene and is dramatically holding both the parties apart.

"Why didn't you tell us this scumbag was going to be here?" Super demands, nodding his head at Ravi.

"Calm down, Super. I didn't know you guys had issues between you."

"Issues? ISSUES? Ask him what he's done to my sister. Just ask him. And you will probably have issues with him too. Sorry to mess up your party, man, but there are a couple of golden rules which when violated will cause me to react, and react strongly. The first golden rule is, no one messes with my family."

Ravi and his cronies push past us and head towards the exit without saying a word. One crony is holding his arm and guiding him out. Sujet turns to Laila and me asking if we are okay. He then quietly hands Super a drink. "Come on in and let's enjoy the party."

* * *

Its noon on Sunday and the three of us are standing in a row before our seated parents, intently examining our feet. Apparently Sujet's mom Reena Aunty telephoned Mom this morning to 'enquire' how we were doing. She conveyed to Mom her version of what had transpired at the party last night.

"Mom, can we at least have coffee while we talk?" Super has always been the least affected by our parents' concern in such matters.

"And *chai*," Laila mutters.

A giggle escapes me before I can stop it. I feel like a kid again, standing with my siblings and being reprimanded for some mischief. We are all still in our pajamas, which somehow makes it more comical. My giggle is infectious and I hear Laila stifling hers. From the corner of my eye I see that Super has a grin pasted on his face, with no attempt to hide it.

"You three seem in a great mood. It must have ended in your favour." I can't tell if Papa is unperturbed, or upset, like Mom.

"Rabdai is making your *chais* and coffee. Can we get serious here for a minute? This is not funny. What happened?"

But by some unspoken sibling code of honour, none of us says anything.

"*What happened?*"

"Mom, nothing. You know how it is. Some guys get excited and someone says something, and someone else hits someone, and boom, a fight has begun." Super gives Mom his Super-sweet grin, the one that always manages to melt our mother. And true to form, she does melt. Papa catches my eye and raises one eyebrow, giving me a knowing, reprimanding, yet indulgent look. I nudge Laila. Super gestures a thumbs-up behind his back. It's a well-coordinated moment of silent family communication. I feel a deep, satisfying, happy feeling starting in the pit of my stomach organically spreading, like nourishment for the deprived. It's because of the belonging that I have here, at home. It's like being bathed in warm sunlight, or wrapped in the softest blanket, or even better than any of those. If only this moment could last forever, everything else can be forgotten.

* * *

We are on the back-porch, satiated with Rabdai's *chai* and *kachoris*.

"Last night was fun. Asshole got his butt kicked. I'd wanted to do that for a long time. Finally got the chance." Super is in an unusually good mood.

"The *honour*," I say with mock exaggeration, and we burst out laughing, even though it's not all that funny.

"Um... I have something to say." Super says.

"What?" I ask.

"I mean I have something to ask... or say."

"You're starting to sound drunk, you know? Is it the drinks from last night?" Laila chimes in. She and I are on the porch swing, while Super is perched on a wicker chair.

"*Starting* to?" I tease. "Laila, let me enlighten you, he was born like that."

"Well, no, I'm serious."

"Yes, please continue."

"No, that's it, I'm serious this time."

"You are making no sense."

"I mean I'm serious about Sonia. Sonia Rathod."

"Huh?" He has our attention now. "Who is Sonia?"

"Yeah, that's what I wanted to tell you. That I'm serious about her now. It's different."

"Dude? You are not hearing something. WHO IS SHE?"

"Oh? My fiancé."

"WHAT? You are engaged? Do Mom and Dad know?"

"Um... no. It just happened."

"When?"

"A few months ago."

"This conversation is really bizarre. Super, you know it's odd that you have not shared this with us, right? I mean, we haven't even met her. I mean, it's great if you are happy, but awful that we don't even know this person. What is wrong with you?"

Super shrugs his shoulders with a sheepish grin.

32

Laila Myna Dutt

I love dressing up in traditional Indian clothes. They are so beautiful. This is how people are meant to dress. I think Western clothes have it all wrong. Meera and I are wearing *salwar kurtas* today – I am in white and gold, and Meera is in aqua and silver. My gold and Meera's silver are intentional – a complementary, twin vision. I love our look in the soft, ballooning *salwar* pants, the short, embroidered *kurta* tops, and the transparent, scarf-like *dupattas* thrown casually over our shoulders. We have jewellery to match. Meera likes long earrings and thick bracelets, while I favor the whole shebang, necklace and all.

Sonia was orphaned at a young age, when her parents died in a car crash. She was raised by her aunt and uncle. They are throwing a dinner party tonight so both families can get to know one another. I can't believe Super is actually going to be married. The wedding date is set for a month from now.

Mom and Papa want to host the entire wedding – they told Sonia's aunt and uncle that it would be their privilege. By Indian standards it's a small wedding, because that's how Super and Sonia want it – not like Meera's, which was so elaborate. Super argued with Mom and Dad about the guest list and brought it down to half, also insisting on a one-day celebration as opposed to the three-day affair that Mom and Dad wanted. I like small and intimate, so I'm glad it's going to be like that, but Mom and Dad worry about offending people who won't be invited to this wedding. I was only fifteen during Meera's wedding and now I am eighteen, which makes it different. I am an adult now and I've seen enough of life myself to really feel like one.

Mom and Papa, Mom especially, found it difficult to accept that Super was engaged to some girl and the family knew nothing about it. She cried and didn't talk to him for a week. Super was upset that finally when he did share his big news, instead of being happy about it, and inviting Sonia to meet them, Mom was angry.

Meera and I played the Switzerland-role. We placated both parties, and generally tried to soothe the friction. We all had a lot of questions. Apparently Super and Sonia had been dating on and off for two years and he didn't tell us about her because he was just not sure about going forward. When Mom heard the two-year part, she was even more furious and indignant. Super finally melted her by saying something about wanting to ensure that Sonia was the girl he wanted to bring home to his mother, for she had to be worthy of that.

"Feeling kind of sick," Meera whispers. We are driving alone, as Mom, Papa and Super have gone ahead in Super's car.

"Huh?"

"I don't know, it could be something I ate. My stomach is just ugh… you know? Like before an exam."

"Oh, drink some club soda when we get there, and breathe. Are you worried about Neel?"

"A bit, yes. We've barely talked since I've come. I don't know what's going to happen... but the whole idea was to give him a break so he can decide what he wants. He's coming for the wedding. He said we'll talk then. Three weeks to go." She squeezes her eyes shut as the car goes over a bump on the road.

"Sorry, Meera."

* * *

Her sick feeling has subsided, thank goodness, and Meera is being the groom's gracious sister, which lets me off the hook a bit. I am content to sit back and let the rest do the talking. My eyes wander around the room. Sonia has three cousins –Deepak, Dhavan and Rohini, her aunt and uncle's children – attending the party with their spouses and families. Sonia seems close with her cousins. She is the youngest among the cousins, and quite the looker, with long straight hair midway down her back, which she's left down with several thin braids in the front to frame her face. The hairstyle is simple and elaborate at the same time, as is her entire look. She is in a subtle peach *salwar kurta* with tiny gold and white beads embroidered into it.

Sonia lets Super do most of the talking for the two of them – which is not saying much at all considering Super is a moody communicator, sometimes so chatty and other times one can't get a peep out of him. He is being the charming groom this evening, though. It's strange for me to see Super with a fiancé. The idea of Meera getting married seemed natural, but with Super it feels abrupt. My impression of him is of the perennial bachelor playboy – never serious about any relationship. I want to get to know Sonia, and yet, I don't know why I am resistant. Sonia is very polite with everyone.

She has a welcoming smile, but the smile doesn't reach her eyes.

"Meera, how are you feeling?" I ask as I catch Meera alone for a moment.

"Ah, absolutely fine now. I don't know what it was."

"Oh, good. So? What do you think?"

"We are going to have to get used to Super being with someone. You know?" I nod furiously, as Meera echoes my sentiment. "And she's guarded," Meera whispers about Sonia before moving away to smile and chat with Rohini.

* * *

"How do you feel, *beta*?" Mom asks Super. Back home after the dinner party, the five of us, out of our finery and comfortable in our nightwear, have somehow gravitated back to the living room.

"We are elated," Papa chimes in, looking like the cat who's swallowed the canary. "Sonia seems like a sweet girl. And all we want is for you to be happy. What more could we ask for?"

"Are you happy?" Mom asks.

"We have to start the preparations right from tomorrow," Papa says.

"Let him answer for a minute, will you?" Mom says, irritated at Papa.

Meera and I are giggling and Super is rolling his eyes. I squeeze Meera's hand.

"What are you three giggling about?" Mom asks, annoyed, and we burst out laughing. Even Super lets out a chuckle.

"You both are classic," Meera says to them.

"So? How was Sonia?" Super asks.

"Quiet. Why was she so quiet? Is that her personality?" Mom wants to know.

"She was very nice. What do you expect, Noorie? Practically the second time the girl is meeting us. Of course she will be quiet. You were very shy when we got married."

"Not today's girls. Today's girls are outspoken and bold. You will not find a girl like me today," says Mom.

"Let the boy speak," says Papa.

And so it goes, the banter in our family.

33

Meera Myna Dutt

I am pregnant. I didn't plan for this. I am sitting on the closed lid of the toilet seat, and I can barely breathe. I did three home pregnancy tests in the last seven minutes and they are all positive. Plus there is the unexplained nausea over the last few weeks. I know the tests are accurate. I know I'm pregnant. It must've been that night Neel and I made love, a couple of weeks before I left to come here. By my calculations I am just under two months pregnant. It doesn't show at all. But what do I do now?

I'm not sure how long I sit there, but Mom's insistent banging on the door shakes me out of my paralysis. I stuff the tell-tale pregnancy tests deep into the waist of my jeans and open the door.

"Are you sick or something, *Raja beta*? She uses that same old endearment from childhood. "You've been in there for over an hour."

"Nope. Just kind of fell asleep."

"Huh? Are you taking *the drugs*?" Mom's eyebrows shoot up an inch and her eyes widen as she carefully pronounces *the drugs*, referring to, in general, all dangerous and illegal mind altering substances in the world.

"Noooo, Mom. I am not taking *the drugs*. I am fine. Let's

go watch that TV movie you said was going to run at six today."

"Oh yes, *beta*. I really want to watch it. It has Mohini in it and she is such a good dancer. I am sure it is a classical, artsy type of movie. Will you like it?"

"Ah! Can I tell you after I watch it?"

"Now don't get smart with me, young woman. Rabdai, will you put on some *chai* please? And then come join us for the movie," she yells out.

* * *

It's night and I'm alone in my childhood room, carrying a child myself. My hand clutching the phone feels clammy. I've dialed Neel's number about six times and disconnected before it can ring. I'm torn about telling him. He leaves New York to head to Delhi in just a couple of hours. Super's wedding is in three days and Neel will be here tomorrow.

Since I came to Delhi we've maintained a once-a-week phone call to ask how each other is doing. And I had the one extra mid-week call to tell him about Super's engagement and upcoming wedding. Our calls have felt superficial and formal. I have no idea how he is really doing, or feeling about our marriage. Mostly I try not to think about it. I know the day will come when we have to talk about things, but until then I don't want to think about it. I pick up the phone again, but my fingers are shaking and they won't punch the numbers. I want to cry, I want to rewind the last five years, and I want Nani.

"Krishna, Krishna, Krishna," I mutter with my eyes closed. Nani said Krishna always comes when you call him.

* * *

Super and I are at the airport to pick Neel. "Why are you so fidgety? Are you excited to see your husband after all these weeks?" Super asks as we stand outside the international terminal. I just give him a dirty look in response.

I think I am so nervous, I am numb. My mind has been jumping between telling Neel and not telling Neel until he tells me what he wants out of our marriage, moving back to India and raising our baby on my own if Neel doesn't want the marriage, aborting? I wonder if it's a girl or boy. I don't know if I can abort. What if Neel wants an abortion? Should I not tell him? But that would not be fair. I am unable to shut down this constant chattering in my head.

"There he is. Your husband, Meera."

Super's voice cuts through my thoughts. I unclench my hands, shift on my feet and mentally brace myself – for what, I'm not sure. I don't know what to expect and it feels so awkward, especially with Super right here. The nervousness stirs inside me and rises as nausea in my throat. I am scared, I am scared for my baby, and I'm scared for my own future as well. This is the first time I've thought of it as 'my baby'. Just then Neel hugs me. "Hi, Meera," he says softly in my ear.

"Hi, Neel." Super and Neel are doing the half-hug, half-thump-on-the-back-greeting that guys do.

"So, marriage huh?" Neel grins at Super.

"What can I tell ya? Another one bites the dust."

"It's not half as scary as it seems," Neel says as he puts an arm around me. Should I read into that? Did that mean something positive for us?

The drive back is mostly Super and Neel talking about the agenda for the next two days. It's going to be busy.

* * *

We are finally alone in my room and I have no excuse to avoid the conversation anymore. "Neel, I... we need to talk, no?" I wonder if I sound scared.

"Yes, I know."

There is complete silence as I wait for him, and he, it seems, awaits some divine inspiration. Finally he says, "We will...."

He's about to say something more when we hear Mom's voice from outside, loud and agitated. We instinctively look at each other, a questioning look in our eyes. It is such an automatic and familiar gesture. I choke up. I feel I am floating between the familiar shoreline and a vast dangerous ocean. I don't know if the shore will allow me on land, and if it doesn't, what will I do?

We step out to see what is going on. Super is sitting on the sofa in the living room, with Laila kneeling down next to him. Mom is on the love-seat, now silent, hand over her mouth. "What's going on?" I ask.

"The wedding is off," says Super in a staccato voice.

"WHAT?"

He silently hands me a yellow manila envelope. It's addressed to him and feels thick and heavy. I sit down next to him, feeling a wave of nausea wash over me. This is bad, I can feel it. Papa is out at the reception hotel addressing some last minute details. In a way I'm glad he's not here so I can assess whatever shocker is in this envelop before it gets to Papa. With Neel peering over my shoulder, I pull out the contents. Into my hands spill about a dozen glossy five-by-sevens, in colour.

"Oh, my goodness." The pictures are all of Sonia, with some unknown man. Kissing, in one picture, smiling at each other in another, and walking into the sunset hand-in-hand on some beach, in yet another. All the pictures are romantic, some more compromising than others. But they leave no doubt that Sonia and this man have a romantic interest in each other. "Oh my goodness," is all I manage in that moment.

"Who brought this envelope? And do you know the guy in the photos? I'm assuming from the reactions that the woman is Sonia." Neel takes charge.

"Yes, that's Sonia. The man is Raghav, an acquaintance." Super's clipped voice is a pitch higher than normal.

"You know him, beta?" Mom asks in an alarmed voice.

"How did you get this envelope?" Neel asks again.

"Someone left the envelope at the front door with this note. I found it," answers Laila, handing the note to Neel.

Sagar, she's marrying you for security, not love. Don't make this mistake. Let her go. She loves me. She will never look at you the way she looks at me. Raghav.

"Now what?"

"Well, let's inform Papa, and start making the cancellations. Please inform Sonia's family as well, Mom." Neel is very matter of fact.

* * *

My conversation with Neel is postponed, for obvious reasons. Papa is shocked, but his usual practical side has taken charge by the morning. Neel is helping Papa make all the necessary cancellations of hotel bookings, caterers, music and video and I don't know what else. Mom's busy returning as many of the ordered or purchased gift items as she can. She spoke to Sonia's family earlier and it was difficult for her to keep the conversation polite. She told them to ask Sonia the reasons why, but that the wedding would not be happening, at least "Not with my Sagar as groom", she had said. She told us they sounded very confused and concerned and that "The scheming girl must have kept them in the dark too. It seems they have no idea about Sonia's double life."

Meanwhile, it's left up to Laila and me to offer some solace to our close family and friends, and make courtesy calls to the distant ones. Explaining that the reasons for the wedding being cancelled are highly personal and we would not be able to talk about things right now, is tedious. They have many questions and no consideration for our request. Yes, they may visit soon; yes, Mom will talk to them soon; yes, Sagar is just fine; For the majority of the calls, it feels like we are consoling them rather than the other way around.

Super is mostly quiet through all the activity. Some of his friends have called, but he does not want to talk to anyone right now. I go up to him in the middle of the day and squeeze his arm. He just looks at me with a haunted, questioning look in his eye that I will never forget. We don't say anything to each other. What is there to say? I am not a violent person, and cringe on seeing violence, even in movies. But if I had five minutes with Sonia right now, I think I could be violent.

In the buzz of activity and emotion my own troubles are forgotten and feel like they belong to another time and place. Neel and I function in a well-coordinated manner in the face of this crisis. It feels almost normal between us and there are moments in the day when I even forget about the pregnancy. I've decided I don't want to tell Neel until he tells me his decision on our marriage. I don't want his decision to be influenced by the news of the pregnancy. The conversation needs to happen fairly soon, though. It is both uncomfortable and unfair to keep this from him. The baby is his too.

Papa is very sad. Sometimes I wonder who is sadder – Super or Papa. Even though Papa doesn't say anything at all, I just know. Sometimes I know deep in my bones how he feels. This is one of those times. He is more saddened by the fact that in this world something such as deception exists, than he is by any personal injury or loss. I have to avert my face so no one can see any reflection of the wave of shame and horror that washes over me. After all, if not deception, what would one call what I have done to Neel?

* * *

After three days of relentless work to try and undo all we have done in preparation for this wedding, there is a lull. Sonia was calling and texting Super every hour for the first two days and then like a switch, all of a sudden her calls and texts stopped. We assume she's finally discovered that her boyfriend left us a little gift.

It's early in the morning and I'm awake, mulling over the different trajectories my life can take at this point. Finally, I get out of bed and wander out to the kitchen. The back door is open, and I see Super alone on the patio swing. I make chai, pour two cups and go join him.

"Thanks," he says and we sit in silence for a while, each seemingly lost in our own thoughts.

"Should I talk to her?" He asks after a while. "I mean, I just want to ask why. You know? I just want an answer why she did this. I mean, was it all pretend? All the things she said to me? We were together for eighteen months, you know? And the pressure for marriage was from her."

"There is no deeper answer to why she did it. You already know why."

"But, why? Raghav's note said 'security, not love'. But what is the point? It makes no sense to me."

"You are a catch, Super. Whether you see it like that or

not, others do. Papa and Mom are very well established and respected in Delhi circles. I hate to admit it, but you are a good looking guy. No one has heard of any girl drama or bad habits associated with you, your career is up and coming – heck, you were featured in an article in the young entrepreneurs' magazine. By most standards, and definitely by Delhi society standards, you are a catch."

"So was none of the emotional stuff real?"

"I'm not saying that at all. Maybe she was fond of you. She probably found you attractive too. And we don't know what her long term plans were. Maybe she thought she would find happiness in prioritizing all the reasons she was with you."

"You don't play with someone you are fond of."

"I know," I say, reminded of my own follies for a long gut twisting moment till I force my attention back to the present moment.

"I've got to ask her. Just once I have to ask her for my own peace of mind."

"I understand that." I say quietly. I recall the burning desperation I had to talk to Ari when he left me and I didn't understand his actions.

"I'll ask her to meet me at Coffee Café."

"I'll tell everyone you've gone to the gym."

"Okay."

I put an arm around Super and squeeze his shoulders, and he uncharacteristically leans in, resting his head against me for a moment. Again the unspoken tenderness that can only exist between siblings, wells in my heart.

34

Sagar Suraj Dutt

She's sitting at the corner table. Her hair is tied up high, the way I like it. Her eyes are red and I know she's been crying. But what the heck am I supposed to feel? Sorry for her? She did this. She knowingly did this. So why has *she* been crying? After cheating and lying, what right does she have to cry over it? She could have been my *wife* by now. Scary! Thank goodness I found out in time. I have to remember that. I walk over to the table, watching her red, wistful eyes track me.

"Hi, Sagar."

"Why did you do this? That's all I want to know. We don't need to talk about anything else. Just… why?" I'm surprised at the contempt in my voice.

She speaks very rapidly, with no pause. "When I was very little and brought to Aunty*ji*'s, after Ma and Pa passed away in the crash, I was very, very scared…"

"What's that got to do with the way you've treated me?" I cut in.

"Please, Sagar. Just let me speak." Her red rimmed eyes silently appeal. Fleetingly I see endless misery in them. It it's almost too much to bear and I avert my gaze.

"Ma and Pa were gone, and I was brought to Aunty*ji*'s, and it was very kind of them to take me. Otherwise I think

I might have been put in an orphanage. And who knows if that could have been even worse. Well, anyway, I was there with my cousins Deepak, Dhavan, Rohini, all bigger than me." She's speaking rapidly again. Like she wants to get it out all at once. "Rohini had to share her room with me, and Deepak and Dhavan, they had their own room. Rohini was not happy about having to share her room and I heard her argue with Auntyji about it. I was scared of Rohini. I felt like I was taking something away from her. They rearranged the furniture in her room to make place for my bed and desk from my home. My furniture didn't match hers and Rohini hated that. I didn't know what to do. Anyway, the second night that I was there, Dhavan came into the room in the middle of the night and slid into my bed. He said this was what I had to do to repay them for moving into their home. He said it was like rent, because I didn't have any money. Rohini saw and knew all this, but she turned over and never said a word, never stopped him. After that he came in the room almost every night for about three years. He said that if I ever told anyone about this, he would kill me. I was only seven and very afraid. I didn't tell anyone. Auntyji and Uncleji are nice people, and if they ever found out about this, it would break their hearts. I got used to the nightly ritual, and it remained a dirty secret amongst us. Rohini always had this superior air, like I was dirty and... anyway. We never discussed it, never spoke about it, never so much as mentioned it. But I could feel it in their eyes on me. I don't know what Deepak knew about what was happening. He's always been kind to me, but distant and disinterested. I'm not sure if he even fully knew I wasn't his real sister.

"When I was ten, and before I turned eleven, Dhavan stopped coming to my bed. It's a strange thing to say, Sagar, but without his visits my sleepless nights were hauntingly empty, and I had to face myself. I was mostly a quiet, sombre type, is what I remember people saying about me. They said my smile had vanished with my parents. I became very studious and topped all my classes. Auntyji and Uncleji praised me and encouraged me, but it made Dhavan and Rohini hate me even more. I think they felt personally insulted that I could stand first even though I was 'sullied'. This made me study even more furiously and I got all those awards over the years, you know? The more I got, the more they hated me. The more they hated me, the more I studied. I could not bear their eyes on me, and when I opened a book, I got lost in it. I forgot about my real life.

"That's how it was, until I was sixteen. By then Dhavan and Rohini were engrossed in their own lives. Rohini was twenty and had a boyfriend who took up her attention. And Dhavan was even older. Deepak was married and Dhavan was next in line. Auntyji would talk about this with her friends. She talked about how she wanted to find a bride for her Dhavan. I could not bear the thought of Dhavan getting married to some innocent girl who knew nothing about him, I couldn't bear the thought of him having children... perhaps having a seven-year-old daughter someday. But I still couldn't tell anyone what had gone on all those years ago either.

"I started going out, Sagar, going out a lot, with every boy who asked me out, and even those who didn't. Once I slept with them, I was done. I don't know what it was, but like a sick addiction I wanted to sleep with and discard every boy I could. It was only years later that I could understand this thing, this... this compulsion. But anyway, this went on for years. Mostly I was discreet, but still the word got around that I was a slut. I didn't care.

"I met Raghav when I was twenty-one. For some reason that I've never understood, I mattered more to him than I ever mattered to anyone since my parents. I know how clichéd this sounds, but he saved me from myself... he really did. He cared. Even though I didn't. Until I began to believe maybe I was worth it. If one human being could care about me that much, maybe I was worth it."

"Why did you date me when you had him? Were the last two years a joke? Or was it just that you couldn't be faithful to one man."

She looks down as she answers. "No. I love you. I... I began dating you because you were so attractive. You and everything you came with. The family, the security, the way you described your home. It seemed so wholesome and pure. *You* were wholesome and pure. I felt like I finally had a shot at belonging to a family. I loved the way you saw me. You didn't know anything about my past. You didn't see me as damaged, or someone who needed to be rescued. It was different from how Raghav saw me. I was drawn to that, Sagar."

"Were you with him when we were dating?"

"I wanted a clean start with nothing about my past standing in the way. When we talked about being exclusive, I broke it off completely with Raghav. I didn't see him for many months. Then one day I ran into him at Bharat Bhavan, and we began talking again. He was hurt. I... I should not have treated him in that way. It started with one coffee and then slowly we began meeting on and off. I told myself I wasn't cheating on you because I didn't have a physical relationship with him then. He said he loved me, but I kept telling him I was with you and that there was no future for him and me. Then you proposed to me. That's what I wanted but I also..."

"You also what?"

"I... I also loved him. I made the choice to be with you. But... I couldn't fully do it. I'm sorry."

"So when exactly did you start cheating?"

"Um... the day you proposed, and I accepted, that evening Raghav asked me to meet him. He was crying on the phone. I met him that night and we talked for a while, sitting in his car. He was a mess, Sagar. I was comforting him, and I don't know how we ended up... you know?"

"The day we got *engaged?*" I thought I could understand a little bit, but really I could not. And I could not bear to look at her, this woman who'd cheated me. Suddenly I just wanted to leave. I didn't want to hear any more of her heart wrenching life-story. "What are you going to do now?"

"I don't know. Aunty*ji* and Uncle*ji* want an explanation. I need to tell them something. I've completely broken it off with Raghav. I don't know. I will figure it out. I don't have a right to ask, but what are you going to do, Sagar?"

"You are right. You don't have the right to ask. I'm sorry you've had a difficult life, Sonia, but it doesn't give you the right to play with mine. I will never share your story with anyone, so don't worry about that. You can give Aunty*ji* and Uncle*ji* whatever explanation you want. Blame it on me, if you like. But do me this favour, don't play with anyone else's heart." With that I push back my chair to leave. Even though I try to avoid looking at her, I catch a glimpse of her eyes, wet with tears. I don't feel anything.

35

Neel Kant Duggar

"Meera, I don't want to wait anymore for the right moment. I want you to know I've done a lot of thinking… I don't want us to end. I think we can make things work. Let's leave the past in the past and move on. I want us to be together because I love you, and I think you love me. I was afraid we might try to work it out for all the wrong reasons, you know? For family and society. But these last few weeks I imagined life without you, and I didn't like it. I like us, I like who we are together and how I feel with you. I know we will have to work hard to make it all right again. I like our history. I… why are you crying?"

"I'm pregnant. And I don't know why I'm crying. It's what I hoped for. I mean you still want 'us'… that's what I'd hoped for. I didn't tell you about the pregnancy before, because I wanted to know what you want. You know, I didn't want it to influence your decision. I… No one knows yet. I've kept it to myself. I wanted you to know before anyone. I… I'm sorry about everything… and…."

"Wait. You're pregnant? I mean we're pregnant. It's ours, right? I mean…"

"Yes, it's ours. It's the one time we were together before I came."

I look at my hands. I dig my nails into my palms and realizing I've never consciously done that before. It's more of a Meera-type of gesture. She digs her nails in her palms to check if the moment is real. I look back up at Meera and in her expression I can see she's waiting for me to say something. I just reach out to hug her. She moves closer on the edge of the bed where we both are sitting, leaning into me.

"I want it all, Meera. I think perhaps finally, we have the chance to be a real family."

EPILOGUE:
TWO YEARS HENCE

Stories Within Stories

36

Rumana Hasan Jana

"Rumana, baby, we've tried it once. Why go down that road again? I mean, what we have now, it's comfortable. No?"

"Yeah, sure. It's comfortable for you. You come and go as you please. I don't know where we stand, Ari. And it's not about Rumi. It's about us. I was finally feeling normal, Ari. I was finally feeling *hopeful*. And you came back with your charm, and said you wanted to get married. Why? I mean it, *why*? Why lie about wanting marriage? Why did you want to get back together at all? You don't like being tied down by anything. You like your variety. I've just been a fool."

"Listen. We can always work out issues. But you will have to trust me and…"

"Well, I *don't* trust you. Just tell me the truth. Did you come back to me because I won the lottery? Just tell me, Ari. You owe me that much. Life with me looked attractive and convenient, right? You never intended marriage. You thought it would be easy to slip back into what we had before. You never intended to give up your outside interests."

"I did. I gave it all up to be with you. It's not about the lottery? Of course it's not. It's just marriage. I don't… It doesn't *mean* anything. To me, in a sense we are married already. Since when did registering it mean anything to you? Trust me..."

"Ari, you will have to earn back my trust. Ah!... I can't believe I still have hope. This is just a replay of the last time around. I know you cheated, so many years of our marriage. I just looked the other way, because I had nothing to offer you. *I was grieving our son.* But that doesn't mean it didn't hurt. It hurt. A lot."

"Baby. What do you want me to change? You know me. You know I love you and Rumi. And you know I lost a son too. Just tell me what you want me to change now, and I will."

"I want you to be faithful and honest."

"How have I not been those things?"

"Oh, Ari. Don't pretend. You like your women. You've made no secret about that. It was different when we had an open marriage and we knew of each other's lovers. But after Roho? After Roho, I didn't want any of it. But you continued your secret life. I didn't understand how you could. But whatever. That time is gone."

"You are mixing the past with the present."

"Now I don't want this live-in thing with you going off whenever you want and having your ready excuses. I want marriage, I want commitment. I want to comfortably grow old with someone, someone I can trust, completely. And if you aren't interested in that, *leave!*"

"Rumana, please don't. Give me some time. I... let me figure this out. I don't want to lose you. But I don't know... Marriage?"

"Either I have a ring on my finger by the end of September, or you need to move out, and I will move on."

37

Laila Myna Dutt

I want to stop thinking about Ravi. It's been almost two weeks since I ran into him at *Sapphires*. He looked wistful and kind of lost. I wish I could help him, but I've to remember I can't. I can't help Ravi. I have to stay away. I have to stay away. I have to stay away. I wish his number was not imprinted in my mind. I'm sure he's got people he can turn to for help if he needs it. I am not one of them.

"*Beta*, Laila, Jugal is here." Mom calls out from downstairs. I realize I am smiling already.

"Coming." Jugal is Sunaina's younger brother, younger than me too, by a year. A few months ago I was over at Sunaina's with a few other friends and he casually asked if, hypothetically, he were to ask me to go out for dinner with him, whether I would consider it. I told him I would. He proceeded to ask me out to dinner. He is so confident, so... so mature in ways. He asked me all this within earshot of friends and Sunaina. I had wondered about his embarrassment had I said 'no'. But he reassured me in his confident, casual manner that he would have been completely accepting of my answer, whatever it might be, and it didn't matter to him that others were there to hear the exchange. I love this about him. He goes about life putting in his best effort without any self-consciousness and without any attachment to the outcome. He says what's important in life is to put your best foot forward, and do what you do with complete commitment to the journey, not the destination.

I knew for years that he had a crush on me, but I thought of him as a kid. Then suddenly I was twenty, and he nineteen, and the difference didn't seem that big in the face of his drop dead gorgeousness, all the attention he gave me, and his gentle, considerate manner. We have been seeing each other for a few months. Mom and Papa seem accepting and happy. I trust Jugal, and so do they. Trusting anyone has been a struggle since the Ravi episodes. But he is not possessive, or jealous, and he just wants me to be me. Meera says he is an old soul. Meera says when she first met Ari, he was nineteen, but very different from Jugal.

We are going to an art exhibit where one of Jugal's friends has displayed his paintings. That's another thing I like about Jugal. He's got an appreciation for art and a wonderful group of friends. All gentle and artistic.

I see him before he sees me. He is engrossed in a deep conversation with Papa. Probably about cars. He is in blue jeans, a sky blue t-shirt and a black blazer. Formal giving the impression of casual. His hair is brown and it flops over his forehead in an effortless manner that's so him. I am happy. At first I was afraid Sunaina would not like me seeing her brother. But if anything, it's brought us closer. Even though evil monsters sometimes make you doubt it, the fairytales... they *are* real.

38

Noorie Varun Dutt (Mom)

I don't have the courage to destroy these, but they can't be found. I hold them to my face. They still have the aroma of a forgotten time. When I close my eyes, I see him as he looked the last time I saw him. So young at seventeen. *Arman was my neighbour before the Janas moved in next door. We spent our childhood together. We were at each other's homes all the time, eating together, playing marbles or cricket, chatting, doing homework or sitting attentively as his grandma told us stories of Ram or Krishna or Allah. Those were such precious times. Arman was my best friend. One summer I was fourteen, and he was fifteen, and things changed. We realized that over the last decade or more we had fallen in love with one another. It was always there, this love. It was always so… we only understood it now. We would look into one another's eyes deep and long, drinking it in. We told each other what the other meant, even though it was so obvious to us it didn't need to be put in words. We could not imagine a life without the other. We had, after all, known each other our entire young lives. But this was also the year that we understood we could never be together, for he was Muslim and I, Hindu. Our families would not accept anything beyond a friendship between us. As though right on cue, this was also the year our families began to monitor our time together at one another's homes. My mother told me I was older* now and must spend less time with Arman, lest it be "wrongly perceived". Mother knew.

I was heartbroken. Perhaps our love was destined to be tinged with sadness. We accepted this fate, but we were still irresistibly drawn to each other. Arman would come into my back yard each night at midnight and we would look at each other through my bedroom window. I would tell him about my day, and he would tell me about his. We never intentionally touched each other. Perhaps as children, while playing, our hands or arms may have touched. I don't recall. But we never touched each other romantically. We did not ever even hold hands. We held each other through our eyes and words only.

Then one day when I was sixteen, Arman came by my window. His eyes were bloodshot red. He had a fever. He told me his family was moving to Hyderabad. Tears seeped down our faces and we could not say anything more to one another. We just looked at each other, drinking in the other's grief in bewilderment. Even though we had accepted fate, we were not prepared for such a parting. It was clear to us that we could not be together against the wishes of our families, but yet parting was not a reality we had considered.

Soon enough, Arman and his family came to our home to say goodbye. Arman's father talked about how the mounting tensions between the Hindus and Muslims was worrisome. How they had a large community in Hyderabad and as an opportunity had come up, it was only wise for them to move. Arman and I avoided looking at each other that day, lest we should cry in front of our families. That night we sobbed as our broken hearts were breaking even more.

Abruptly these nightly visits stopped as Arman had moved. I battled a fever on and off for six months. No doctor could diagnose the cause. But I think Mother knew my ailment was a broken heart *and nothing else. Arman and I were never to speak again, or see each other, except through our letters.*

We began writing letters to one another. Our letters were innocent – telling one another about the happenings of our lives. There was never any talk of love in them. Mother would quietly bring these letters to me. She asked to read the first one that came. After that she didn't ask again. I think Father didn't ever find out about these letters. I don't know how Arman explained my letters to his family. I never asked.

When I got married to Varun, Arman and his family were already settled in Pakistan. Arman was engaged to be married to Jasmeen. We described our chosen respective spouses to each other. We continued to write over the years. I told Varun that Arman was a childhood friend, and Varun, in his generosity and confidence, never questioned the three or four yearly letters. I don't know why. I didn't ask Arman how he explained my letters to his Jasmeen.

The letters feel heavy in my hands as I clutch them to my chest. I have a bundle with one thousand, three hundred and one letters. The letter I just received from Jasmeen lies open in front of me. Arman is dead. He died of a massive heart failure a month ago. In her letter she tells me she knew about me since before their marriage. He had told her he would always love me in a way he could not explain, but he would always be faithful to her. She must marry him only if she can accept this. She writes that Arman was a wonderful and gentle husband to her, and a loving father to their two children. And that I must be someone very special for her Arman to hold me so dear. She says she has not found my letters among his possessions, and that if she ever does, she will destroy them without reading them. He told Jasmeen more than I could tell Varun. I am grateful to her for her acceptance, for her letter, for loving Arman. Arman is dead. My Arman is dead.

I dry my eyes and silently go out to the backyard, still holding the bundle of letters to my chest. I kiss the bundle, inhaling the scent of decades old paper. I raise it to touch my forehead. Then I dig a deep square pit in the corner of the yard and lay the bundle in it. I cover it up with mud. I pick up one of the pots – the one with the succulent cascading over the edges. And I place it carefully over the place I had buried the letters.

39

Varun Manu Dutt (Papa)

There is a swing hanging from the branch of a large neem tree and Noorie is swinging on it. She is so young. She looks barely sixteen; beautiful and innocent, smiling and radiant. She is wearing Indian clothes — a yellow salwar kurta. I've never seen my Noorie like this. A young boyish-man appears and helps her off the swing. He's a foot taller than her and well dressed. They embrace. I'm watching silently, rooted to my spot, unable to move. I don't think they can see me, half hidden by shrubbery. But suddenly they begin walking towards me, hand-in-hand. The boyish-man takes my hand and places Noorie's hand in it. He conveys to me with his eyes that she is very special. He waves good bye to us. Noorie is crying, but smiling through her tears. Suddenly he disappears, like thin smoke. I wake up, startled. I don't usually dream. And this is an especially strange one. Ah, I just need a cup of *chai* and today's papers to clear my head. "Rabdai…"

I dress with extra care today. After all, it's that day of the month. Noorie looked distracted. I'll talk to Ruma about Noorie and that strange dream. It is a long way through winding traffic to Ruma's office in Gurgaon. Only Shawn knows about Ruma. After the accident, the shaking began, and then with what happened with Laila, I could not bear it, and I could not talk to Noorie. Shawn insisted I meet

Ruma one time. It's been three years since my first visit with her. I tell Noorie I'm going to the factory when, every first Thursday of the month, I go to see Ruma.

"Hello, Varun."

"Hello, Ruma." I ignore the excitement I feel. Ruma is my psychotherapist, and my crush on her is certainly unplanned. I finally admit it to myself. My heart lights up when she smiles in that soft, benevolent way. I don't think she can tell how much I look forward to our monthly visits.

"How are you?"

"Very well. Thanks to you." I smile. "Everything is going well."

"I would like to talk to you about the sessions."

"Yes."

"I think it's time we stop."

"What? Why?" I feel a sadness come over me.

"Varun, as you know, therapy is a treatment, it is not a lifestyle. You came here during a difficult time in your life. Your anxiety was circumstantial, not physiological. You are doing well now. You have been an exemplary client and I enjoy our time together, our philosophical conversations, a lot. But it is my ethical duty to tell you that it's time to stop."

"Don't I get to determine that?"

"I must share my professional opinion. Of course you can call me anytime if you need to. If anything else shows up. But, tell me honestly, do you think we have successfully addressed everything you came here for?"

Outside the window I can see the street hawkers sell *chanachor* doused in lemon and coriander. *Chanachor* is a childhood favorite. I don't know this yet, but from now it will remind me of this day in Ruma's office.

"Varun, now I don't speak as a therapist, but rather as

someone who has got to know you, and appreciate you over the last few years. You are a good person. Your family means the world to you. I understand that. Sometimes contradictions exist. Under different circumstances we could have been friends and shared coffees and jokes. But I must respect my professional boundaries. I just want you to know I understand your feelings."

"Ruma, you are a very lovely person and an astute doctor."

"It's my profession." She smiles at me.

"I respect your advice. And I understand what you have conveyed. You are a generous person with so much to contribute to so many. Thank you."

I have an hour and a half drive back home. Ruma knows about my attraction. She addressed it without judging it. And she conveyed that it cannot go anywhere. My sadness is bittersweet, but I also feel relief. The relief of knowing contradictions do indeed exist. And really the relief of going back to Noorie, fully. I am happy and I can't understand it. I look forward, more than I have in a long time, to sharing the evening with Noorie.

40

Rita Ashish Batra

"Lallu Jivan saw me in the market about three years ago. He had the guts to walk up to me and say to my face that he likes me and do I know that that means. I just turned the other way and walked off without answering. At that time I didn't know who the fellow was. Then on and off for a few months I would spot these youngish looking men in black hanging around in various places, but I didn't think much of it. Then for a while – almost a year – it cooled completely. There was nothing. No youngish men in black and no Lallu. But then unfortunately, I ran into Lallu Jivan again at a restaurant. He was at another table and as soon as he saw me, he sat staring and smiling at me in a lecherous way the entire time I was there. He had a smile plastered on his greasy face…ugh! Then I began spotting the men in black again. I see them randomly at the market, the street corner, even the airport when I flew to Delhi. I know they are his goons; they have this certain look about them. They are watching me. I don't think they will do anything, but this Lallu Jivan gets his kicks out of keeping tabs on me or something, it seems.

"Six months ago I saw them hanging around outside Rani's school. Imagine that. I went to pick Rani and I spotted them. I tried to hide her from their line of vision, put her straight in the car, and told Sukhdev (our chauffeur, you know?) to put his foot on the gas. I mean, I'm a wife, a mother, for goodness's sake. What does Lallu Jivan want from me? Just because he is some big shot politician in Rajasthan doesn't mean he can get away with this kind of behavior, does it? He should move on to someone who will respond.

"That's the day I went to the police station. Rohit *ji* is a kind old cop. He told me there was no point in filing a formal harassment complaint. It's not like he's done anything to me, and there is no evidence these men are his and they are stalking me. Nothing would be done to Lallu Jivan even if I had evidence, because of who he is. He said the best thing to do is to wait it out till someone else catches his fancy. That my best protection is that he would not risk hurting me, because that would lead to a scandal which would rock his candidacy. Rohit *ji* was apologetic about the state of things."

"And Ashish knows all this, right?" Meera asks.

"No, no, I can't tell Ashish. He would get so angry."

"What? Rita, you must tell Ashish. None of this is your fault, why would he get angry?"

"Ashish is possessive. I never told you that all these years. But, Meera, I've concluded that the whole male race is sort of, a bit, you know... faulty? So this is Ashish's one flaw – he's the jealous type. What can I do? He's good to me. We are good together. Unless and until someone shows interest in me. I don't know what happens to him then. He just turns into this angry, unreasonable man. It's happened only twice in all these years. But it was really bad, and I'm afraid of that aspect of him.

"So once in Subhash's party, like four or five years ago, this random guy was drunk and flirting with me. It was harmless. But Ashish flew into a rage and threw a punch at the guy.

We had to hold him back. He blamed me for attracting that fellow. I was so shocked. I don't know. Slowly things went back to normal between us, but it took a while. Then a year ago it happened again, when one of our good friends was overly complimentary about my looks at this beach party we had gone to. I admit this guy went a bit overboard with the compliments, but again it was no fault of mine. Ashish didn't say anything at the party (thank God), but when we got home, he was absurdly mad at me and we had one of the biggest fights ever. We didn't speak to each other for almost a month. I can't tell him about Lallu Jivan. I don't know what he would do. Lallu is dangerous too."

"Oh Rita, I don't feel good about this. Do you want me to talk to Ashish? I'm worried about your safety. And if Ashish has a problem with possessiveness, he needs to get over it."

No, no. Promise me you won't tell him. Promise me. I just know if he finds out, it will end badly somehow. I just know it."

"I'm worried about you."

"I know. I'm going to be fine. We have *chawkidar* and Sukhdev and *bai*. I promise nothing will happen. The thing is, Lallu Jivan can't risk a scandal, you know? I'm more afraid of Ashish's reaction if he finds out all this than I am of Lallu."

"If anything happens, if you even for a moment feel you are in any sort of danger, promise me you will call Chintan right away. I'll give you the number once I get back to Delhi. You must keep his number on speed dial and always have your phone with you. Chintan's a guy who was with Neel and I back in school and he lives here now. I never really liked him, but Neel kept in touch over the years. He is very well connected and has his own political aspirations. He will know how to handle such a situation. I'm going to tell Neel

about all this and have him let Chintan know, in case we ever
need help. Okay?"

"I'm glad you visited."

"Me too."

41

Rupa Pawan Singh

I almost told Meera the evening we went drinking after Darryl, but then I didn't. It's just not easy to share or explain this part of my life. We don't need to know everything about one another to be best friends. She doesn't need to know that the one weekend a month when I go 'home' I actually go to visit my 'brother' Alex in prison. The same Alex who presumably is responsible for the death of his parents – the parents who adopted me from the orphanage when I was three years old. She doesn't need to know that I don't know who my biological family is, or whether they are alive, or that Alex – the only family I know – is the one person I hate.

I love him because I've loved him ever since I remember, and now I don't know how not to. Alex and I were two peas in a pod. When the Coates found after having Alex – their miracle baby – in their forties that they could have no more children, they decided to adopt a little girl. I was fortunate enough to be that little girl. I was three and Alex five when I became a part of his family. We did everything together, from playing with his wooden railway set to riding bikes in the autumn-hued streets of our suburban neighbourhood, to competing with the neighbourhood children in stamp collecting. He took his older brother role so seriously, taking me under his wing and leaving no doubt in anyone's mind that if they tried to mess with me, they would first have to contend with him. The Coates kept for me the name that was registered at the orphanage, and sometimes I got teased for having a different last name. But soon enough Alex put a stop to all the teasing. He told me I had a different name only because I was very, very special. The Coates were always very open and forthcoming about my adoption. They always welcomed my questions and took the sting out of the fact that I was not biologically their child. They explained that relationships were made from more than just biological connections, and I was as much a part of the family as Alex. They were the gentlest people I knew. And then that fateful day everything changed.

The Coates were close to their sixties then. Settled, comfortable and content. Mr. Coates... Dad... had a top notch post with the Food and Drug Administration and often worked long hours. Mrs. Coates... Mom...dear, kind Mom had taken early retirement after several decades of working part time at the local library. She loved to cook and potter around at home, and was always doing little home projects. She kept our home immaculate.

I got home from school that day and the house was eerily silent. There was no fragrance of fresh food from the kitchen to greet me. "Hi Mom," I had called out. "Mom, where are you? Is Alex home?" And then I'd noticed the soft sobbing coming from upstairs.

I found him sitting inside the bathtub in his bathroom. He was hunched over and I immediately ran to him, trying to hold him and comfort him. All he could say over and over was "Mom, Mom..." He was inconsolable.

I finally went to Mom and Dad's bedroom and found Mom

passed out in their bed. There was no breath, no pulse that I could find. The lamp on her bedside table was knocked over, and there were angry red marks on her throat. I had this intense urge to straighten the lamp and the sheets, because she liked everything neat in its place. But somehow, instinctively, I knew I must not to touch anything.

It felt like it was happening to someone else, and a part of my consciousness was perched up on the ceiling, observing the scene. The other part, the part that was in high functional mode, made 911 call, and then a call to Dad, asking him to rush home for "a medical emergency". The rest is a blur. There were paramedics and police all over the house. Dad came home and buckled to his knees as soon as he saw Mom surrounded by the paramedics and the police. He had a massive heart failure right before my eyes, collapsed and died there in their bedroom. Alex was handcuffed and taken away. In a moment, my entire family was gone.

I cried till I had no tears left. I visited Alex in prison and pleaded with him over and over to tell me something about what happened. But I got no answers. He said he had no memory of it. He came home from school and everything was fine. He went into his room and the next memory he has is of being in Mom's room, kneeling over her, realizing she was not breathing, and finding his hands around her neck. He thinks he choked his mother, but he doesn't why. And he has no actual memory of doing it, but the evidence was overwhelming.

I wasn't sure I believed he did it. But he worked on convincing me. There were funerals and attorneys. I kept pleading with Alex to remember something. Anything to indicate he did not do it. But there was nothing. And the worse part was that he believed he did it. He was a tortured man. I don't know if he was more tormented, or I. Those months and years passed in a blur. There was nothing to indicate he was innocent of the heinous crime of taking his mother's life and Alex was convicted on first degree for thirty years.

There was plenty of money and Alex and I were named as inheritors of everything. The Coates had left huge savings accounts and trust funds for us. A significant amount went to Alex's defense lawyers, but there was more left than I knew what to do with. I hired a financial manager, who made me wise investments. I sold the house as soon as I could and moved to the city, where I was relatively insignificant and not recognized as the poor girl who lost her family in one insane instant. I focused on finishing my education and drowning myself in writing and in work. I isolated myself for a long time. I had no friends. I worked, spent hours at the gym, and fell exhausted into bed each night. I visited Alex once a month. For the first few years I still had a lingering hope that he would still remember something. But then I accepted that this is how it is going to be. Alex in prison, Mom and Dad very dead, and me out living my life.

I finally began dating again after six years of relative solitude. Now it's been over decade since that horror. And I have worked hard to be healthy and normal in every way that matters. I take Alex books and food when I visit. I don't know him anymore. I don't know who he has turned into. But I miss the brother I still love so much. He has turned to religion. Something I don't understand. But I suppose we each have to find our way to survive. I survive by the love I have for him and by the hatred I have for him. Though a glimmer still lingers. Perhaps he didn't do it.

42

Sagar Suraj Dutt

"Pari is forty-two, and I am thirty," I announce to no one in particular.

"We know how old you are, Sagar," Mom says, the irritation apparent in her voice. After almost two years of dating, I finally invited Pari to meet Mom and Papa over dinner at a *Bhaiji's*, a restaurant in Connaught Place. I mean, I knew it would be difficult for them to accept our relationship, but they are reacting like I've committed murder. I hope she can't tell how upset they really are. She's so astute though, I'm quite sure she has an idea.

"Look, Pari dear, in our family this kind of thing just doesn't happen."

"MOM!"

"It's okay, Sagar. I understand. It's difficult to accept. And then I have Geeta too," Pari says calmly.

"Which Geeta?" Mom asks confused.

Pari looks at me. "You haven't told them?"

"I... ah, um... Mom, Papa, Geeta is Pari's five-year-old daughter. Don't worry, the father is not in the picture. And of course, when we marry, Geeta will live with us."

"When you *marry*? You are *marrying*?" Mom's jaw has dropped open. Why would I introduce Pari to them if we weren't planning to marry? Sometimes Mom's logic ability is incredibly missing in action.

Papa isn't saying much, and Mom has become very, very quiet after her outburst. She keeps her eyes downward cast, barely moves, or speaks, and has a martyr-like expression. This situation has fast deteriorated and none of us have much appetite. I hope Pari isn't offended. I've known her to be patient and mature, forgiving and kind. But women as a whole are so unreliable, who knows when she may flip. At her age she must be nearing menopause too, so I must remember to be prepared for mood swings and erratic behavior, I suppose.

Suddenly Mom looks up straight in my eye and says "Why? Just tell me why you want to do this?" Her voice is tremulous and her eyes look watery.

"Mom, really, let's not get dramatic."

Papa finally speaks, "Sagar, this is a question any Indian mother would ask, *beta*. Pari, no offense to you. We don't mean to be rude, and you must excuse us. We are understandably shocked, you see? You are a lovely young woman…"

"Not so young," Mom mutters.

"MOTHER!" I am ready to get up and leave, but I want to hear the rest of what Papa is about to say, so I don't.

"Now, now… Pari, you are a lovely woman. You know our son is younger and perhaps he's taken a bit after his mother in his fickleness. You must find a steady life for yourself and your son."

"FATHER! What is wrong with you both? I am marrying Pari because we love each other. I am not fickle. And besides, she has a daughter, not a son."

Pari is staring at me, with a slight smile on her face. She turns back to Mom and Papa and says, "I am not offended. I understand this relationship is difficult to accept and you both are shocked. I'm sure you are protective of Sagar. But please believe we are in this for the right reasons. We really do love each other."

"Well, you know love is not all that you imagine it to be. And it's not enough to build a marriage on. Society can be very cruel. We just want you both to be aware of the other things to consider. Where did you both meet?" Papa asks.

"My cousin introduced us at a party. And you must understand, uncle, that our generation thinks different. For us, love is enough," Pari answers.

"Well," Papa changes his approach. "How long were you married before?"

"Actually, I didn't marry. Geeta's father and I had a live-in relationship six years ago for a year. It ended while I was pregnant."

"Oh! Um… does that man know he has a child?"

"Yes."

"So why do you want to marry our son now?" Mom interjects.

"Well, I'm okay with not marrying. Sagar prefers to marry," Pari says. It's true. She prefers a live-in relationship, but I know that will be even more unacceptable to Mom, Papa and their circle of Delhi people. So I suggested we just continue dating. But Pari wants to either move in together, or move on. She says she's too old to 'just date'. She wants to cohabitate. That's why I threw in the marriage card. It's the only way our relationship will ultimately be accepted by Mom and Papa.

"Oh, don't worry," Mom says. "We will convince our son to not marry you."

"Well then, I would prefer living together." Pari responds immediately, before I have a chance to say anything in protest of Mom's offensive declaration. This is not going well. I think I'm going to need Meera and Laila's help to win this one. Or, rather than deal with those two, maybe I can just elope and then announce it to the family.

43

Ari Hassan Jana

Really? A lawsuit? Gosh, and all I want to do in life is to enjoy my beer, admire beauty, work for HENNA, spend time with Rumi and call it a day. I mean... that's all the good stuff in my life. At this stage, or really at any stage, a lawsuit is a hassle. I mean... I'm almost fifty. Still young and happening, mind you, but done with such disturbances. Shit!... Shit, shit, shit! This is such a hassle. And if Rumana finds out, it's going to be a big issue for her... and for me. I'm being accused of sexual assault, specifically aggravated rape... *aggravated rape*? I don't even remember this chick... this Bobby Leo. Apparently she was a secretary at the company. What a name, Bobby Leo. I would remember Bobby Leo if I'd heard it before, right? Well, I know, my memory has holes, but this is big. Bobby Leo claims I raped her in 1996, ten years ago. I was forty and high on my espionage work. She claims I used my power and position. Why would I? I had the world at my feet. I could have whoever I wanted. I mean, I was married then, but still. We had a comfortably open marriage.

It seems I asked her to come back to my office after a happy hour on the pretext of some work, offered her a heavily laced drink. Okay, I could have done that, but I would not have without her consent. And then I brutally forced myself on her on my office couch, which makes no sense. I mean not the office couch part, because that was put to good use, I recall, but the 'brutally forced' part. I've never forced sex on anyone, brutally or otherwise. Never had the need to, and never would. But according to her, she said "no" four times and I did not take heed. She got pregnant, had an abortion, got very depressed, went to HR at the agency, but they squashed it and found some pretext to fire her within the year, and she was in therapy and on medication for six years. Nice! She's even managed to get professionals to support her story! The memories of the actual incident were repressed and only emerged towards the end of her therapy and so she could consider a lawsuit only much later. How convenient. And they are calling this aggravated rape because of the laced drink and she says I had a broken glass in my hand, which made her afraid that I would hurt her. This just does not ring true.

I wonder if she's someone I slighted and now she's after some sort of vengeance. Even if she loses this hoax of a case, I wonder if what she really wants is to smear my character by telling her story, going after my reputation, forcing me 'hear' her and respond. Or I wonder if she just wants to harass me, or wants my attention. I wonder if she actually has a crush on me. Hmmm...

Get real! I'm fucked! I'm sure she has therapist's records, abortion records and goodness knows what else. I don't recall this incident at all, so how do I defend it? I think the defense has to be that this just didn't happen. I'm honest in saying I have no recollection of it. So as far as I'm concerned, it is a complete fabrication. I mean, it's just not happened in my history. Maybe, just maybe she has me mistaken for someone else. For fuck's sake, I don't even recall her. Yeah, maybe I don't need to worry about this and it will go away. It's my word against hers. Do I even need to defend this thing? I mean, what about the statute of limitations? I wonder what she even has to get so far as to filing the lawsuit ten years after the alleged incident. This is a mind fuck. First thing, I need to get myself a lawyer through Rufus's connections. Next thing, I need to put all this out of my mind and open a beer. And maybe I need to talk to Rumi and Rumana and prepare them there's a lawsuit, but it's not a big deal…Yeah, that's what I need to do.

"Hey, Rumi, you ready? Let's go, darling. Got to get back down the mountain before the sun sets."

"Coming, Dad." She comes out hurriedly, her mop of thick curly hair falling over one eye.

"Rumi, what would you say if I told you someone's accused me of sexual harassment?" She's almost eighteen, and maybe this is a good way to work towards preparing her.

"I would say don't let Ma find out about it," she answers with a chuckle. I can't help but laugh at her astute answer.

"You would, would you now?"

"Dad, you can handle anything, except if Ma's pissed at you, then you just really go berserk."

Really? The little twerp! "What do you mean by I go berserk?"

"You mess up. Mostly to do with women. I was younger, but heard things, you know. You guys had an open marriage and that's all fine and good and Ma's explained things to me. But then you also did other things outside of that. And these women weren't always… like… safe, you know? And you always do these random things with random people when Ma's mad or sad or something."

"What? This is all new to me. This is a bizarre theory, Rumi. You really think so?"

"Yeah, but look, I don't know. I mean it's not like I've tried to study you guys."

"Have you told Rumana?"

"Ma? Nah! She probably already knows this about you."

"You ladies! Really, Rumi? *Beta*, I had no idea you were sitting and analyzing me."

"I was not sitting and analyzing you, Dad. Not at all. It's just... you know... visible."

Someday I will tell her about all my escapades and see what she makes of the whole story, or what I recall of it.

44

Neel Kant Duggar

Dear Meera,

On our anniversary I want you to know that I have finally been able to put everything behind me. I am finally moving on, fully. This is what you have wanted for the three of us. You, me and Karam. You are right that we don't need another entity in between us. What you don't know Meera, and what I need to tell you, is that there were not one, but two other entities between us – your past and also my past. My past is not a clean slate either. And perhaps you are the bigger person for having told me everything first and on your own accord. And perhaps I'm not for having carried my 'stuff' for this long. The reason it didn't even occur that I must tell you about this is because I wanted to protect you and because I didn't think it mattered between us... but it does.

So here it is – all those work happy hours I went for... as you know I met a bunch of colleagues there. Most would have a couple of beers and leave. But this guy – Joe Digamma – would stick around for hours. Often he and I would be the last to leave, sometimes we would shut down the bar. You've met Joe once at the first annual company dinner. You didn't like him. He's slightly overweight and you said he smiled too much and smelled like a brewery. Well, Joe can outdrink most people and he is a great storyteller. Often when I knew you were out with Ari... well... and I guess I also knew you were angry and sad and I didn't want to face that – those days I would just sit around with Joe for hours after everyone left. I would sip my beer and he would do some serious drinking while bitching about everyone and everything. He would mostly tell me old scandalous company stories, stories about his ex-wife and their gory divorce and custody battle, and his current dating exploits in which the girls he dated turned out to be inevitably, ridiculously inferior. The drunker he became, the more entertaining his stories became. We soon got into this routine, and developed an understanding that when his head would start to drop on the bar table, it was my cue to put him in a cab and pre pay the driver to take him home.

One day, during those first few months, Joe was not at work as he had court – it was a custody hearing. But he'd messaged me to say he would join us for happy hour. He'd said in his message, he would in fact probably really need a drink after the hearing. I was looking forward to his sarcastically comical take on his situation.

But he didn't show up until it was time for us to leave. This was unlike him and I hoped he was okay. The last few of us were about to leave when Joe came rushing in. He didn't look like himself. His face was white as a sheet and his eyes were bloodshot. He was sweating profusely. I tried to read his eyes and he seemed to be gesturing me wait until everyone had left. After the goodbyes were said and people were finally gone, I turned to him. And Meera, this is what had happened.

He'd been in a car accident. Actually, he'd caused the accident. He was drunk. He'd begun drinking straight after his hearing, right there in the court house. It was snowing and dark that afternoon. He'd begun driving to go back to his apartment, drop his car and then head out for happy hour. And he'd run his car over the sidewalk. He'd run straight over a few homeless people huddled on the sidewalk. He didn't know how many people. It was snowing. It was close to Christmas time. You know how dark it gets that time of the year, even in the daytime.

He'd stopped when he heard screams, and felt something squash and crunch under his car tires. Stumbling out, he'd found there was blood everywhere, and a bloody blanket, and blood in the white snow, and black eyes staring at him from a black face twisted in pain, while some voices screamed. He'd looked around and through the whirling wind and snow, it seemed he was seen only by those haunting black eyes. His car is a common black, the tracks would soon be covered by the falling snow, and the blood would be washed away or frozen into drops of unrecognizable evidence, and vision could be mistaken in that weather. This is what he'd counted on as he'd reversed and sped away as fast as he could.

He told me all this with dry, choking sobs after downing two shots of whiskey. He'd been drinking for a while; his words were starting to slur. In that one shocking moment of clarity I saw his cowardice for what it is. His lack of willingness to take responsibility in his life finally became apparent to me, and it was ugly. For reflected in it I saw my own weakness, my inability to face the truth, my desire to escape your reality, my seeking momentary relief in his stories mocking his ex-wife, gossiping about ex-employees of the company, or making fun of the women he dated. I would laugh at others with him, and I didn't look at what was going on with us.

Meera, I never told you before. But this is my failing. This is the ugly part of me. Now you know the best and the worse of me. I didn't do anything. I let him talk and talk and talk. But that day I took no action, I didn't try to talk him out of hiding his crime. In fact, I told him to get a good night's sleep when I put him in a cab and sent him on his way home.

But I was horrified at what I had done, and angry that Joe put me in that position, and kept waiting to hear the hit and run being linked to him. But day after day Joe Digamma came to work like nothing had happened. After that day we avoided each other, and that's when I stopped going for happy hours, if you recall.

Finally, about a month later, I could not sit with the guilt anymore. I hired an attorney and told him the situation. He managed to work out an immunity deal protecting me against any legal repercussions if I were to come forward with information about a hit and run. After that I told the local authorities everything I knew. I hid all this from you for so long.

We were going through therapy at that time and it felt like everything was crashing down around me. Things were supposed go a certain way and follow a certain direction and that was not happening at all. It was then too that I knew for sure I wanted to work things out between us. I knew I could not give up without trying. And I wanted for us to move back to India.

Meera, I took my time to tell you all this us because I wanted to be certain. And I came to see you in Delhi only when I knew I could bring a healthy and strong me to you. I hope, my love, you understand this part of my story that I have not shared with you. I'm sorry I've held on to all this for so long. Can you forgive me?

This is all there is, though.

Neel

45

Meera Myna Dutt

I haven't been close to Neel's family. I believe it's a two-way street. In the first year of marriage, I tried – God knows, I tried. But the outcome was disastrous. Neel's parents are somewhat old-fashioned and conservative in their thinking, and Neel himself is not very close to them. His older sister Sarika is somewhat a replica of his parents and initially tried to be over-involved in our business. His younger brother, Fahad, is a complete deviant, wanting as little to do with the family as possible. It's been a blessing they've always lived in the suburbs. In the first year, Mom and Papa tried to socialize with them. But the styles were so different that eventually efforts on both ends fizzled out, and what remained was cursory contact at the time of occasions, life events, festivals and such. What astonishes me is how Neel is still unassuming Neel, in spite of having grown up with his parents and sister, and has retained his gentle kindness and forgiving nature, and yet he doesn't shy away from his family like his brother does.

Since we moved back to Delhi just before Karam's birth, and even more so since we've had Karam, I've had the typical Indian wife complaint that my in-laws interfere in our lives. I don't know what it is about daughter-in-law and mother-in-law relationships, but there's an element of antagonism in the best of them. Very rare are those that escape this and I can't boast of having seen any first hand. Neel's mother adores Karam and if she had it her way, she would gladly evade me and take over the job of raising him... if I let her. But I suppose I have it better than the vast majority. We don't live together and don't intend to.

Anyway, I turn my attention back to Neel, and after a long time, Ari. Life has a strange sense of humour. I know it must have taken Neel some struggle to write me that letter. And when he says he's finally been able to put everything behind him, I know he truly means it. It is all the more ironic that I've received an email from Ari after years, the very same day Neel handed me the letter. Ari's email is short and non-committal. It simply states:

How are you? It's been a while. Would be nice to catch up. Where are you these days, anyway?

It's irritating that Ari has not shared anything further. Not that I want to know about him anyway. But it's irritating he has the nerve to write me such an email out of the blue after the disappearing act he pulled on me, after no contact for two years! How dare he? What is he expecting? He thinks he still has some magical hold on me! He thinks I will write back! Maybe I should write back and tell him exactly what I think of him. Tempting, but no way! I'd have to tell Neel and I just won't open that chapter again. It's not fair for Neel, or for us. I must just delete the email and delete it from my mind as well.

"Ma..." I look up from my thoughts, suddenly aware of my nails digging deep in the palm of my hand, and yet there is a smile on my face at hearing Karam call out to me. My son's voice invariably pulls me to the sunniest part of my life. I love Karam so much. And so does Neel. And that binds us tighter. I get that children must not be the reason for a marriage, but my child has added meaning and dimension to mine. Neel and I mostly get along these days. That his work takes up so much of his energy and attention still bothers me. But he's better than before. And Dr. Mona said, people's basic nature does not completely change. With a lot of effort and commitment, one can change to an extent.

"Ma..." Karam is pointing proudly to a mount of sand he has patted with his little hands into a tiny little hill in the sandpit he is playing in. He's stuck a small twig at the tip of his hill. He's almost two now. I clap my hands for him and smile broadly. Karam is the most mature little two-year-old I know. To be fair, I don't know a lot of two year olds really, other than the ones in Karam's nursery where he goes for three half-days of the week. But I still think Karam is incredibly mature and able to gauge our thoughts and feelings beyond what I would expect from a two-year-old.

"Maa...aaaa," Karam is clapping his plump little hands excitedly and smiling at his masterpiece construction as I take delight in his delight and hurriedly fish out my phone to capture the moment so I can text it to Neil at work. Suddenly I stop what I'm doing midway and stare at Karam, who at that moment has his eyes squeezed shut, his face turned up, and a wide grin on his face. There is an unmistakable cleft in his chin. How has this cleft never made its appearance before? Could it be that it's just developing? Neel doesn't have a cleft. Neither do I. Ari does. I gasp at the horror of the possibility. *But it cannot be. I checked dates. It just can't be. I know. Someone in the family tree must have a cleft. There has to be a genetic explanation. Wait! Didn't Neel's great aunt have a cleft? NO! It was a hair lip. This can't be. It must be coincidental.*

Karam is looking right at me and smiling his gleeful smile, eyes shining and hair slightly ruffled by the play and wind. I detect Ari in him. All of a sudden there is a resemblance. It's not just the cleft, but also some mannerisms. It's the way Karam holds his head to one side when he's thinking, and something about how his face and eyes light up with his smile. And now the cleft! How did I not see all this before?

I'm breathing heavily now and the familiar dread is in the pit of my stomach. Is one more disclosure in store between Neel and me now? Do I get a genetic test done to determine my suspicion? Could I have been wrong about the dates? What's this going to do to my precious family? We are just about healing so well.

I call Mom, my eyes never leaving Karam for a moment, following his every movement, silently saying sorry to him over and over in my mind.

"Hi beta, everything okay?"

How does she always know? I choke on a deep sob before I can say anything.

"Beta, what's wrong? It will be okay, whatever it is. Tell me, what is it?"

And out tumbles the whole entire story, a full confession to Mom, for the first time, from there on that park bench.

"Beta, go home. I'm coming over. I will see you there in half an hour." I have heard her this assertive on rare occasions. On my wedding day, when she told me how I made a beautiful bride, and when Super's engagement broke and she told him he was going to be okay. I feel unusually calm as I gather up Karam and his sandpit toys, and head back to the car to drive home. I look at Karam – it feels like for the first time, as he comfortably snuggles in my arms and buries his head in my neck for a moment. He looks back up in my face with a quizzical, comical expression. Possibly wondering why I am staring at him in this strange manner. He tentatively touches my cheek, reassuring me that he is still him. I smile back at him, deep into his eyes. A reassuring smile. He *is* still him, and I am still me, and nothing can take that away from us.

* * *

Mom's already over when I get back. She's let herself in with her key that she has to our house, and she has a pot of chai going on the gas. Delightedly she takes Karam from me, giving me a quick hug.

"Go wash up, beta. I will give Karam a bath." What would I do without her?

In my bedroom, alone, I lean my head on the wall for a moment. I pull up Ari's email on my phone. Does he deserve to know? If indeed Karam is his son, must I let him know this? Is it fair to Karam if I don't? Is it fair to Neel if I do? I hit delete and then go to my trash bin and permanently delete Ari's email.

By the time I wash up and go out, Karam is bathed and happily eating warm *khichri* in his highchair. Mom pours me some chai and signals with her eyes that we must wait to talk till Karam is napping. Karam is a happy baby and a sound sleeper. Soon he is done and sleepy. As I take him to his room to put him down in his cot, I take in his warm baby smell. Again the horror and panic strike me. I cannot let this hurt my child.

Finally Mom and I are sitting at the kitchen table. "How do you know for sure?" Mom asks.

"I don't know for sure, but I see it in his face."

"So you are not sure?"

"No. And as I think back, it still does not make sense with the dates. But the cleft?"

"Could Karam have a feature that neither of you has? One that's not in visible on either side of the family?

"Yes, I suppose."

"Are you happy in life now, beta?"

"After a long time there is a settled feeling, and confidence. I don't think about the past anymore. I think Neel doesn't either. It feels fresh and clean." I swallow the lump in my throat. "Now it will all go away again, Mom."

"It doesn't have to, does it?"

"What do you mean?"

"Do you know that Karam is not biologically Neel's?"

"I mean, I don't know for sure. Only genetic testing will tell."

"What you don't know, you don't have to tell."

"You mean... you mean..."

"Yes, I mean we will never speak of this again."

"But..."

"Think about it, Meera. Think about the pain and upheaval something like this – if at all it's even true – would cause. Not just to you, but to Karam and Neel too. Forget the families. These would be scars for life. And if this is not the case, then all this angst for nothing. Think about the love Neel has for Karam. Do you want to take that away from them? Isn't Karam Neel's very own son in every imaginable way?"

"But is that fair to them?"

"Who was with you at Karam's birth? Who wakes up at nights when Karam wakes up? Who has changed countless diapers? Meera beta, don't cause distress in your precious family. These relationships are delicate. Once damaged, the crack remains forever. Who knows this better than you?"

"So it's okay to just continue as though everything is fine?"

"Everything *is* fine."

"But I will keep wondering…"

"That's your burden to bear. Don't put it on them."

"So you really mean its okay to just keep all this to myself and never, ever do anything about it." I hear the relief in my own voice.

"Yes, it is okay. Karam is your and Neel's child, and grandchild to us and Neel's parents, and what you were momentarily considering would cause immense distress to a lot of people. So let it be. Do not question…"

"What about Ari?"

"What about that man? Hasn't he done enough? You owe him nothing and it would be best for you to wipe him completely out of your system. I don't want to hear that name on your lips ever again. I don't want you to think that name. He does not exist for us. Promise me, Meera."

"Yes, you are right."

"So you promise?"

"I promise, Mom."

Acknowledgments

Anita Jain, for being my most rigorous critic, first editor, voice of reason and closest friend. Thank you for your generosity of spirit. Without your tough love, wise counsel and incredibly sharp insight, this book would not have been this book.

Purvi Shah, for being magical and making me believe I can be magical too. Bela Labovitch, for being my loving sisterhood of safety. Richa Jain, for the poignant shared times since I was three feet tall.

Sheela Mehta, for your zest for life, indelible wit and for being my mentor over the years.

The numerous clients for their trust and the profound privilege and honour of allowing me in.

My parents' in-law Pushpa and Naresh Patel for your unwavering support and constant supply of delicious food over the years. My sister in-law Neena Patel, for being a sounding board and having my back when I needed it.

My brats, my childhood co-conspirators: my brother Sumit Mehta, for giving me my first and only black eye; my brother Amit Mehta for selecting the biggest, juiciest strawberries for me. Love you crazies! My sister-in-law Monica Becerril Ugalde for smilingly joining in the mad Mehta clan.

My Mami and Mama, Nirmala and Yogi Durlabhji, for being beacons of shining light in my life.

Dadiji, Dadaji, Ba and Bapuji, for guiding me from the other side. I miss you and feel your presence often.

All those whom I haven't named here, for contributing to me in countless ways.

Bimal Patel, for being my rock, enduring my idiosyncrasies and never not believing... even when I faltered.

Krisha Patel, my secret reader, for your humour and your pure love. Thank you, deeply, sincerely for inheriting the 'mad'.

For really making it happen, heartfelt thank you to the dynamic *Write Place* and *Authorsupfront* crew: Anup Jerajani, for establishing gracious first contact; Indur Vaswani, for seeing it through every step of the way; Manish Purohit, for striking editorial oversight; Ramya Sarma, for astute editing; Niyati Joshi, for capturing the story's essence for the cover art.

"Victory" for survivors of violence seems as unattainable as world-peace. And yet, how can we ever give up our attempts to end abuse of any kind from the face of this earth? To that end respect, support, and encouragement for the survivor are vital.

It is important for us to share our stories, anonymously or openly, for you never know whom you may provide the courage or inspiration to find a path to a violence-free existence.

— *Sheela Mehta, LCSW*

Made in the USA
San Bernardino, CA
20 September 2017